Praise for Catherine Cavendish

'If there is a crown for queen of Gothic horror,
[Catherine Cavendish] should be wearing it.'
Modern Horrors

'Cavendish draws from the best conventions of the genre
in this eerie gothic novel about a woman's sanity slowly
unraveling within the hallways of a mysterious mansion.'
Publishers Weekly on *The Garden of Bewitchment*

'Well-rooted in classic gothic traditions, the novel doesn't
furiously spill the blood like most modern horror, but
it maximizes its unique advantages. [...] An atmospheric
and gently scary tale that will appeal to horror fans and
Brontë enthusiasts alike."
Booklist on *The Garden of Bewitchment*

'Cavendish sets the scene exceptionally well and the book
is atmospheric and spooky throughout.'
The British Fantasy Society
on *The Haunting of Henderson Close*

'Cavendish breathes new life into familiar horror tropes
in this spine-tingling tale of past and present colliding.
[...] The story of female resilience at the heart of this
well-constructed gothic tale is sure to please fans of
women-driven horror.'
Publishers Weekly on *In Darkness, Shadows Breathe*

CATHERINE CAVENDISH

THOSE WHO DWELL IN MORDENHYRST HALL

This is a **FLAME TREE PRESS** book

FLAME TREE PRESS
6 Melbray Mews, London, SW6 3NS, UK
flametreepress.com

US sales, distribution and warehouse:
Simon & Schuster
simonandschuster.biz

UK distribution and warehouse:
Hachette UK Distribution
hukdcustomerservice@hachette.co.uk

Publisher's Note: This is a work of fiction. Names, characters, places, and incidents are a product of the author's imagination. Locales and public names are sometimes used for atmospheric purposes. Any resemblance to actual people, living or dead, or to businesses, companies, events, institutions, or locales is completely coincidental.

Thanks to the Flame Tree Press team.

The cover is created by Flame Tree Studio with thanks to Shutterstock.com.
The font families used are Avenir and Bembo.

Flame Tree Press is an imprint of Flame Tree Publishing Ltd
flametreepublishing.com

A copy of the CIP data for this book is available from the British Library and the Library of Congress.

PB ISBN: 978-1-78758-821-9
ebook ISBN: 978-1-78758-823-3

Printed and bound in Great Britain by Clays Ltd, Elcograf S.p.A.

CATHERINE CAVENDISH

THOSE WHO DWELL IN MORDENHYRST HALL

FLAME TREE PRESS
London & New York

For Colin
I told you that *Country Life* subscription was a good idea!

CHAPTER ONE

You have probably visited many a village in your lifetime, but I can pretty much guarantee you have never been to one like Cortney Abbas. For your sake, I hope you never will.

Oh, to a cursory glance it looks like any other Wiltshire hamlet. A main street bordered by stone-built cottages that have stood there for countless generations and are likely to remain for many more, unless the developers come along, of course. There's the church, with the pub next to it. The village shop and its post office supply most of the villagers' day-to-day needs. Goodness alone knows, those are simple enough. Most local folk are self-sufficient, at least in terms of eggs and vegetables. Every day, people who can trace their ancestry back hundreds of years meet, work, and live their lives as they always have done. There are few cars, quite a few horses and ponies, and most of the men work on the farms, stopping at lunchtime for a bite to eat at the pub or tucking into sandwiches made by their hardworking wives or mothers.

On Sundays they put on their best clothes and troop off to church to hear the rector preach about the errors of their ways and to sing that verse in 'All Things Bright and Beautiful'. The one that goes:

'The rich man in his castle, The poor man at his gate, God made them, high or lowly, And ordered their estate.'

So, everyone is reminded of their place in life and, just in case they remain in any doubt about it, there, at the edge of the village, are the imposing Gothic towers of Mordenhyrst Hall.

Mordenhyrst Hall is my reason for being here in Cortney Abbas. Not that it was in my family's heritage. Far from it. I came here because, in the first few weeks of 1928, I met and fell in love with the heir to the earldom – Viscount Simon Mordenhyrst.

Simon was unlike anyone I had ever met before. He made me laugh, swept me off my feet, and made me feel special in a way I had never experienced before. How young and naïve I was then! When he held me close, I felt intoxicated by his presence. In short, he was everything I had ever dreamed of.

Of course, it would have been too much to hope that his family would be the same. I soon learned he had a father who spent most of his time in the south of France with a girlfriend young enough to be his granddaughter, and one older sister. His mother had died in tragic circumstances when Simon was a small child.

But it was his sister who was to make the greatest impression on me. And not in a positive way.

You see, of all the people I have met in my life, Lady Cecilia Mordenhyrst holds first prize in the cruelty stakes. She and her precious coterie of sycophants represented the over-indulged, spoiled products of their age. They were the Bright Young Things of the 1920s and by the time I met them had their personas down to a fine art. They lived for pleasure, themselves and their class. To hell with anyone else, especially one who didn't belong. One who had an accent, worse still, a *Yorkshire* accent, and whose lineage could only be traced back to members of the working class. In a nutshell, me. Grace Sutcliffe, daughter of Acton Sutcliffe, a self-made man who owned a carpet manufacturing mill in the West Riding, deep in the heart of the industrial north of England.

I knew Cecilia would be trouble when Simon first introduced us. He insisted a party be held for us at his ancestral home, Mordenhyrst Hall. We had known each other for such a short time, and I wasn't ready for all that went with living his life. For all I had found Simon easy to fall in love with, his family was another matter entirely.

Simon had met my father once – on the same day he met me. I had conspired with Father's sister, my Aunt Penelope, to go and stay with her in her flat in Belgravia. I craved the bright lights, Harrods and dinner at Claridge's. Father hated the bustling capital city and resolutely insisted on staying at our not-inconsiderable home near Leeds as much as he could.

"I could never abide London," Father said. "It's full of criminals and swanky overblown aristocrats with empty heads and full coffers. Nay, lass, give me good old honest Yorkshire muck anytime. It were good enough for me father and it should be good enough for thee. Find yoursen a farmer with a few acres to his name. Settle down and raise a couple of bairns. That'll see thee right."

Frankly, I could think of nothing worse than settling down and becoming a broodmare. This was the 1920s after all. The war and all its misery were behind us. Mine was the generation that lived for today and to hell with tomorrow. It might never come anyway. Not that you'd know anything had changed, stuck up in my Yorkshire backwater. I doubted anything had moved on since Queen Victoria was a young bride. Of course, I couldn't voice my thoughts to my father. He had my best interests at heart, and was trying to protect me, but I was young and headstrong. Life was passing me by, and I was determined to do something about it.

Eventually, much against his better judgment, or so he told me, Father caved in and agreed. I believed it was actually to put a stop to a simple but effective pincer movement mounted by my aunt and me. When he saw me off on the London train, there were tears in his eyes.

"It's the damned smuts from the engine," he said. But I knew different.

Aunt Penelope was my father's younger sister and, thanks to his generosity, lived in a handsome apartment full of her many knickknacks. She was happy to put me up for as long as I wanted. I always loved Aunt Penelope. She was the one I turned to when Mother died. Her hugs and reassurances helped me cope with my bewilderment and loss. Fathers were supposed to be strong and carry on, and Acton Sutcliffe did just that, hiding his grief from everyone, including me.

Those first couple of weeks in London were a whirl of visits to museums, art galleries, afternoon tea at Gunter's and Fortnum & Mason and trips to the theater to see the latest musicals. All accompanied by my aunt, who proved to be excellent company.

Then, Father came down to stay. He had business in London and couldn't avoid the visit.

"There's nowt else for it, lass, I have to drag myself away from God's own country down to your neck of the woods. I shall only stay the one night, mind. That den of iniquity's enough to blacken a saint's soul."

I smiled to myself, wished Father a safe and pleasant journey and handed the telephone receiver back to my aunt.

When he arrived a couple of days later, he surprised me by asking me to accompany him on a business appointment. It turned out to be a visit to the bank where my father had recently transferred both the business and the family accounts. It was a sizeable piece of business and demanded the personal attention of a senior manager.

That role fell to Simon, who introduced himself to us. The instant I felt the warmth of his hand as he touched mine when he greeted me, I felt a connection. When I looked up into his eyes, I knew he felt it too. He behaved impeccably, of course. First, he asked my aunt if, in her role as my temporary guardian, she might allow him to call on me one afternoon, my father having returned to Yorkshire. With some reservations, she agreed. From the way I simply wouldn't shut up about him, she knew this was no mere flight of fancy and we would conspire to meet – with or without her consent.

Not that it meant she liked the idea, especially as our dates grew ever more frequent. She began by dropping not-so-subtle hints. "Don't you think he's a little old for you, Grace?"

"He's only twenty-seven. Seven years isn't a lot of difference. Besides, I prefer a more mature man. Boys my age can be real pillowcases."

That bit of flapper slang raised a perfectly arched Aunt Penelope eyebrow. "I don't know where you picked that term up from, Grace, but I suggest you put it back where you found it."

On another occasion, when I announced that Simon and I were going to the cinema to see *Metropolis*, she tried again. "Does your father know you two are walking out together?"

"Not as such. No."

"When were you thinking of telling him?"

"When I see him next."

"And when will that be?"

"I really don't know, Aunt."

"Best tread carefully when you do. Your father won't like you taking up with someone like that. He's out of our class, Grace." She shook her head sadly. "I'm sorry, but I think it's doomed to failure. Any girl marrying out of her class is asking for trouble."

At that moment I was literally saved by the bell as the front doorbell rang and, seconds later, Ethel, Aunt Penelope's maid, announced Simon, and he and I trotted happily off on our latest date. I felt like the bee's knees walking out on Simon's arm. He was attentive and funny. He even taught me how to smoke, although I never really took to it.

"That's because you don't inhale. Look, you do it like this." He took a long drag, inhaling deeply before exhaling a cloud of aromatic smoke.

That evening, we enjoyed a delicious meal at Simpson's on the Strand. All around us, the chatter of the upper classes, clattering china, tinkling crystal glasses and delicious smells were accompanied by an army of bustling waiters attending to our every need. The moment I extracted a cigarette from Simon's silver case, a waiter appeared at my shoulder ready to light it. I copied my boyfriend's actions to the letter with the inevitable result that I collapsed in a fit of coughing and choking that caused heads to turn and disapproving glances to be directed at me. This only made me worse, and Simon laughed so hard, tears streaked down his face. A tall glass of water arrived, and I drank it down. My coughs subsided and Simon dried his tears on a pristine white handkerchief he replaced in his top pocket.

He clasped my hands in his.

"Oh, Grace," he said softly. "I know we've only known each other a few weeks but I'm falling in love with you. You're all I can think about. Do you think you could possibly find it in your heart to love me too?"

I couldn't speak. I nodded, smiled, and eventually trusted myself to speak, as realization hit me like a sledgehammer. "I love you too, Simon."

The rest of that evening passed in a blur. I saw the film but took none of it in. All the while, Simon's hand entwined with mine sent shivers of joy running up and down my spine.

By the time he saw me safely to my door, I had to tell someone. Aunt Penelope was reading in the drawing room when I burst in.

"Oh, Aunt, he loves me. Simon told me. He's in love with me."

With barely a flicker, Aunt Penelope placed her bookmark in her novel, closed it, and laid it on the small table next to her. Now, it appeared, was the time to ratchet things up a notch.

"Sit down, Grace. I have something to tell you about Simon's family."

I told myself that duty once again required her to warn me of the dangers of mixing with someone from his elevated social class, so I obediently heard her out.

"There's a history of insanity in that family," she said. "The mother – God rest her soul – killed herself, you know."

"Simon told me. She must have been desperate to do such a thing. Especially with children."

"It's the father. The earl. He may be titled and privileged but he's a ne'er-do-well. A philanderer of the first water. There are rumors he's fathered numerous children in the village where Mordenhyrst Hall is situated. I'm told there are an inordinate number of young people and small children bearing a noticeable resemblance to him."

"That seems to happen in all these society families."

"True enough, Grace, but in this case, there's more to it than that. Countess Mordenhyrst – Lady Elise, the one who killed herself – may actually not have committed suicide. She may have been murdered. At least that's the story I heard. Or, at the very least, something in the house itself drove her to take her own life, which amounts to the same thing in my book."

"Oh, that's superstitious stuff and nonsense," I said.

"Be that as it may, but Mordenhyrst Hall has seen generations of that family come and go and the stories abound. Be very careful, Grace. It's no place for you. No place for anyone not born to it."

I looked at her curiously. "They are people, Aunt. People like you and me."

"That's the point. They're *not* like you and me. Far from it – and this time I'm not merely talking about their social status. A friend of mine, an impeccable source of information on that family, told me. There's something not right about the Mordenhyrsts. So much tragedy and heartbreak in one family...." She paused and shook her head. "Suffice it to say, I know I can't stop you seeing that young man, but I would much prefer that you leave him alone. He may be charming, chivalrous and handsome, but when it comes down to it, he's one of *them* and always will be. Mark my words, Grace. You're heading for trouble if you persist with this relationship."

A wave of righteous anger threatened to spill out of me. How dare Aunt Penelope ruin my moment of joy? I marched to the door. "I'm off to bed, Aunt. Good night."

I resisted the urge to slam the door. After all, I was a guest in her home but, in my room, I raged at my reflection. Then, adrenaline abating, I took a good hard look at myself. I wasn't bad looking, fashionably slim so I could wear the new fashions without having to bandage my breasts flat against my chest. My light golden-brown hair was shingled. My cheekbones were sufficiently prominent to give me a half-decent profile and my makeup was fashionably dramatic. Maybe my wardrobe could do with a little updating but, apart from that, while I was no head-turner, I was at least passable.

Of course, with his good looks, title and position, Simon could have had anyone he chose. So, a worrying thought began to trouble me.

Why, of all the girls at his disposal, had he chosen to fall in love with me?

CHAPTER TWO

We had known each other nearly three months when Simon proposed. As with his declaration of love, it occurred on the spur of the moment.

May has always been my favorite month, maybe because it's my birth month, and that day was its zenith. Birds sang in cheerful choruses, a cloudless sky, bright sunshine and the mingled scents of spring flowers and new leaves warmed my soul. Simon and I were strolling around Kew Gardens when he suddenly stopped under a large and ancient oak tree, took me in his arms and whispered, "Darling Grace, will you do me the great honor of marrying me?"

I was glad he was holding me, or I would have in all probability lost my balance. Had he really said that?

He released his grip so we could look into each other's eyes. Had he really just delivered the best birthday present I could ever have wished for?

In my head, a niggling concern tugged at me. *Why me?* I suppressed it. "Yes, Simon. Oh yes. I love you and want to marry you more than anything in the world."

He swept me up and spun me around. Luckily there was no one in the immediate vicinity to witness this display or they might have thought us mad. Or simply, utterly, in love.

"I will have to do the decent thing and ask your father for your hand, of course."

"Of course," I said, sounding more confident than I felt. This would come as a total surprise to him unless my aunt had already told Father about our courtship. "Will you telephone him or go up to Yorkshire?"

Simon hesitated. "No chance of him coming to London then?"

"Not likely. Maybe once every year or so, but no more than that. It's only a short time since he was here. It'll take him months to recover." I laughed.

Simon pondered for a few moments. "Then I...we...shall travel up there together."

★   ★   ★

Aunt Penelope was almost speechless. She mumbled insincere congratulations, gave me a peck on the cheek, and shook Simon's hand while pasting on the fakest smile I had ever seen on a person's face.

If Simon was nonplussed, he didn't show it and I decided not to raise the subject with him later.

I bit my tongue around my aunt, too. To give her credit, she didn't try to dissuade me. Maybe she thought that her efforts thus far having failed, she would leave that up to my plain-speaking father.

He had obviously been warned of what was coming by Aunt Penelope. All *I* had said was that I was coming up for a whirlwind visit and bringing Simon with me. Father asked no questions on the telephone and, when we arrived, greeted us with a kind of cold courtesy that was not typical of him and made me feel as if an icy wall had sprung up between us.

The interview between my father and Simon was a private affair but lasted no more than five minutes, after which Simon made his way straight out to the garden and I was summoned to my father's study.

He was standing by the window, looking out toward the moors beyond. He turned as I entered. "Well, lass, so it's come to this, has it? I feared it would. You go down to that heathen place and catch yourself a man with wealth, privilege and a title to boot. Very commendable, I must say. There's only one problem."

My heart pounded. My father only sounded this cold when he was really angry, and it wasn't a sight I had witnessed more than twice in my life. Neither had been an enjoyable experience. Neither had, unlike this time, been directed at me.

"Penny warned me you'd become mixed up with yon viscount and I asked her to do some digging for me. Turns out that's the last family any father would want his daughter marrying into."

"I don't understand, Father. The Mordenhyrsts are an old and distinguished family—"

"*Distinguished!* They're rotten to the core. Every last man Jack of them. Oh, I can't stop you marrying him. You've just turned twenty-one so you can do as you please. And I know you will. But I'm begging thee. Think on. Think about what you're doing. Is there no shred of doubt in your mind about this man?"

I swallowed down the anger I felt, the hurt, the pain of my own father taking against my decision so badly, denying my future happiness. "I don't know what you mean, Father. Simon is a wonderful man. He's not a womanizer, or...." I couldn't use the word in front of my father.

"I never said he were. If he were a womanizer or a nancy boy that would be one thing but this.... Young lady, I've heard things about this family that would make your hair curl. If you still had any left to curl."

"But what are you talking about? I wish you would just come out and say it. What is the problem with the Mordenhyrsts?"

I had never seen Father so lost for words. "I can't tell you details, Grace. It's not fitting for a young lady to hear of such things, but I am your father and I'm asking...*begging* you to listen and obey me for once."

"It's 1928, Father. Not 1828. You can't shock me."

"Can't I? Really? Can't I? Then the world has come to a pretty pass, that's all I can say. If young ladies can't be shocked anymore, I don't know what the last war was all about."

"That doesn't make any sense. The last war was a terrible waste of millions of young men's lives sacrificed on the altar of political ambition and military bloodlust. William...." I stopped. The pain in my father's eyes at the mention of my poor dead brother was too much to bear. Captain William Sutcliffe. Blown up by a hand grenade at the Battle of the Somme. He was just twenty-three years of age.

Father picked up a heavy book from his desk and threw it down on the floor. I swear he would have thrown it across the room if he could have been certain of not hitting me with it. "That's enough, Grace. Go on, marry the bastard. But don't invite me to the wedding. I shan't be giving you away like a lamb to the slaughter."

Simon and I caught the next train back to London.

"He'll come round," Simon said, twining his fingers with mine. "It's just been a shock for him, that's all. He's from another age and finds it difficult to adjust. My father's the same. Class is everything in their world. Everyone should know their place and stick to it. They're not ready for the modern age. It's our turn now. You and I will have a wonderful wedding and, one day, your father will reconcile himself. Once he sees how happy we are. How happy I make you. And I will make you happy, Grace. I swear it."

I believed him. Every word. I was so in love with this man, I got a lump in my throat whenever I looked at him, especially when he smiled at me, and his deep brown eyes seemed to draw me in and cosset me in a delicious sensual warmth.

Aunt Penelope continued to let me stay with her, although it was noticeable that whenever Simon was expected, she always had some important and urgent errand to run.

"I'll give him your regards, shall I?" I would say, knowing she would feign not to have heard me.

Of course, it was inevitable that Simon would want his new fiancée to meet his family and so we embarked on my first trip to the village of Cortney Abbas and the grandest of grand houses, Mordenhyrst Hall.

*   *   *

I will never forget that first drive along the seemingly never-ending private road, past acres of farmland where cows grazed, paddocks where thoroughbred horses were being put through their paces ready for the hunting season and then, that first glimpse of the mighty house itself. Turreted, its gray stone walls soaring into the sky, it took my breath away. One day, Simon would inherit all this. As the only son, he would also inherit the title that went with it. Earl Mordenhyrst of Mordenhyrst. One of the oldest hereditary titles in the country.

But there was something that scared me about Mordenhyrst Hall, for all its magnificence. I told myself it was purely its palatial grandness. My home wasn't small by any means, but it was built of solid local stone and exuded a welcoming promise of warmth and safety. Mordenhyrst Hall wasn't like that. It wasn't like that at all. The windows seemed to stare at me with something approaching malevolence. I told myself it was my imagination. I hadn't really seen figures moving behind the glass of that upstairs room. I hadn't really glimpsed a face that wasn't really a face at all. Something menacing. Inhuman. *Nonsense*. I shook myself.

The gleaming black Rolls-Royce drew up in front of the servants, amassed and ready to greet us. My heart pounded as reality dawned. This would be my new life. My destiny would be to stand at Simon's side as Countess Mordenhyrst, whereupon I would take precedence over his own sister.

I surveyed the neat uniforms of the butler, valets, ladies' maids, cook, housekeeper, parlor maids, footmen, kitchen maids, laundry maids, gardeners.... How many of them were there? A sea of expectant faces. There must have been thirty, forty or more. And they were all there to check out the soon-to-be new addition to the family. I would be expected to learn all their names and roles in running this house. In due course I would also be expected to issue orders appropriately. God forbid I instructed the butler to perform a task suited to a footman. Nothing would be more guaranteed to set tongues wagging downstairs as to my suitability to be chatelaine of Mordenhyrst Hall.

Right at that moment, Simon seemed to sense my hesitation and trepidation. He squeezed my arm. The lightest of touches but the smile that accompanied it, along with the slight wink, reassured me.

"Come on, Grace, turn on that smile of yours. It won me over and I know it will win them over too. They don't bite, I can assure you, even if Buckingham does look like a fierce bulldog. I'm told he has problems with his dentures."

I already knew that Buckingham had been the family's butler since the turn of the century. I would need to get him on my side if I were ever to be happy at Mordenhyrst. That weekend would set the tone for what was to come. I returned Simon's smile, took a deep breath and, as the liveried chauffeur opened the car door, took my first step onto Mordenhyrst soil.

$$\star \quad \star \quad \star$$

Cecilia was waiting for us in the drawing room. She didn't rise as we entered, but remained as she had arranged herself, dressed in an elaborately embroidered Chinese silk robe, her feet clad in fashionable embroidered mules. She was draped over a chaise longue and smoked a cigarette through a long, slim, black holder. Her hair was a dark chestnut bob that gleamed and seemed to reflect the sunlight that poured into the room. She had painted her lips in a deep crimson bow and blackened her eyelids with kohl. One leg rested casually over the other, revealing a slim pair of stocking-clad legs. She looked every inch a Hollywood movie star but exuded the air of the aristocrat she was.

Her eyes met mine briefly as she appraised me. The coldness in those blue eyes chilled me.

"Darling Lia," Simon said as he leaned over and embraced her. "It's been simply ages. But here we are at last, and here...." He stepped aside and indicated me. "Here is my lovely fiancée, Grace. She's been longing to meet you."

Cecilia cast him a swift glance that said, 'I doubt that.' She was right. She exhaled a plume of smoke before getting to her feet in one smooth, well-practiced move. In those heels she towered a good three inches above me.

I forced myself to move a few steps closer and she held out a slim arm. I shook her proffered hand, noting the tapering fingers, professionally manicured and painted in a shade which matched her lipstick. The color of blood. Her grip matched her gaze. Frozen.

"So, you're little Grace of whom we have heard so much and seen so little. In fact, nothing at all until today. Simon that was really too, too naughty of you. You know I hate it when you keep secrets from me. Remember what I used to do to you when you were a child and tried to hide things from me."

Simon laughed. "It's true, Grace. Lia used to lock me in the gardeners' potting shed, miles from the house, and then deny all knowledge of my whereabouts for hours until either one of the gardeners found me, or she tired of her game." The smile suddenly died on his lips as if he had recalled something that disturbed him. But the hesitation was fleeting, and he was soon all smiles again.

Meanwhile, I was being mentally appraised by his sister. She didn't approve of what she saw. Was it my clothes? Hardly. In the short time since becoming engaged to Simon, I had purchased an entire new wardrobe from London's and Paris's top designers. Simon had insisted on footing the bill and had opened up accounts for me at Harrods and other leading stores. Cecilia could have no problems with my family's financial status but, of course, for people like her, money meant nothing. It was all about power, position, titles and heritage. Once again it all came down to social class.

Cecilia took another deep drag of her cigarette and blew the smoke out in my direction. It could only have been deliberate. I struggled not to cough but the effort brought tears to my eyes. A result which, judging by the twitch of her glossy lips, amused her.

How dare she put herself above me simply through an accident of birth? But I knew it didn't matter how much my inner self railed at her perfunctory treatment of me. This was the way it was, and would continue to be, in Simon's world. If I were to marry him, I had better get used to it and I had better start fast. After all, I couldn't say I hadn't been warned.

Cecilia's attention diverted to her brother and the knowledge that she was no longer appraising me felt like a noose loosening.

"Grace looks tired," Cecilia said, as she removed her cigarette from its holder and stubbed it out in an onyx ashtray. "I'll ring for her maid to show her to her room. I expect she has everything unpacked and put away by now. I have given her Nell, Simon."

Simon frowned. "Nell? Should I know her?"

"Of course. Old Tom Fletcher's youngest. She's been in service here since she was thirteen years old. High time she moved up the hierarchy and Grace will be just the thing for her. Not too demanding."

Spoken by someone else that could almost have been a compliment but issuing out of Cecilia's mouth, I knew I had just been insulted. Demeaned.

Simon appeared not to notice the slight. "Oh yes, I remember little Nellie Fletcher. I'm sure she will do splendidly."

Cecilia pressed a bell at the side of the fireplace and the door was answered almost immediately. The butler entered.

"Fetch Nell, would you please, Buckingham? Miss Sutcliffe is tired after her journey."

Buckingham gave a light bow. "Very good, My Lady." He shut the door quietly behind him.

"Actually," I said, wishing my voice didn't crack at that point, but my throat was so dry it felt like sandpaper, "I'm not really tired at all. I would love to see around the house and get to know my surroundings."

Was it my imagination or was Cecilia stifling a fit of giggles? What had I said now?

She turned away and picked up an ornament on the mantelpiece – an action that, from my perspective, seemed completely unnecessary.

Simon stepped in again. He took my hand. "Plenty of time for exploring later. Have a rest now and we'll do all the orientation you like tomorrow. Cecilia's right. You do look tired. Your eyes are quite heavy."

Did he know that I had guessed he was merely placating his older sister? Was he so in her thrall that he had to agree with everything she said? And what was the truth of her behavior toward him when they were children? She was four years older than him but, because of ancient traditions of primogeniture, could not inherit the estate. For a strong-minded modern woman like Cecilia, that must have rankled. I fleetingly wondered why she had never married. She must have been a debutante and had her season some years earlier. With her credentials suitors would surely have been beating down the doors. Maybe her inclinations led in other directions? I had heard of lesbians but, so far as I knew, had never actually met one.

This was not the time to pick a fight or stand my ground. Anyway, it might be a good idea to get some rest. Something told me I was going to need all my wits about me and plenty of energy to deal with whatever slings and arrows Mordenhyrst Hall in general, and Lady Cecilia in particular, might care to throw at me. Then, of course, there was the Absent Earl, as I had learned he was often called. Simon told me he was arriving from Nice that weekend, no doubt to check out his prospective future daughter-in-law, but as yet there had been no sign of him.

The door opened and a slight young woman of around twenty entered. She was dressed neatly in a black high-necked, long-sleeved dress. Her hair was styled traditionally, in a neat bun at the nape of her neck.

Cecilia inserted another small cigarette from a silver case into her holder. "Grace, meet Nell. Nell, this is Miss Sutcliffe, and you will attend to her requirements. She has had a long journey and needs to rest. We shall see you at dinner, Grace," she said to me. "We meet down here for cocktails at six-thirty, and we shall dress this evening in honor of your arrival. Nell knows what to do and will look after you."

That was it. I had been dismissed just as surely as Nell had. My new personal maid opened the door and stood aside for me. Simon stared out of the window, apparently lost in his own world and oblivious to me. I suddenly felt cut off and alone and, to my horror, tears pricked the back of my eyes, but nothing on this earth would permit me to cry in front of Cecilia.

My first sight of the room that Nell had prepared for me was a mixture of surprise and delight. Sunshine streamed through the floor-to-ceiling windows. A soft breeze ruffled the net curtains and provided a welcome, refreshing breath of air. It helped to blow away the feeling of being stifled that I only then realized had been gradually overwhelming me since I crossed the threshold of Mordenhyrst Hall. Maybe it was all the painted eyes in the portraits of stern and haughty ancestors adorning the walls of the marbled entrance hall, or the sensation of being watched that refused to leave me – a growing sense of menace I knew was irrational but which I couldn't let go of.

Set against all those centuries of history and tradition, this room – I suppose I should learn to call it *my* room now – made a refreshing change. The pale lemon walls, modern furniture, luxurious and inviting bed, the exquisite mirrors and lamps in sculpted frosted glass…Lalique, surely. I picked one up and examined it. Sure enough, there was the signature, and I recognized the subject. The beautiful iridescent figure of a nearly nude, dancing nymphet, draped only in a diaphanous robe, was one I had admired when Simon had taken me on a shopping trip to Harrods. He had offered to buy it for me, but I felt the price too extravagant. A warm feeling wrapped itself around me like the softest of embraces. He had bought it anyway. He wanted to make me feel welcome in my soon-to-be new home.

"This is a beautiful room, Nell."

"Yes, miss. They call it the Lemon Room. That's what it says on the bell in the servants' hall."

I glanced again at the walls. "Most appropriate." A stronger breeze billowed the net curtains and, just for a second, it looked as if someone was behind them, pushing them aside as she walked. She? I shivered and turned away.

Nell busied herself putting out my clothes for dinner. Her soft voice brought me back to reality. "I thought your beaded peacock-blue dress would be just right for this evening, miss."

I smiled at her. "Perfect, Nell. Thank you. I think you and I shall get along splendidly, don't you?"

Nell smiled and almost instantly lowered her eyes as if her expression had been a little too familiar, too forward from a servant on such a short acquaintance. Well, to hell with it. She may have become used to all this stuffy upstairs/downstairs nonsense, but I wasn't nearly so comfortable with over-deferential servitude. My father had never forgotten his upbringing in a small coal mining community. His father, grandfather and generations before had seen the Sutcliffes go down the pit. Acton Sutcliffe was the first to break out of its grip, and he had been saying 'to hell with it' ever since. Every time one of the 'toffs' as he called them, looked down their long noses at the forthright Yorkshireman, he took great delight in outbidding them at auction, winning the next big export deal or turning down their offer of a prestigious membership of some exclusive men's club or other.

"Those sorts of shenanigans are not for the likes of us, my girl," he would say to me. "They'll be asking me to join the Freemasons next!" His great booming laugh was as generous as the belly from which it issued. Of course, the Freemasons were about the only ones who didn't knock on his door.

I watched Nell as she smoothed down my chosen dress and hung it on a padded hanger. It looked so light and delicate, but the intricate beading made it quite a heavy article to wear. It skimmed the knee with an undulating hem and my midnight-blue silk shoes set it off perfectly. I was about to suggest them when I noticed she had taken them out and was examining them for any scuff marks.

"Thank you, Nell. Exactly what I would have chosen."

"Thank you, miss. Would you like me to turn down the bed for your nap now?"

I stifled a yawn. "Yes, please."

"I'll draw the curtains too, so you can get some proper rest. I'll come and rouse you at five-thirty, so you have plenty of time to have your bath and be ready to go downstairs at six-thirty."

I let her help me undress down to my slip and she held back the sheets for me as I sank into the cozy embrace of my bed. I wanted to find out more about this woman who would play an important role in my future life. Back at home in Yorkshire, our servants were almost like part of the family. We celebrated their birthdays, bought them presents at Christmas, laughed and cried with them. I wondered just how much interest the Mordenhyrsts took in their servants. If Cecilia was anything to go by, I suspected very little.

★ ★ ★

Nell helped me look my best. I was never going to be a conversation stopper like Cecilia, but with makeup and hair styled by Nell's skillful hands, the reflection that stared back at me from the mirror was that of a confident young woman. It caused me to briefly wonder who she was.

"Thank you, Nell. You've done a lovely job."

"Thank you, miss." She stood back, and held out my shawl, made from the same fabric as my dress.

She draped it loosely around my shoulders and I was ready to go.

I made my way down the stairs feeling calmer and more collected than when I had ascended them. The door to the drawing room was slightly ajar and voices drifted out into the hall. I heard my name and stopped. Cecilia was holding forth.

"My dear Simon, you can't possibly be serious about marrying her. I mean, have you heard that awful voice? She sounds like a scullery maid Mama employed once. Can't remember the silly girl's name but she managed to get herself pregnant by one of the footmen. Naturally, Mama sacked her and threw her out."

"I can assure you, Lia, Grace is not pregnant and, yes, I do intend to marry her."

Simon's affirmation warmed my heart. Then an unfamiliar male voice, that of an older man, added his opinion.

"Seems like you've been swept away by a pretty face and a well-turned ankle, my boy."

"Papa's right," Cecilia said. "Bed her by all means, but you don't have to wed her."

The older man didn't like that. "Cecilia!"

"You have no room to talk, Papa. How is little Ernestine or whatever her name is?"

"You know perfectly well her name is Eglantine and she is currently sunning herself on Lord Fairleigh's yacht in the Bahamas. She needed a holiday."

"I'll bet she did," Cecilia said.

"Lia. Don't." My fiancé, the peacemaker.

All my brittle confidence shattered, but the clock struck the half hour and it wouldn't do for me to add tardiness to my list of shortcomings. I gritted my teeth, took a deep breath, and forced my head upward. I gave a slight cough to announce my impending presence and opened the door.

Three heads turned in my direction. Simon smiled, advanced toward me, and planted a light kiss on my cheek. "You look beautiful, darling," he whispered. "Come and meet my father."

The seventh earl had a physique to match his voice. Not overly tall and with a gut to rival my father's, he was dressed in immaculate white tie and tails, as was his son. He peered at me over half-rimmed spectacles and the look was almost lascivious, as if he were imagining me naked. I extended my hand as convention demanded and wished I didn't have to.

"Papa, this is Miss Grace Sutcliffe. Grace, my father, Earl Mordenhyrst."

The earl's bewhiskered upper lip grazed my proffered hand, and I was glad of the silk gloves Nell had put on me. The thought of skin-to-skin contact with that man revolted me. How such a lecher could have fathered a man with the charm and personality of Simon was beyond me. Maybe age had taken its toll. He was nearing seventy, but tales of his profligacy, relayed to me by Aunt Penelope in increasingly graphic detail, not to mention his fecundity, reached back more than fifty years. His latest mistress, Eglantine DuBois, was only nineteen years old. She was a former chorus girl whose real name was almost certainly neither Eglantine nor DuBois. Her holiday in the Bahamas was probably only the preface to an ending of the current arrangement in favor of a more lucrative one with a younger man. I had heard of Lord Fairleigh. He was only thirty-five and recently widowed with not only a considerable wealth of his own but also from his late wife, who had left him a castle in Scotland and an estate in Norfolk along with a portfolio of property in Mayfair. Eglantine was evidently no slouch when it came to sniffing out the money.

I managed to extricate my hand from Earl Mordenhyrst's clinging grasp.

"Welcome to Mordenhyrst Hall," he said, as if suddenly remembering his lines. "I don't believe I know your father."

Cecilia's lips twitched and she took a sip of her martini. I opened my mouth to speak but she got in before me.

"Grace's father owns a carpet factory. That's right, isn't it, Grace?"

"Sutcliffe's Carpets is internationally renowned for exceptional quality," I said. Why did I sound as if I was defending myself?

"I'm sure your father would be proud of his daughter's skills as a saleswoman," Cecilia said. "It must come in handy when customers come calling."

"Lia. Stop it." Simon's voice held a warning note. Cecilia seemed about to add another catty comment, saw his expression and settled for another sip of martini.

Simon handed me a glass. He knew how I liked my cocktails. Not too strong, well chilled and, as this was a martini, furnished with an olive. I thanked him and took a much-needed gulp. The fiery liquid burned my throat. I coughed.

Cecilia made no attempt to hide her pleasure. "Oh dear, I'm afraid I added another drop of the hard stuff. Simon makes such weedy drinks. I prefer something with a kick in it."

Simon handed me his handkerchief so I could mop my eyes, trying as best I could to prevent my mascara running. By the sight of my reflection in the overmantel mirror, I appeared to have succeeded.

Sadly, the handkerchief was probably ruined. I handed it back to him with a mumbled apology. He gave me a reassuring smile and tucked it away in his trouser pocket.

"You should warn people when you do things like that, Lia," he said. "We don't all like to drink something with a kick of a mule."

Cecilia shook her head. "Oh Sy-Sy, whatever's happened to you? You used to be so much fun. You've turned into an old fuddy-duddy. I can't think why." She glared accusingly at me.

The door opened. Buckingham entered. "Dinner is served, My Lord."

"Jolly good," the earl said. "I shall take you in, Miss Sutcliffe." He took my arm. I had no choice. This was protocol. Simon followed us, escorting his sister.

Dinner consisted of seven courses, all served formally by a flotilla of male servants. I was so unnerved by the way the evening had gone and the crass rudeness of my future sister-in-law that I ate little. I needn't have worried though as no one appeared to notice. Not even Simon. The conversation excluded me entirely and revolved around the upcoming London Season; Cecilia regaled her father and brother with her latest exploits with her friends. They sounded a vacuous lot, leading futile existences, whose idea of living a fulfilling life consisted entirely of scavenger hunts, designed to humiliate people of 'lower' classes. Stealing a policeman's helmet, or even his bicycle was a 'jolly good wheeze'. Even the resulting appearance before a magistrate was 'ripping good fun'.

Simon and his father discussed financial matters relating to their bank. Simon was destined to be chairman one day when his father stepped down from a role he already devoted little or no time to. Such conversation went over my head and clearly bored Cecilia, who soon found a way of diverting attention back to herself. When she finally declared that she and I should leave the menfolk to their cigars and port and adjourn to the drawing room, it was almost a relief. Except that I would now have to endure something like twenty minutes alone with a woman who had set herself firmly against me.

She was already lighting a cigarette when I joined her. I looked around, contemplating where she might decide to seat herself. It wouldn't do to select the chair *she* wanted. Cecilia took a long drag on her cigarette holder and blew out a cloud of smoke before arranging herself on the chaise longue she had occupied earlier.

"Sit down, Grace." She indicated a chair, so I deliberately chose another one. I was now directly opposite her. The one she had selected for me would have involved me sitting awkwardly, perched at an angle on the edge. Judging by the frown that wrinkled her otherwise flawless forehead, she did not appreciate my flash of independence.

Our eyes locked for a few seconds that made me feel as if I were staring down a cat. The first to break eye contact would be the loser. I wasn't going to be that person.

In the end, she needed to reach for an ashtray – the perfect way to break the deadlock without losing face. She tapped her cigarette, and the small column of ash landed neatly in the onyx dish.

"You know, of course, that you cannot possibly marry my brother."

There it was. At least she had afforded me the courtesy of coming straight out with it. I decided to return the compliment.

"Simon has asked me to marry him, and I have accepted. We are engaged, Cecilia, whether you like it or not." I surprised myself. I certainly surprised the woman in front of me. Her eyebrows couldn't have raised any higher and her cheeks flushed an angry red under the ivory makeup.

"You've got guts, I'll say that for you. Plenty of guts but, unfortunately, no class. I believe you stand to inherit a considerable amount of money when your father kicks off this mortal coil. Money, yes." She traced a tick in the air with her forefinger. "Class, no." She shook the same finger. "A future Earl Mordenhyrst needs both in abundance. This old pile costs a lot to maintain in the condition to which it has become accustomed, and a certain poise, elegance, demeanor and breeding in the chatelaine is equally important. Society demands it. That's why it's imperative that Simon marries the right girl. There's a glut of rich American heiresses in London society these days. I'm quite sure he will find his future wife among their number."

"You make it sound like a cattle auction."

Cecilia gave a brittle laugh. "You're right, Grace. It's exactly like a cattle auction and my brother is one of the top ten most desirable bachelors in Britain at the moment. The Prince of Wales is number one, of course, although he seems to prefer them mature and married. No doubt he will find a suitable bride before long."

The way she said it convinced me that she would consider herself firmly in the running should the prince's wandering eye ever land on her.

"Surely Prince Edward will be expected to marry royalty. One of the European princesses."

"Since the war there aren't all that many of them left and those that are eligible tend to be Roman Catholic or absolute dogs. No, I think he will be encouraged to look closer to home. To Britain's landed gentry. We have the breeding, know how to behave and some of us even have royal relatives. Did Simon tell you, a distant ancestor of ours was a Plantagenet?"

Simon had omitted to furnish me with that little snippet. I didn't bother to ask which side of the blanket *that* well-connected ancestor had sprung from.

Voices outside the door. Simon and his father sharing a joke. His father's deep belly laugh echoed in the marble hall.

He was still laughing when the two entered, swiftly followed by Buckingham.

"Brandies all round I think," Simon said.

I nodded.

"Rather," Cecilia said. "And soda for me please, Buckingham. Oh, and don't forget the rocks."

"Rocks, My Lady?"

"Ice cubes, Buckingham. Can't abide warm brandy and soda."

"Very good, My Lady."

He left, closing the door behind him.

Simon sat in the chair next to me. His father stood by the mantelpiece, lit a cigar and puffed aromatic smoke, which briefly settled like a small blue cloud around him.

"So," Simon said. "How have you two been getting along?"

He looked at me, but his sister replied first. "Oh, I think it's safe to say we know each other better now. I was thinking of hosting a Saturday-to-Monday in a couple of weeks. Just a small affair. No more than ten people. It'll give Grace a chance to meet our friends and for them to get to know her."

"Sounds like a topping idea," Simon said. "What do you say, Grace? Are you up for a bit of socializing with our set? They're a friendly bunch, and don't usually bite."

Cecilia laughed. "Except for Lilo. I've heard he thinks biting is quite the thing."

"*Cecilia.*" The earl's disapproval was written all over his face.

"Oh, Papa, don't be such an old spoilsport. I'm quite sure you've heard far worse."

"Not from one who purports to be a young lady. My *daughter* nonetheless."

Cecilia made a dismissive gesture with her hand, and I couldn't help thinking how my father would have handled the situation if I had ever dared to speak to him as Simon's sister had to the earl. I shuddered at the thought. Middle class we might be, but it seemed we were way ahead in showing respect for our parents.

Buckingham returned with a silver tray bearing a decanter of brandy, jug of water, ice bucket and soda syphon. He proceeded to pour generous measures of cognac and hand them round, along with the ice, water and soda for us to add what we required. I noted Cecilia added the merest splash of soda but piled in the ice so that her glass chinked loudly every time she touched it.

"You'll like Lilo," Simon said to me as I took a sip of my drink. "He's a bit wet but don't take any notice of Lia. He wouldn't hurt a fly."

"That can't be his real name surely," I said.

Cecilia laughed. "Lionel Smythe-Leverton. Actually, he's an Honorable. Don't know where his nickname Lilo came from, do you, Sy? You were at Eton together."

"Can't remember. The 'Li' bit was from Lionel obviously, but the 'Lo'? Haven't a clue. I think he was already called that when he started school. He had an elder brother there. Dennis, I believe. Killed during the war."

As were so many. An image of William flashed into my mind. What would he have made of this situation? Not a great deal, probably. He couldn't abide snobs any more than my father.

The atmosphere in the room had grown somber as each of us sat immersed in our own thoughts. Cecilia smoked incessantly. Her father stared up at a portrait over the fireplace that depicted an elegant woman of around thirty, dressed and styled in Edwardian fashion. Her eyes gazed benevolently out over all who observed her. Right now, the earl seemed almost bewitched by her and I could swear his lips trembled.

Simon sprang to his feet. "Come on, everyone, let's liven things up. I'll put some music on the gramophone, and we can have a go at perfecting our Charlestons."

"Not for me." The earl broke his gaze from the lovely face he had been staring at for almost five minutes. "I shall retire and let you young things dance yourselves into a frenzy. Good night, one and all."

Our 'good nights' delivered, the earl quit the room, closing the door behind him.

"I should have asked, Grace," Simon said. "Are you happy with your room?"

I nodded. "It's beautiful."

"Which one did you give Grace, Lia?"

"Mama's. The Lemon Room."

"You did *what*?"

I nearly dropped my drink. Whatever mischief had his sister committed now?

Her eyes wide, she appeared the picture of innocence. Clearly a bad sign. "It's a beautiful room. Grace said so herself. Mama loved it and it's such a shame it is so rarely used these days."

"Cecilia, you and I know it's rarely used for a damn good reason. Now I insist that Grace be moved out of there immediately."

"I'm fine, Simon," I said, but the anguish on his face as he met my eyes shocked me.

"I'm sorry, Grace, this is something you don't understand. You couldn't be expected to."

How could I have been so unfeeling? "I'm so sorry, Simon. Of course, it's your mother's old room."

"It's not that. It's—"

Lia slammed her drink down hard on the small table next to her. A cube of ice shot out of the glass and landed on the carpet. "I don't know what you're making such a fuss about, Simon. Grace is perfectly happy where she is. Let her stay there. It's high time you put all that nonsense behind you."

"It's far from being nonsense, and you know it. You've seen what happens. You were there when…." His voice tailed off. A warning frown from his sister had shut him up for some reason. Yes, he was right, I didn't know what was going on here, but I was damn certain I was going to find out. If not tonight, then tomorrow at the latest. Meanwhile, there lingered the small issue of where I was going to sleep.

"How about if I stay in that room tonight and then move out tomorrow morning? It's getting late and I don't want to put Nell to all the trouble of moving me out, making up a new bed and so on."

An exasperated sigh from Cecilia told me I had committed another innocent *faux pas*.

"It's not Nell's job to make beds. She's a *lady's* maid. One of the *house*maids will move you, assuming there is any need for you to be moved."

"Yes, of course," I said, wishing I didn't sound so feeble. "I don't want to disturb them either. They have quite enough to do in a house of this size without me adding unnecessarily to their tasks." I touched Simon's hand. The troubled look on his face told me he was less than happy with the compromise, but....

"Very well. Tonight you stay where you are, but I mean it, tomorrow morning you move to the Mauve Room. You'll be in the same wing as me."

"And me," Cecilia said.

Simon shot her an angry glance. At that moment he looked as if he could have cheerfully strangled his sister. "Indeed," he said.

Cecilia lit another cigarette and poured herself more brandy. She didn't offer to freshen anyone else's glass, so I performed that task myself, topping up Simon's and mine, adding the correct amount of water and one ice cube, just the way he liked it.

Simon excused himself at that moment. After he had gone, I grabbed the opportunity. "Why is Simon upset that I'm staying in your mother's old room? It isn't because of her, is it?"

Cecilia stared at me for a moment. "Simon was very young when Mama passed away. Shortly afterwards he began having vivid nightmares. I would wake up in the middle of the night, hearing him screaming. Every time I went to investigate, there he would be, cowering in Mama's old room. When Nanny asked what the matter was, he didn't seem able to speak. He would always point up at the same spot on the wall opposite him. Nanny would pick him up, comfort him and take him back to bed. I would follow on behind. No one took any notice of me, of course. I was four years older and expected to deal with my mother's unexpected death like an adult. I was ten years old."

All these years later, the bitterness and resentment she carried with her seemed not to have dissipated. At that moment, I saw why she had cultivated such a defensive persona. The seemingly poised, self-assured woman was no more so than me. Barely concealed under the surface lay the same scared little girl, still grieving for her loss. I actually felt sorry for her.

Before I could speak, the door opened. Simon was back, and Cecilia's face resumed its usual well-practiced mask of perfection. She offered her brother a cigarette from her silver case, and he took it, lighting it with his monogrammed lighter – a birthday gift from his father, he had told me.

I caught myself fiddling with the hem of my dress. A bead came off in my hand, leaving me with the awkward decision of where to deposit it. In the end, I settled for opening my purse and sliding it in, removing a handkerchief to conceal my clumsiness. I dabbed my nose with it. Cecilia didn't seem to notice, while Simon was too busy inhaling and exhaling clouds of smoke. The awkward silence lengthened until he finally stubbed out the cigarette.

"Is anyone else in that wing with Grace?"

"Only her maid."

"Then why did you choose to put her there?"

"Oh Simon, *do* stop carrying on about it. Clearly, I made a mistake and tomorrow Grace shall be moved to the Mauve Room as you wish. I'm quite sure that if Grace is willing to endure the rigors of Mama's bedroom for one night, you can put up with it."

Simon looked from one to the other of us. His jaw was set firm, and he seemed agitated to the point where he looked as if he would dearly love to smash one of the expensive vases that adorned the shelves and cabinets in this museum-piece of a room.

"Very well," he said. "Then I shall move into that wing for the night."

"No, Simon." I grabbed his arm as he made to get up, no doubt to summon his valet. "That doesn't make any sense. I shall be perfectly fine for one night. Nell will be on hand if I need her and then, in a few hours' time, she will move me. It's one night. Eight, nine hours maybe. What's the problem?"

Simon grasped my hand on his arm. "Oh, Grace, you don't understand. That room...."

"Stop it, Simon." Cecilia stood and poured herself another drink. "You'll frighten Grace, so she'll start imagining all sorts of things. What you thought you saw was simply the product of a child's fertile imagination. You were only six, remember."

Simon put his hands to his head. "But I can still remember it. Even after all these years."

"You're only recalling what your mind conjured up. Remember what the doctor said."

Simon lowered his hands, but his face was racked with fear. "Doctors don't know everything. I didn't manufacture what happened all those nights. And you saw it too, Lia. I know you did."

"Rubbish. I was only humoring you because you wouldn't shut up about it. Now stop it."

Simon grabbed his sister by both arms and shook her.

I cried out, "*Simon!*"

He dropped her arms and stepped back. "I'm...I'm sorry, Lia. I don't know what came over me."

Cecilia glanced at me and then back at her brother. "Forget it, Sy. It was a traumatic time for you. For both of us. Even Papa in his way, I should imagine. You were her little prince. Apple of her eye. It's only natural you would feel it in different ways to the rest of us."

Was that a note of bitterness in her voice? Hard to tell. Her face retained its composure and, despite the shaking, not one hair had drifted out of place in her immaculate coiffure.

★   ★   ★

I retired to the Lemon Room at around eleven-thirty. Nell was there, with my nightdress laid out ready.

"Oh, Nell. I'm so sorry," I said. "I should have told you I would manage for myself tonight. I didn't mean you to stay up so late."

"That's quite all right, miss. I'm happy to do it."

"Well, in future, I'll get myself ready for bed. You need your sleep too."

Nell hesitated. "I'm not sure that would do, miss. I mean Mr. Buckingham's awfully strict on these things, and then there's Mrs. Bennett...."

"The housekeeper?" Learning all the names would be a nightmare, but at least I seemed to have got the senior members of the household memorized.

"Yes, miss. Mrs. Bennett doesn't tolerate any slacking, and when Lady Cecilia gave me this position, she told me she would be keeping an eye on me specially. To make sure I did things for you proper."

I smiled. The young woman, so close to me in age, but so separated by protocol, class, privilege and all the baggage that went with it. "I would say, Nell, that you and I are going to be learning together. No doubt Mrs. Bennett will be keeping an eye on me too. After all, if I am to marry into this family, I'll have a lot to live up to. I'm sure Mrs. Bennett will have her own opinions as to my suitability for the role. So, if she has any problems with my instructions she can come and raise them with me herself. And you can tell her that from me."

Nell's eyes opened wide. "Oh, miss, I daren't do that. She'd have my guts for garters for insolence."

I couldn't help but laugh. Nell looked so shocked and the whole situation struck me as ridiculous.

A teeth-rattling crash exploded close by. I jumped. Nell let out a scream.

"What on earth was that?" I raced to the door and wrenched it open. The corridors were dimly lit by gas wall mantels. There was no electricity in this wing yet and their light lent itself to gloomy shadows and writhing reflections on the walls. It would be all too easy to imagine ghosts. Even the silence seemed leaden. I looked both ways. Nothing.

Back in the room, Nell cowered by the bed. I shut the door and dashed over to her. I put my arms around the trembling woman. "Whatever's the matter?"

Nell shook her head. "I thought I saw.... It was stood right next to you.... But then you turned and it...and it...."

"What was it, Nell? What did you see?"

She clung on to me as if letting go would spell certain disaster. Her teeth chattered.

"Nell, please. I need to know what you saw. Was it a person?"

"Oh, miss, I…don't know."

"Tell me what you saw. Please."

"A shape. A tall shape. Like a human but…it didn't…."

"Sit down beside me, Nell. Come on." I steered her round and sat her on the bed. I sat next to her, still holding her. "It was like a human, but it didn't…what?"

This seemed to take a supreme effort of will. "It didn't have…a face. It had the shape of a face, but there weren't no eyes, mouth, anything that makes a face."

I looked over to where Nell was still staring. In the limited light afforded by the oil lamps in the room, the walls revealed nothing but shadows above and below the ray of illumination. In this light, the normally bright room was dark. And that struck me as odd, because the walls were papered in a pale-lemon patterned paper which should have reflected lighter than it did. Even where the lamps were at their closest proximity, an observer could have been forgiven for thinking the decorations were in dark browns, ochers or deepest violet. A shiver shot up my spine.

Nell shifted in my arms. "I'm so sorry, miss. It's all gone now. I'm fine."

I relaxed my grasp and she stood, her composure at least partly restored. She smoothed her dress and hair. "Now, as I'm here, let's get you ready for bed."

She wouldn't get any argument from me. Besides, we still had no clue as to what had caused the big bang we had both heard only minutes earlier. "Where are you sleeping, Nell?"

"Right next door, miss. Normally I would be on the top floor, but Her Ladyship thought it would be better for you to have someone else sleeping in the wing. Especially as this is a strange house and all. I mean, strange to you. Of course, we were all surprised she wanted you in here. Nobody sleeps in this wing unless Her Ladyship has a Saturday-to-Monday or some other big event. And even then, well, this is the last room that ever gets occupied."

"Why is that, Nell? Why does no one sleep here?"

Nell paused in brushing my hair. "On account of…well…like that bang we heard. People hear things here. And they see things." She shuddered and almost dropped the brush.

"Like you did?"

Our eyes met in the mirror's reflection. "Yes, miss. I think so."

"Does anyone know what is making the noises?"

Nell shook her head and placed the brush down on the dressing table. "Mr. Buckingham says it's all poppycock and all old houses shift their timbers, especially at night, with the air cooling and whatnot."

"That may be true but what we heard was no house shifting its timbers. That was the sound of something large and heavy falling very nearby. Maybe in the corridor, only I couldn't see anything there. Or maybe it was in one of the rooms either side. Or even the one directly above us."

I stood and Nell followed me to the bed, where she turned the sheet down for me. "What's your theory, Nell?"

"It sounded closer than that. It sounded like it came from this very room."

"But we both know that's impossible, don't we?" I swung my legs into bed and Nell settled the sheet over me.

"Yes, miss. I suppose we do. Shall I leave a lamp on for you? Or would you prefer to sleep in the dark?"

I hesitated. Right now, I didn't feel sleep was an option any way. My nerves were jangling and the hairs on the back of my neck prickled at the sound of my own breathing. "Leave the lamp on near the door, please. I'll turn this one off when I'm ready." I indicated the table lamp.

"Very good, miss. Good night."

"Good night, Nell. Thank you."

She closed the door with a soft click. I leapt out of bed and raced to it, fumbling with the key in the lock. Only when I heard the satisfying clunk of the lock engaging did I breathe out.

The lamp near the door flickered and sputtered. It dimmed and gave life to the shimmering shadows on the wall behind it and adjacent to the window. I stared at the writhing tendrils as they clung to each other, separated, and clung again, engaged in some macabre dance. I heard a whimper and realized it was me. The lamp sputtered back into life. Gone were the writhing tendrils. Glimpsed through the window, the jutting wall, covered in Russian Vine, seemed almost alive, its tendrils like the thinnest of fingers, but it was merely the breeze ruffling the leaves. Could that have been what I saw in the gloom? I had to believe it was. I had to believe it for my sanity's sake if nothing else.

I climbed back into bed and turned the bedside lamp down to its lowest, deciding to retain a modicum of light, but not enough to keep me awake. It took a long time, but eventually my eyes grew heavy, and I drifted off.

When I awoke, Nell was busying herself in the room, drawing the curtains to reveal a bright and sunny new day. A cup of fragrant tea had been placed on my bedside table. I noticed it was strong, just as I liked it. Nell had done her homework.

"Good morning, miss," Nell said, a bright smile lighting up her face.

"Good morning, Nell." I sipped the steaming liquid. "Delicious tea. Thank you. Most people put far too much milk in, or don't leave the pot to mash long enough."

"Lord Simon told Mrs. Bennett how you like it."

I caught sight of the door. The lock. The key was there. But....

"Nell, how did you get in here this morning?"

Nell looked as if I had mysteriously sprouted another appendage. "Through the door, miss."

"I know that, Nell. But I locked the door last night. After you left."

Nell shrugged. "It was open this morning, miss."

I studied her face. She gave no indication that what she was saying was anything other than the truth. "Thank you, Nell. That will be all," I said, and she left, closing the door behind her.

My heart thumped painfully. Images of the previous night flashed through my brain. The loud thump that seemed to have precipitated it all. Nell's fright at what she alone could see on the wall. Nell leaving, closing the door. Me locking it. I *knew* I'd locked it. There could be no mistake.

Then there was that vine.... I pushed back the bedcovers and marched up to the window. It was slightly open. Nell must have done that when she drew back the curtains. I stared at the Russian Vine. Overnight it had grown. I was certain of it. I was no gardening expert, and only recognized the Russian Vine because we had some covering one wall of Caldwell Grange. It grew fast but not this fast. The thing was trailing onto the windowsill. It had even pushed its way under the window and was clearly intent on invading the room. I opened the window wider, meeting resistance from the vine. The leaves rustled and it seemed to grow another inch or two. I tugged at the longest tendril, intending to snap it off, but it wrapped itself around my hand. I used my other hand to free myself and dashed to the bathroom. In seconds I was back, clutching a small pair of nail scissors. I gasped as I saw that in that short time, more tendrils had crossed over onto the inside windowsill. Scared and furious, I hacked away. Leaves and tendrils fell onto the sill, where they writhed for a few seconds before withering. When I had cut off the most invasive parts of the plant, I swept the debris out of the window and closed it firmly.

An offensive smell of rotten vegetation invaded my nostrils and I glanced down at my hands, stained with green ooze. The scissors too were coated in it. I would never use those again. I raced back to the bathroom, dropped the scissors into a waste bin, and scrubbed at my hands with soap and hot water.

Finally, the smell had gone and I breathed calmly. I could tell no one what had happened, they would think me mad. Maybe I was. Perhaps it was my imagination again. Whatever the reason, I had to get on with the day. I must behave rationally, but it wouldn't be easy. Not in Mordenhyrst Hall.

I hardly noticed which clothes I put on. Nell had not consulted me but had decided a sensible, below knee-length tweed skirt, simple but well-tailored pale blue silk blouse and long, buttoned cardigan were appropriate for the day ahead. Or at least the morning. I already knew I would be expected to change at least twice more as the day progressed.

Later, I sat in front of the dressing table mirror as Nell styled my hair. Her actions were calming. They soothed my troubled soul.

"Do you know what plans have been made for today?" I asked.

"Mr. Buckingham said Her Ladyship wants to take you out in her motor car. She gave instructions that you were to dress warmly even though the weather is quite clement for this time of the year."

I smiled. 'Quite clement' was not a term that issued naturally from Nell's lips. That one had come straight from Buckingham himself. "Is Lady Cecilia's car open to the elements then?"

Nell gave a little shiver. "I'm afraid so, miss. It's what they call an open top and she drives it very fast. Nearly knocked my poor old dad off his bicycle a couple of weeks back."

"Oh heavens. Was he all right?"

"Oh yes, miss. It takes a lot to topple Dad. He cursed a bit and had a few bruises, but they soon healed. Fit as a fiddle now, he is."

"I'm very glad to hear it. I expect it must have given Lady Cecilia a bit of a fright."

Nell's lips pursed. She avoided my eyes and stepped back so I could no longer see her expression, but I could hear the annoyance in her tone. "Yes, miss. I expect it did."

I stood and made my way to the door. Nell opened it for me, and I paused to inspect the lock. I turned the key this way and that. It moved smoothly and firmly into place. Now there could be no doubt. Someone had entered my room and unlocked my door before I awoke that morning.

In the dining room, breakfast was laid out buffet style. Ornate, covered silver serving dishes lay in a straight line, serving forks and spoons arranged next to each. As I lifted each lid, new aromas awakened my appetite. A real country house breakfast awaited me. Everything from deviled kidneys, kedgeree, bacon, sausage, mushrooms, scrambled eggs, kippers, to a tureen of creamy porridge. I helped myself to a couple of slices of bacon, a spoonful of eggs and some mushrooms and sat down. I was alone for maybe five minutes except for the ever-attentive footman on hand with fresh warm golden toast and delicious coffee.

Inevitably my peaceful repast ended with the door opening. Relief shot through me when I saw Simon's smiling face. I stood and he put his arms around me in a loving embrace.

"How was it last night?" he asked, and the dark circles under his eyes told me he had slept worse than I had.

I decided not to tell him about Nell's fright, but the thump was something else. Maybe he had heard it?

"It was so peculiar. Both Nell and I heard it distinctly, but we have no idea where it came from. It sounded close by, though. As if someone had dropped a heavy piece of furniture or maybe it had toppled over somehow. Did you hear anything?"

Simon released his hold on me and picked up a plate, ready to serve himself breakfast. This also gave him the opportunity not to look directly at me as he answered. "I didn't hear a thing. The walls are so thick in this place, I doubt you'd hear an earthquake from one wing to another."

His plate duly loaded, he sat opposite me and accepted coffee from the footman. "No toast, thank you, Joseph."

The footman moved away.

"So, what have you got planned for today?"

"After I've helped Nell move my things to the Mauve Room—"

"Let me stop you for one moment, Grace. You must understand, this is a traditional house run along traditional lines. We have our place and the servants have theirs. If Nell needs any help moving you out of Mama's room, she will ask one of the servants to assist. It isn't your role."

"But I—"

"No, Grace. You'll only make Nell feel uncomfortable and it may even cause her to be in Mrs. Bennett's bad books. Isn't that right, Joseph?"

"Yes, My Lord."

"You see? Joseph knows. He knows his place. He's been working here since.... How old were you when you came here first?"

"Thirteen, sir."

"Boot boy, I think?"

"Yes, sir."

"At everybody's beck and call, I should expect."

Joseph gave a slight, wry smile. "Oh yes, sir."

"And now there's some other snotty-nosed thirteen-year-old performing those tasks. Am I right, Joseph?"

"You are, sir."

"There you are, Grace. Everyone in this household knows their place. Even my sister. Has she been down yet, Joseph?"

"Yes sir, she was up and out early. She wanted to take Snow Prince for a ride."

"Ah yes, Snow Prince. Temperamental horse but, for some reason, putty in her hands. Papa wanted to sell him a couple of years back, but Lia wouldn't hear of it. Had a fierce tantrum about it. Went on for days until Papa relented. The next day she was riding Snow Prince to hounds and Papa was off back to the South of France to recuperate." He leaned closer to me. "Word to the wise, Grace. Don't cross my sister. She has a wildness in her, and a temper to match."

He returned to his rapidly cooling eggs and a frown crossed his face. *As if he knows he's spoken out of turn.*

We finished our breakfast in almost total silence and it felt awkward. Unnatural. On top of all my other misgivings since entering this house, I felt as if I had been drifting away from the closeness Simon and I had always enjoyed. Since the day we met, in fact. It seemed like a lifetime away now.

CHAPTER THREE

The car was an MG14 two-seater and was not, as Nell had said, an open top, but a convertible, one of the new breed of all-weather cars.

"Racy little thing," Cecilia said as I tried, unsuccessfully, to negotiate my way into the passenger seat while maintaining at least a shade of decorum. For a moment I thought she meant me. "This one's been upgraded. Thirty-five horsepower. Think of that, the equivalent of thirty-five galloping stallions under the bonnet."

I tried to imagine it but settled for a smile instead. After all, it was her money and a considerable amount of it had clearly been lavished on this vehicle of vivid scarlet and eye-wateringly gleaming chrome.

As I closed my door and settled myself into the seat, Cecilia leapt in, and the chauffeur grasped the starting handle. He cranked up the engine and it fired almost immediately.

"Right," said Cecilia, "off we go."

The chauffeur was used to this, judging by the deft way he sidestepped Cecilia's roaring MG as the full power of the thirty-five horses was unleashed and the car jerked forward. I caught sight of Simon, standing on the steps, smoking a cigarette and laughing as we set off. He must have seen the horrified look on my face. I was wishing I hadn't indulged my love of bacon and scrambled eggs for breakfast. Why hadn't I stuck to plain toast instead?

At least I had had the sense to take Nell's advice and wear the long scarf she suggested, wrapped around my head and neck and carefully tucked into my coat to stop it flying around me. Once it had become clear there was no way I could scheme my way out of this trip, I had reached for my hat as usual, but she had warned me off.

"Probably best not, miss," Nell said, handing me the attractive gift from Aunt Penelope, which I had fortunately thought to bring with me. "It can get a bit windy when you're motoring at speed, or so I'm told."

I had hesitated but agreed and let her arrange the scarf around me so that it looked both fashionable and practical. Now I welcomed it. My hat would have blown off within the first ten yards.

Even in profile I could tell Cecilia was relishing every moment of my discomfiture. I tried to hide it, but it's difficult when your insides are threatening to erupt in a most unladylike manner. A sharp turn sent us whizzing round a bend and I swore we circumnavigated it on two wheels. The combination of speed and the stench of oil and petroleum made me gag. I reached into my purse for a handkerchief and held it over my mouth. Who cared what Cecilia thought? I was far more concerned about preventing a torrent of vomit from shooting up from my stomach.

The engine roar made conversation difficult. In my case, downright impossible. Cecilia laughed. "I can see you're not used to speed, Grace. In my family we all love it. Horses. Motors. Simon's a devil on a motor bike."

Was he? I had no idea. In fact, the more I thought about it, the less I was beginning to know about the man I had agreed to marry. Agreed to marry? I had jumped at the chance. I loved him. This wonderful, charming, attentive, intelligent man who found me attractive enough to go against the wishes of his family and make me his wife.

Cecilia spun the wheel as we negotiated another tight corner. I clung on to the door. She laughed and the sound of it grated on me. This was no mirthful jolly laugh. This was cruel, harsh. Born of someone who enjoyed inflicting discomfort on others. Maybe more. How far would her enjoyment of seeing others suffer go? Did it extend to actual physical violence? Simon had warned me not to cross her.

We roared into the village and screeched to a halt outside the pub. The Mordenhyrst Arms. Was there anything in this area that didn't have to share its name with the local gentry?

A cloud of dust and smoke billowed around us and made me choke. A few villagers stopped, saw who had disturbed the tranquility of their morning and, their suspicions confirmed no doubt, soon moved on. Cecilia opened her door and swung her perfect legs out in one smooth gesture.

"Come on, Grace. I need a drink."

I refrained from protesting that it was only ten forty-five, and I doubted the landlord would have opened up yet. I scrambled out, trying to control my skirt, which had ridden up and seemed hellbent on revealing far more of my legs than was seemly, even for 1928, while she thumped loudly on the door with one hand and rattled the handle with the other.

From inside, a male voice protested that it wasn't opening time yet.

"Oh, but you'll open up for me, won't you, Sykes? It's Lady Cecilia and I'm parched."

I joined her by the door. On the other side of it, bolts were drawn back, and the key turned. The door opened to reveal a tired-looking man in shirt sleeves and corduroy trousers. "Sorry, Your Ladyship, I didn't realize it was you."

"Quite all right, Sykes. Mind you, I did make quite an entrance. Woke up any village late sleepers at any rate."

"I was out back. In the...."

"Yes, I'm sure you were. Now, this is Grace Sutcliffe. She is staying at the Hall for a few days. What will you have to drink, Grace? I don't think Sykes has quite mastered the art of cocktail-making, even though my friends and I persevered with him. You remember that night, don't you, Sykes?"

"Yes, Your Ladyship."

"Oh dear." Cecilia gave a light laugh, so different to the one she had treated me to in the car. "Poor Sykes probably hasn't recovered. It was one day last spring. We had been to the races and felt like celebrating. I think it was five o'clock in the morning before we finally left, wasn't it?"

"Nearer six as I recall."

"Yes, well, we all had a ripping time and there wasn't too much damage, was there? A few glasses and such like. Never mind. Less to wash up." She laughed again. Sykes exchanged a look with me. Of course, it would never have occurred to Cecilia that each broken glass had to be paid for.

"I'll have a small sherry, please," I said.

"Oh, bugger that. She'll have a *large* sherry. Dry, if you have it. I'll have a Scotch on the rocks."

"I'm sorry, Your Ladyship, I don't have any ice."

"No ice? Oh dear, how tiresome. Oh well, I'll make do with a splash of the coldest water your tap can produce. Let it run for a minute or so."

Sykes poured Lia's Scotch and reached for a bottle of sherry of somewhat dubious origin. He uncorked it and poured me a generous glass. He then left us and returned soon after with a small jug of water.

I followed Cecilia to a table by the window and sat down.

"Chin-chin," she said, raising her glass.

I took a sip of my drink and my taste buds wrinkled in disgust. Maybe there wasn't much call for sherry among the villagers.

"You can see all human life from here," Cecilia said, indicating the view from the window. "All human life pertaining to the lower classes at any rate. This must all be quite new to you, Grace."

"In what way?" I asked.

"Well, you're surely not used to living in a grand house with servants at your beck and call. Each one knowing their place and happy to stick with it."

Anger boiled up inside. The urge to slap that too-perfect face almost overwhelmed me. I struggled to control my voice. "Actually, I *am* used to living in a large house with servants. Granted, Caldwell Grange isn't as grand as Mordenhyrst Hall, but it's a beautiful house set in stunning scenery. As for everyone knowing their place, my father's employees are happy to labor for him and they work extremely hard. In return, he provides decent wages and housing."

"How...charming it must be. Up there in rural Yorkshire. All those sheep would drive me mad. I've heard you eat with your servants. Is that true?"

"If you mean do we share the same table then, as a rule, no, we don't. Only at Christmas when, before the war, there was a tradition that the family served the staff their Christmas dinner on Christmas Eve. Sadly, after my brother was killed and my mother died, the tradition petered out. We also don't have as many servants as we used to. It's difficult to find young men and women who are prepared to enter service. I'm sure you face the same difficulties, Cecilia."

She didn't reply. Instead, she fixed me with a blank stare before opening her purse and extracting an enameled cigarette case and a telescopic holder. Next came the small, dainty lighter, monogrammed with her initials. She lit her cigarette, casually blew smoke in my direction and resumed her gaze out of the window. "I see the rector's being nobbled by Mrs. Chesterton. Really, the old biddy should be put out to grass. She's such a meddlesome old witch. Spreads the most fearful rumors. It looks like she has a particularly juicy tidbit to impart this morning. Oh dear, the poor rector."

Cecilia collapsed into fits of giggles. I observed the reverend looking as if he would welcome anyone to tear him away from his current ordeal. Mrs. Chesterton, meanwhile, seemed hellbent on telling her tale, whatever his reaction. Then she glanced over to the pub. She saw us in the window, pursed her lips and shook her head. So, *we* were her latest target. Maybe it was Cecilia's noisy entrance she objected to, or maybe.... The rector's expression changed as our eyes met. It turned from one of exasperation to one of concern. Cecilia was oblivious. Far too busy giggling. Mrs. Chesterton stormed off, head held high, straw hat firmly rooted to her head.

The rector lingered for a moment, then tipped his hat to me and moved slowly away. He stooped a little and I couldn't be sure if it was due to his advancing years or to the fear I had read in his face.

Cecilia had recovered herself enough to make an announcement. "I'm going to pop over to the post office to make a telephone call.

Too many ears at the Hall. At least Mrs. Prentice has a private room. You'll be all right here for a few minutes, won't you?"

Without waiting for my reply, she stood and was gone. The landlord came over, eyed my mostly full glass, and smiled. "Not very good, is it? Can I get you anything else, miss?"

"I think a nice glass of tomato juice would be just the ticket," I said.

"I'll get it for you." He took away the offending glass of sherry, along with Cecilia's drained whisky glass, and returned shortly with my drink.

"Thank you," I said. "May I ask you something, Mr. Sykes?"

"Yes. Miss?"

"Have you lived here all your life?"

"Yes, miss. I was born right here in the village. My mother was the postmistress before Mrs. Prentice and my father was the blacksmith."

"So, you know everyone and everything that goes on here. Especially owning this pub."

"Oh, I don't own this. Lease it. From Earl Mordenhyrst. He owns everything around here. The entire village in fact. The buildings, I mean. As for what goes on here…. Yes, you could say I pretty much know what's what."

"So, you would know about the late Lady Mordenhyrst."

Mr. Sykes sighed. "Such a tragedy. She was a lovely lady. Always had time to ask after your family. She took the trouble to know everyone in the village, everyone's name, what they did, whose children belonged to whom…. And she always took part in the activities. The May Queen, Summer Fete, Empire Day, all of that."

"It must have been a great shock when she died. Especially in the circumstances."

"It was, miss. Many of us couldn't believe it. I mean, we all knew that she and His Lordship, the earl I mean, hadn't been getting along too well, but that happens in the best of families. She had been looking a little pale, and I heard she hadn't been sleeping. When she did, she had nightmares."

"Nightmares? About what?"

"Oh, I don't know if I should pass that on, miss. It's just hearsay and it doesn't sound possible. Reckon old Mrs. Chesterton got her hands on a perfectly innocent story and gave it her usual embellishment."

"Nevertheless, Mr. Sykes, I would be grateful if you would furnish me with the details."

He hesitated. I was sorry to put the man in such a quandary, but I had to know. Especially after my own night in her late Ladyship's room.

Eventually he took a deep breath, leaned closer and spoke. "She would lock her door at night, and in the morning it would be open, even though the key was still in the lock on her side. And I heard she saw shadows on the wall that couldn't be there, and—"

The door opened and Cecilia breezed in. The landlord straightened. A brief look of annoyance flashed across Cecilia's face.

"I do hope you haven't been divulging all my family's worst kept secrets, Sykes."

"No, Your Ladyship. I mean...I don't know any secrets—"

Cecilia gave a dismissive wave of her hand. "Get me another drink, will you?"

"Straightaway, Your Ladyship."

Reeling from the similarity of the landlord's account with my own experience, I busied myself with adjusting my scarf while Cecilia sat down and scowled in the landlord's direction. I took a sip of my drink.

"I see you changed your mind about the sherry," she said, grimacing. "Can't abide the stuff, myself. I swear Sykes brews it up in his bath." She leaned closer. "You shouldn't pay too much attention to his ramblings, you know. This is a small village and there has been a certain amount of interbreeding. It probably accounts for the fact that there are a lot of people with similar facial characteristics."

Yes. And it's strange that so many of them bear more than a passing resemblance to the Mordenhyrsts. I tried to push the thought away but there was no denying that the same slightly jutting chin and deep-set eyes that enhanced Simon's features so effectively also had mixed effects on a number of people I had already seen, either working at the Hall or in this one short visit to the village. So, Aunt Penelope appeared to be right on that score, at least.

Sykes returned with Cecilia's drink.

She barely acknowledged him, added a little water and immediately took a healthy swig. "That's better." She placed her empty glass on the table. "Well, we're all set for two weeks' time, Grace. My friends will be coming. Just a small house party. The twins, of course, and Lilo. Pip D'Arcy and his new chum, Coralie Duquesne. Then there's Sy, me, you.... Just a cozy Saturday-to-Monday. A chance for everyone to meet you."

And give me the once-over, no doubt. I could hardly miss the cruel twist to Cecilia's mouth, but I chose to ignore it. "The twins?"

"Fleur and Persephone Montague-Tarleton. We were all at finishing school in Switzerland together. Percy called it being 'finished off'. She was probably right." Cecilia laughed. "Of course, I was a little older than those two, but we hit it off the day they started there. Been best friends ever since. Oh, I've also invited Billy Standish and his sister, Candice. She's emerging from the most unhappy love affair with Baron somebody or other. He's minor German royalty from one of their unpronounceable houses. Went off with an Italian contessa twice his age but loaded, of course. Sy's old chum from Eton, Fitz, will be coming. He had a thing for me once. Poor Fitz. He always misses his mark somehow. Percy's dotty about him and he can't see it. They would make the perfect couple. Simply divine. I shall do a spot of matchmaking. It could be quite amusing. Now, have I left anyone out? Oh yes, Dorcas Merryman. She'll make sure we don't have odd numbers. Can't abide odd numbers, it makes the seating arrangements so awkward. It does mean we shall be seven girls and five men but that can't be helped. Curzon Barchester was due to come but he's a no-show now thanks to his father cutting off his allowance. Some fuss about unpaid gambling debts so the poor boy's been recalled back to the family pile in Ireland. I'm afraid Dorcas is a frightful bore, and she has a face that would stop an express train, but at least we shall be an even number. I always call Dorcas 'Old Faithful'. She may be tedious but she always turns up."

I forced a smile and hoped it didn't look as fake as it felt. Out of twelve people invited for what was supposed to be *our* party, I would know precisely two. But at least I wouldn't be the only 'new girl' at this shindig. "Who is Coralie Duquesne? She sounds exotic."

"I really don't know. Other than she's American. Pip said we would all be in for quite a surprise. Personally, I already am. I always believed he was batting for the other team."

"Sorry? I don't understand."

Cecilia raised her eyes. "You really are sheltered up there in the wilds of Yorkshire, aren't you? Pip, my darling, is not as other men. Well, most of them anyway. He prefers the company of men of a certain disposition to ladies. You've heard of Greek love, I suppose? Now do you understand?"

I felt my cheeks burn. "Yes. I understand. Perfectly."

"So, you can see how surprised I was when he asked if he could bring her along. Of course, his family want him to marry well so maybe he's just caving in to the pressure. They're terribly well connected, but no money. I suspect Coralie, whoever she is, has tons of the stuff. She'll replenish the family coffers and make sure the D'Arcys can continue to live in the manner of splendid indolence and luxury to which generations of them have become accustomed. Anyway, time to make tracks. Finish your drink and let's get back to the Hall."

I took a final gulp of tomato juice and followed Cecilia to the door, thanking Sykes as I did so. It was only when Cecilia had driven off that I remembered.

"We didn't pay the bill."

"Of course not. We never do. It is Sykes's privilege to serve us. We bring custom to his quaint little hostelry."

If that were true, I wondered if any of them paid either.

Back at Mordenhyrst Hall, Simon was waiting for us in the drawing room. As we entered, he laid down his copy of *The Times* and stood to greet us. He kissed Cecilia warmly on the cheek and planted a more formal peck on mine. Once again it felt as if a drawbridge had been raised, separating us.

I sat, unwound the scarf around my head and neck, folded it and placed it beside me on the chair arm.

"How have you two girls enjoyed your morning?"

Cecilia blew out smoke from a cigarette she had just lit. "The same boring people in the village. Poor old rector looks on his last legs. Mrs. Chesterton was regaling him with some gossip or other."

Simon raised his eyes to heaven. "That woman is a menace. Honestly, Grace, she is a stalwart of the church. Flowers, cleaning, polishing brass, you name it.... If there's a roster for anything, it has her name on it and everything has to be done her way or there's hell to pay. Every Sunday you can hear her twittering at the back of church before the service, ruining reputations left, right and center. Five minutes later, she's singing 'Abide with Me' with the rest of the congregation as if butter wouldn't melt. Terrible old besom."

The door opened. Nell rushed in, white-faced. "I'm so sorry to interrupt, My Lady."

"Well, what is it, Nell?" Cecilia's irritation rankled me. The maid was clearly upset.

"Do you need to speak to me about something, Nell?" I asked.

Nell cast me a grateful glance and nodded.

"Very well. Excuse me," I said, and stood. The others said nothing, but I could feel their eyes burning into me. Outside the door, Nell's lip was quivering.

"Whatever is it?"

"I think you need to come and see," she said.

Whatever had happened, I had the strongest feeling I wasn't going to like it. Nell led me to my new room in the east wing. As she opened the door, I quickly saw why it had been named the Mauve Room. The color was everywhere. Walls, carpet, curtains, bedspread. Only white gloss paintwork had been added to break up the uniform color. Only that and....

"What *is* that?" I stood and stared at the wall opposite the window. It was smeared with strange swirls and sweeps of dirty charcoal. "It looks like some sort of bird got in and flew repeatedly at the wall."

Certainly, the patterns *looked* like they had been made by feathers. As I moved closer, I could see the distinctive marks made by many vanes and the less distinct trails of the downy barbs and after-feathers. In some places it looked as if a large bird had flattened itself against the wall after cloaking itself in ash. There were no beak marks and, mercifully, no blood. I touched the wall and examined my finger. It too was now coated in the lightest of ash that disintegrated when I rubbed it with my thumb.

"Honestly, miss, I don't know how this happened. No birds were in here, I swear. I came up this morning after you went out, and everything was fine. I put your things away, made sure everything was clean and tidy, bed made and so on, and then I thought it would be nice if you had a vase of spring flowers from the garden, so I went out to pick some. When I came back…. Well, it was like this."

On the dressing table, the vase of yellow freesias, red tulips, white gypsophila and blue columbine broke up the overwhelming mauve. The gentle scent, and vibrant colors…such a contrast to the inexplicable and disturbing images behind me.

I struggled to find an explanation. "But a bird must have flown in while you were out, Nell. It's the only explanation."

"I thought that, miss, but when I told Mrs. Bennett, she said it wasn't possible. No bird that big was in the house. At least—" Nell stopped as if she realized she had said too much.

"At least what, Nell?"

She looked up at me and shook her head. "Nothing, miss. Mrs. Bennett said no living bird could have got in here and done that."

"So, she's seen this, has she?"

Nell nodded, twisting her hands in front of her.

"And what was her explanation?"

"She didn't have one, miss."

By the way Nell avoided my eyes, I knew she was lying but it wouldn't do to put her in the position of having to choose between whether to betray a confidence of the housekeeper or obey me. I would speak to Mrs. Bennett myself.

I dismissed Nell and only after she was safely back belowstairs did I make my way down to the study and ring the bell. I guessed that, coming from that room, either Mrs. Bennett or Buckingham would answer. I was right. Mrs. Bennett seemed surprised when she saw who had summoned a member of staff.

"Mrs. Bennett, I understand Nell asked you to look at a wall in the Mauve Room earlier today."

"Yes, miss. She did."

"And do you have any idea what could have caused such a mess?"

"No, miss. I can't say I do." She was almost wringing her hands. I didn't believe a word of what she said.

"On the contrary," I said, doing my best to sound commanding, "I firmly believe you do have a very good idea as to the culprit. Would you please tell me your suspicions?"

Mrs. Bennett shifted her weight from one foot to the other, trying to conceal her action and failing in the attempt. "Has that Nell been saying anything?"

"No, she hasn't. Nell is a loyal member of staff, but I believe you voiced a suspicion to her, and I would also like you to voice it to me."

Mrs. Bennett shook her head. "I couldn't, miss."

"Whyever not?"

"Because…. Because it's family business. The Mordenhyrst family, I mean, and you not being a member of the family…. It wouldn't be right. Lady Cecilia wouldn't like it. She wouldn't like it at all."

"Never mind Lady Cecilia. I am shortly to become a member of this family and I must ask you to tell me what it is you suspect. After all, it was my room that was damaged in that way."

"I have instructed Nell to move you to another room."

"Lord Simon specifically requested that I stay in the Mauve Room."

"Mr. Buckingham is explaining to Lord Simon and Lady Cecilia what has happened."

I was getting nowhere and only succeeding in alienating someone whose help I would no doubt need in the weeks and months, years even, to come. "Very well, Mrs. Bennett, I will ask Lord Simon what he thinks."

"Probably best, miss. If that's all?"

"It is, Mrs. Bennett. Thank you."

A heavy crystal paperweight sat on the desk in front of me and I had the strongest urge to pick it up and smash it against a wall. In fact, the urge was so great I had to get out of there before I acted on it.

Back in the drawing room, Simon stood in front of the window while Cecilia lit yet another cigarette. Neither acknowledged my entrance. Both seemed lost in their own thoughts. I would put a stop to that.

"So, I take it you both know what happened in the Mauve Room?"

Cecilia glared at me. Simon turned and came toward me. He took my arms and steered me to a settee, where we both sat. It was the tenderest gesture I had received from him since we arrived.

"I'm so sorry, Grace. It never occurred to me that…. Look, it's a silly superstition—"

"Simon. Be careful." Cecilia's warning was an order, not a request.

"Dammit, *no*, Lia. Grace has a right to know."

"You're playing with fire."

"She *needs* to know."

"I need to know what, precisely?"

"You've seen our family crest? The falcon on the shield?"

"Yes."

"It's part of our heritage. Hundreds of years ago, an ancestor returned from the Crusades to find his wife had been unfaithful to him and had borne a son to this man. Needless to say, our ancestor was furious and vowed to hunt the man down and kill him. He banished his wife to a nunnery and the child was handed to one of the villagers to raise as their own. For years Sir Edmund de Mordenhyrst searched, and then, one day, twenty years after his betrayal, he discovered that the man who had cuckolded him was Lord Walter de Montagne, who owned most of the land around and was an expert falconer. Despite the difference in rank and the fact that both men were quite elderly, a duel took place. The concession was that each should choose their best falcon. It would be the falcons that dueled. To the death. Sir Edmund's falcon won. Lord Walter was devastated at the loss of his favorite bird and cursed Sir Edmund that his bird would haunt him and his progeny down through the ages until finally the line became extinct. Sir Edmund decreed that our falcon be added to our family crest as a sort of protection."

Cecilia laughed. "It's all a load of poppycock."

Simon turned on her. "If it's poppycock, Cecilia, why did you warn me not to speak of it just now?"

Cecilia shrugged.

I intervened. "But Simon, I'm not part of the family. Not yet anyway. Why would it target me, at this time?"

"I don't know," Simon said.

Cecilia made a noise somewhere between a chortle and an expression of disgust. "Maybe to stop you marrying into the family in the first place. Prevention is better than cure, after all."

"*Cecilia.*"

"Does your father know about this?" I asked, realizing I hadn't set eyes on the earl all day.

"Papa left earlier, while you and Lia were out. I was in the library. He came in, announced he was returning to France and left before I could even say goodbye. He's not even coming to the party."

"Isn't that a bit odd?" I asked. Not to mention rude.

"Not really," Cecilia said. "When Papa decides he has had enough, off he goes."

"But did he know about the wall?"

"I really have no idea," Simon said. "Possibly. No one mentioned it to me until after Nell came to get you."

"What time did he leave?" I asked.

"About half an hour before you returned."

The door opened and Buckingham entered. "Luncheon is served, My Lady," he said.

"Thank you, Buckingham," Cecilia said, standing and straightening her skirt. The butler bowed and turned to leave. I called him back.

"Buckingham. Did you tell the earl about the wall in the Mauve Room before he left?"

"Yes, miss. I thought he should know."

"And he left shortly after that?"

"Yes. He asked for his luggage to be sent on. His Lordship seemed in something of a hurry. Urgent business, I expect."

"I expect so," I said as I watched Simon and his sister exchange expressions I wished I could fully comprehend.

Once again, my things were moved into another room. As the décor was predominantly pinky-red I was unsurprised to learn it was called the Rose Room. It lived up to its name with wallpaper adorned with rosebuds, curtains of a soft red to match the bedcover and a deep-pile rose-red carpet. A feminine room that I would never have chosen for myself.

Nell performed her tasks diligently and without complaint, but I could see she was scared by what had happened. I also felt Simon slipping away from me more and more over the following days.

It had all changed in such a short time. That morning, he hadn't even joined me at breakfast. In fact, the previous night, instead of a loving embrace in the corridor before making our way to our separate rooms, he had wished me a perfunctory, "Good night," landed a peck on my cheek which was more dutiful than amorous and then immediately strode down to his room and, without a backward glance, opened it, entered and closed it behind him.

There was no escaping the fact. Everything had changed since we set foot on Mordenhyrst soil a few days earlier.

Now I wished with all my heart that we could leave, go back to London, and pick up our lives as if this trip had never happened. As if Cecilia didn't even exist.

When Simon wasn't up in London at the bank, he seemed to choose his sister's company over mine at every opportunity. They went on interminable rides together to which I was not invited. On the rare occasions I could get him on his own he appeared stiff and guarded. He never came to me in my room and the nearest he came to showing affection was the odd chaste peck on the cheek.

As for me, I walked in the gardens, picked flowers, arranged them, read *Country Life* and books. Fortunately, Mordenhyrst Hall boasted an extensive library of anything from Dickens through to Oscar Wilde, with the odd thriller thrown in for good measure. New crime writers like Agatha Christie and Dorothy L. Sayers rubbed shoulders with Sir Arthur Conan Doyle and kept me entertained during the long afternoons.

Two days before Cecilia's much vaunted Saturday-to-Monday, I finally grabbed the chance to speak to Simon. The last thing I wanted was to come across as a whiny, clinging woman, but I needed to know what was in his mind.

We were in the drawing room after lunch. Cecilia had gone up to London shopping for a dress or two for the weekend. Simon sat opposite me, smoking and drinking coffee.

"Can we talk?" I asked.

He frowned. "What about?"

"Us."

That frown again, this time accompanied by a slight shake of his head. "Us?"

"Yes. Our future. This is practically the first time we've been alone since we arrived. Did you know that?"

"I doubt that's the case but if you say so...."

"You can't deny you've been avoiding me."

"I certainly have *not* been avoiding you. I have been working and I've just been busy with other things. As have you, I should imagine."

"I hardly call reading, picking flowers and wandering around the garden keeping busy. And that's how I've been spending my time, Simon. You forget, I don't know anyone here."

"You know Cecilia, and she's been bending over backwards to make you welcome and include you in things."

I stared at him. Did he really believe that? "Cecilia has gone out of her way to make me most unwelcome. She has seized every chance to show how unworthy I am to be mistress of Mordenhyrst Hall – a role which I am quite certain she sees herself best prepared for."

"Now, that *is* absurd. My sister has done a marvelous job of stepping into the breach after Mama died but she will no doubt marry one day and then she will be off to manage her own household, which I am sure she will do splendidly."

"Do you really believe that? She's thirty-one years old, for heaven's sake. Most women of her age and position are already married with a brace of children. Honestly, Simon. I don't know what's happened to you since you got here but you're not the same man I met in London."

"And you're not the same girl. That Grace was fun-loving, carefree…. Now? You don't even look the same. That new hairstyle doesn't suit you, for a start."

I put my hand up to my shorter bob. Nell had cut my hair closer to my scalp so it didn't blow into an untidy mop whenever I went anywhere. It also fitted more snugly under the new cloche hats I had recently bought on an outing to the nearest town with Cecilia. She had commented on the way my hair insisted on sticking out however much I tried to tuck it under. Only a close cut would do, she insisted. Nell provided the solution. It was exceedingly short, and I had deliberately avoided the Louise Brooks helmet look favored by Cecilia, who had, for once, complimented me on my change of style. Had she just said that, knowing Simon would hate it?

And hate it he did. In no uncertain terms. "It makes you look like a bluestocking. Especially with that side parting."

"*What?*"

"I'm sorry, Grace, but someone had to say it. You look almost masculine. If it weren't for the makeup, you could be taken for a boy. A pretty one, but a boy no less."

I squirmed inwardly and hoped the feeling didn't translate into the physical. "That's uncalled for," I said.

"Is it? Honestly, Grace, I don't know what you're trying to prove, but I'm at a loss to know where I am with you anymore. I admit I haven't been as attentive as you might have liked. I have a lot of work at the moment. Some important new business has come my way rather unexpectedly, so I've needed to attend to it. I'm sorry for that but when I told Cecilia, she told me not to worry and she would take you under her wing."

"Simon, don't you think it would have been better if you had spoken to me yourself, rather than discussing me with your sister? I might well have decided to return to London, which would, I'm sure, have been preferable to her. She's made it quite clear she doesn't like me or the fact that we are engaged. If indeed we still are."

"Of course we are."

"Then why don't you behave like it? Not one word of concern after that first night of my stay here when both Nell and I were frightened half out of our wits. Not one word after the incident in the Mauve Room. Now I'm in a room halfway down the corridor from yours but do I see you? No."

"It would hardly be proper for me to come to your room after dark, would it?"

"Whyever not? The rest of your set – your sister included – seem to think it's perfectly acceptable. I've heard Cecilia planning who shall sleep where during her Saturday-to-Monday to make sure no one has to wander too far and get lost or, worse still, stumble in on someone they haven't planned to spend the night with."

"Don't be ridiculous."

"Am I? Ask her yourself if you don't believe me. My location is proving really troublesome for her. Evidently Persephone – or Percy as she likes to be called – has a thing for your old schoolfriend, Fitz… whatever his name is, so she wants them to be close together and because another friend, Pip D'Arcy, has elected to bring a female friend, who, Cecilia is sure, will want to be near her beau. My room is slap bang in the center, ruining her arrangements. She's made it clear how tiresome it is."

"Look, Grace, I'm not prepared to sit here discussing my sister's party arrangements. It's bad enough she has to bring these tedious people here in the first place. They hardly possess one brain cell between them and have no conversation worth entering into. But she's doing it for you so you can meet people of your own class."

"That's just it, she doesn't believe they *are* my class. In her opinion, I rank well below any of them. Not only that, she has never once referred to this house party as being in our honor. As far as she's concerned, it's one of her regular get-togethers."

Simon stood abruptly and jammed his cigarette into the ashtray, sending flakes of tobacco flying onto the highly polished side table. "I'm going out for some fresh air. I need to clear my head from all this nonsense."

"I'll come with you."

"No, Grace, I'd rather be on my own for a bit. I need to think."

At least he didn't slam the door behind him, but the atmosphere remained heavy in the room after he'd gone and it wasn't solely due to the smoldering, ruined cigarette in the ashtray.

Tears pricked my eyes and I blinked them back. I would not cry. I wouldn't give that sister of his the satisfaction.

I trudged upstairs. I needed some time to collect my thoughts and make some sense of why I was even here. I was passing the Mauve Room when I heard a noise. I stopped. It came again. A scurrying. A fluttering of wings?

My mouth dry, I clasped the door handle and turned it, careful not to make a noise. It opened smoothly and I sidled in.

Sunlight filtered through the net curtains covering the closed windows as I took stock of the room. On the wall, a ghostly yet distinctive silhouette of a large bird made me gasp. It must be a stain. A patch of damp maybe. But it looked so familiar. I thought of the family crest. That falcon. Were there falcons around here?

A sudden noise made me jump. Something was tapping at the window. It sounded like a claw. I switched my gaze and saw a large bird take to the wing and fly off. I dashed to the window in time to see it circling and swooping. It must have been at least two feet in length, with ghostly white speckled plumage. Its wings were tapered and its wingspan…maybe four feet. It turned and its eyes met mine. There was something in those dark eyes that made me look away. For one second, I felt I had stared into the depths of hell.

But that was impossible. I was being fanciful, lured by an old superstition. It was a bird. A big one. But a bird nonetheless. And if it was a falcon, so what? Maybe someone kept them locally. I resolved to ask Nell about it and forced myself to look back at the bird, just in time to see it soar upward and fly off into the distance.

I don't know how long I stayed there, staring. Waiting for…I didn't know what. The bird to return? The marks on the wall seemed to take on a life of their own. The ashen silhouette of the large bird's wing seemed to flutter before my eyes. At the same time, I felt a rush of air pass by me as if it had taken off and flown too close. I flinched and put my hand to my cheek. A touch, like a kiss of feathers, had stroked my face while a half-seen image of a ghostly bird flew across the room.

And a voice. A woman's voice. Soft, modulated, her words indistinct…then a sigh, so soft it barely registered, but I knew I had heard it. And I knew it wasn't my imagination.

I grasped the door handle, pulled it open, and left the room, as a waft of expensive perfume tickled my nose, gone as soon as I closed the door.

Later, alone in the Rose Room, I studied my reflection in the mirror. I turned my head this way and that. Did I look like a boy? If I had to be honest, Simon did have a point. The side parting particularly.

I combed my hair forward, obliterating the severe parting. The transformation was instant. Now my look could have been designed in Hollywood. The only trouble was, the resulting helmet of hair á la Louise Brooks was pretty much identical to Cecilia's. Would she think I had deliberately copied her and be flattered?

Oh, to hell with her if she did.

I patted my hair down in its new style just as Nell entered. She caught sight of my reflection and her startled expression told me she hadn't expected what she saw. Doubt crept in. Had Nell restyled my hair under Cecilia's orders? She had certainly encouraged it. Was Nell someone I really could trust after all? One thing was certain. Any conversations about falcons would have to wait for now.

★　★　★

Fleur and Persephone Montague-Tarleton were the first to arrive, alighting from their Hispano-Suiza with the practiced air of women who have studied deportment. They were non-identical twins, although they did their best to counter that by dressing, if not identically, then in similar style. Their dresses today were sheer violet silk, glittering with silver metallic thread woven into intricate swirls and sat slightly above the knee. Silk-clad legs culminated in matching pairs of high-heeled satin shoes with silver bow-buckles. Their hair, obviously dyed, was platinum blonde for Fleur and fiery red for Persephone.

"Call me Percy or I shall die. Simply die," she said when Cecilia introduced the sisters to me.

"We've heard so much about you," Fleur said, eyeing me up and down as if she was appraising a horse at Ascot. "Haven't we, Percy?"

"Oh yes, darling. Absolutely loads." Her sister laughed, revealing even white teeth behind lips of vivid scarlet.

Both women wore their hair Marcel-waved, and each sported a glittering headband augmented with a white ostrich feather. Both accepted martinis offered to them on a silver tray by Joseph. They moved away from me and entered into deep conversation with Cecilia, punctuated by affected, girlish laughter that rapidly grated on me.

Beside me, Simon handed me a martini and I took a generous swig. If I was going to derive any pleasure from this evening, I might as well enlist alcohol to help me relax. I was so on edge, my fingers trembled when I raised the glass.

Simon must have noticed. "It's all right, you know. Their bark is much worse than their bite." He squeezed my free hand and winked at me. I squeezed back and winked at him. It was as if a chunk of ice fell off the massive iceberg that had come between us.

The door opened and we all looked to see who had arrived. Buckingham announced, "Mr. Lionel Smythe-Leverton."

"Lilo, darling!" Cecilia rushed to greet the tall, slim young man, who bore more than a passing resemblance to Cecil Beaton. His mannerisms were wide and exaggerated and he moved in short steps as if his shoes were too tight.

"Dearest Lia. Simply wonderful to see you." They kissed on both cheeks, but I doubt their lips touched skin. Lilo's wandering eyes rested on me. He released Cecilia and sidled toward us.

"Simon. Looking handsome as ever. And this must be Grace, about whom much has been said but little understood."

Simon gave a light laugh while I wondered what on earth he was talking about.

"Lilo, always a pleasure to see you. May I present Grace Sutcliffe. My future wife."

How good that sounded, and I realized I hadn't expected him to introduce me like that. It warmed and reassured me with a rush of heat that I'm sure made it to my cheeks.

"Simply delightful." Lilo leaned in and I realized I too was about to get the continental kiss. I submitted and returned. The man certainly smelled good. Gardenia, I thought, and some perfumed pomade he put on his hair to make it gleam like a black mirror.

Once again, the door opened and our attention was distracted. The latest guests were arriving.

"Mr. William Standish, Miss Candice Standish and Miss Dorcas Merryman."

"Darlings!" Cecilia greeted them, arms spread wide. Simon moved forward, his hand cupping my elbow.

Air kisses abounded as Cecilia welcomed her friends before waving her arm vaguely in my direction. "This is Simon's new friend, Grace Sutcliffe. She's from Yorkshire, as you will soon tell the moment she opens her mouth to speak."

"I'll make the introductions," Simon said, his voice tinged with annoyance. "Grace, this is Dorcas Merryman. Dorcas, may I present my *fiancée*, Miss Grace Sutcliffe?"

The plain, rather horsey-looking woman had kind eyes and she used them on me now, giving me a smile that conveyed a mix of friendliness and sympathy. I smiled back.

"A pleasure to meet you, Grace," she said in a cut-glass accent that, like Cecilia's, sounded forced and practiced.

"And these two reprobates are Billy and his baby sister, Candice Standish."

Billy laughed and his sister gave a girlish giggle.

"Happy to meet you, Grace. About time Simon here was caught and bagged. Time to stop sowing those wild oats, eh, Mordenhyrst? Mind you, marriage never stopped your father, did it?"

"*Billy.*" Candice's shocked expression stopped her brother in his tracks.

Simon tutted and then burst out laughing. "Same old Billy. Tactful as a bull in a china shop."

Billy blushed. "Sorry, old chap. Mouth ran away with me."

Simon turned to me. "And that's *before* he's had a drink. You should see him when he's downed a few." To Candice, he said, "Try and rein him in, Candy. There's a good girl."

Candice nodded and the couple moved off in search of martinis.

Buckingham entered again. "Mr. Peter Fitzroy."

"Fitz, old bean!" Simon left my side and dashed over to greet his old friend. They shook hands warmly and Simon slapped the smiling man on the back. "Good to see you. It's been far too long. Cowes last year, wasn't it?"

"I think so. Yes, it must have been."

"Come and meet Grace."

Fitz fixed me with a smile that didn't quite reach his eyes. He also seemed to be looking slightly over my left shoulder. My instant reaction was one of distrust. Something about this man didn't fit. Nevertheless, I held out my hand and he touched his lips to it.

"Charmed," he said. "I say, Simon, is that who I think it is?" He nodded to someone behind me. "Of course, she had long brown hair the last time I saw her."

"Yes."

"Dashed awkward, old chap. In the circumstances, I mean."

I must have looked enquiring because Simon saw fit to remember my presence at that moment. "Fitz and Fleur had a bit of a thing a few years ago."

"I say, steady on, it was more than that. We were pretty much engaged, only her father put the kibosh on the whole shebang. I wasn't good enough for his precious daughter. He was holding out for a title and a fat lot of good that's done him. He's still got both his daughters on his hands and no title in sight."

Simon leaned in. "I have it from an impeccable source that Daddy Montague-Tarleton is pretty much ready to give either or both of them away to anyone who'll have them these days. Provided they have enough dosh to foot their bills at Harrods, of course. Fancy trying your hand again, Fitz?"

Simon's friend screwed his face up. "I think I have done sufficient paddling in that particular pool," he said. "Of course, if she gives any encouragement, a short dalliance might be pleasant."

Simon laughed. "You old dog. You never change."

Fitz winked at me, and I wished he hadn't. I felt suddenly dirty, and a sour taste filled my mouth. Fitz moved off in Fleur's direction. He tapped her on the shoulder, she turned, gave an exclamation of feigned surprise, and kissed him warmly on both cheeks. I guessed that would be one set of feet I would hear padding down my corridor later.

The door opened once again, and the chatter died down as Buckingham cleared his throat.

"Mr. Phillip D'Arcy and…companion."

Pip bounded into the room looking as if he had just left the tennis courts, had changed into a dark suit, white shirt and bow tie and then charged straight over. His energy was infectious. "Hello, everybody. I want you to meet…Miss Coralie Duquesne, my good friend from New Orleans in Louisiana, America."

It seemed everyone in the room froze as the tall, slender woman entered. She was immaculately dressed in a scarlet gown with fashionable drop waist and matching satin high heels. Diamonds glittered at her throat, wrist and in her ears. Her hair was elegantly styled, short and crowned with a scarlet headband also embellished with diamonds. But it was none of this that made everyone in the room stare speechless. It was something she was born with.

Coralie Duquesne was Black.

Simon broke the silence. "Pip, bring your friend over here. I want you both to meet Grace."

Pip took Coralie's hand and came over. Meanwhile, chatter gradually started up again. It was clear who was the topic of conversation, and it wasn't me.

"Grace, this is an old school chum, Phillip D'Arcy, but we always call him Pip and…would you like to do the honors, Pip?"

"What? Oh, yes. This is Coralie."

"Pleased to meet you," I said, holding out my hand and smiling. Coralie smiled back, an expression that only served to enhance her beauty. I guessed her heritage might be mixed as she had the high cheekbones of a Cherokee man I had once met briefly who had been part of a traveling show over from America.

"Why don't I fetch you both a martini?" Simon said. "Or perhaps you would like something else?" he said to Coralie.

"Martini would be just fine," she said.

Simon nodded and moved away to get the drinks.

"Pip. Oh, do come and tell us all your latest news." Cecilia linked her arm through Pip's and steered him away. He didn't put up any resistance. "You will excuse us won't you, Coralie? We're old friends and have so much to catch up on." Before Coralie could respond, Pip was halfway across the room, being expertly maneuvered toward Fleur, Fitz and Percy. That left me alone with Coralie.

"Is she always like that?" The woman's soft Southern drawl was tinged with the slightest of French accents. "Oh, I'm sorry, is she a particular friend of yours?"

"Hardly. She's my future sister-in-law, although if she has anything to do with it, that will never happen. I'm afraid that where manners are concerned, Cecilia doesn't feel they apply to her."

"I guess from your accent that you're feeling as much out of step here as I am."

I warmed to Coralie instantly, although quite what she was doing with Pip D'Arcy was anyone's guess. Coralie had an easy manner, but she exuded a sensuousness and an exotic air that, if rumors about Pip were accurate, would be entirely lost on him. Simon arrived with her martini, saw us exchanging a conspiratorial laugh and left us to it. I realized that was probably the first time I had laughed since I arrived at Mordenhyrst Hall.

"Come on and let's sit a spell, over here." Coralie indicated a vacant settee with a table for our drinks. Once we had settled ourselves, she leaned closer. "I don't want to say this too loudly, but do you see auras?"

"Auras?"

"Everyone gives off an aura. Different colors represent different moods or characteristics of a person. A sort of illuminated signature if you like. It's a spectral field that surrounds them. Some of us have the gift of being able to see them. When I look at these people, I see a whole spectrum of colors emanating from them. Of course, there are many layers, but to put it simply, I don't think I have ever been in a room where there have been so many people emanating black in their aura. Not your fiancé though. He has a lot of red in his, so he is stable, grounded. At least...." She frowned, then shook her head. "Pip is the only other one with no black, but as for the others...." She made a rocking gesture with her hand and raised her eyes skyward. "Cecilia's is the worst. So much black. I can barely see another color in there."

"And what does that mean?"

"Well, it ain't good, honey, let's put it that way. I wouldn't cross her. In fact, I would have as little to do with her as possible. That lady is one great big piece of bad news."

"That's going to be a little difficult, if Simon and I do eventually make it up the aisle."

Coralie touched her temple with her hand and winced.

"Are you all right?"

She looked as if she was about to faint. Her eyes closed and she swayed slightly. Then she seemed to recover herself, took a deep breath and a swig of her drink. "Whew, that wasn't pleasant."

"What happened?"

"Someone trying to get in, or...something. I couldn't tell. It was there and gone too quickly. Close call though."

I hadn't a clue what she was talking about, and it must have shown in my face because she suddenly laughed. "I'm so sorry, Grace. You must think I'm insane. A lot of people do."

"Can you explain it to me?"

"You look at me and you see a Black woman, right? Oh, they call us all sorts of names, some acceptable, most not, but essentially people would say, 'Coralie Duquesne? You mean that *Black* woman? How did she come into so much money?' Or words to that effect. The fact is, I have more nationalities in my heritage than the League of Nations. On my mother's side, there's African, Cherokee, even Irish, I believe. On my father's, Caribbean, French – that's where the Duquesne name originated – Romanian and Armenian. As for our fortune.... Well, that's a long story involving a diamond mine in South Africa and a gold mine in California, plus a succession of extremely astute businessmen on my father's side and a whole lot of shenanigans in the last century that are best not spoken of in polite society. So, here I am. The last in the line and expected to make a good marriage. I have a handsome dowry and stand to inherit a whole lot more when Pa finally moves on to his happy hunting ground. He is determined that before that happens, he'll see me married to an English aristocrat with a title to bestow on me. It's his final ambition and, as Pa isn't too well these days, I thought I should at least give it a try."

"I don't think Pip has a title, does he?"

"Pip?" She laughed. "Oh, you don't think…. Oh no, Grace. Not Pip. We're not together. It's convenient for him to have me on his arm at social events. Stops awkward questions, although this time around, it was at my initiation. Bless him. He's not the brightest, but he is my introduction into your polite society. Mind you, from what I've seen, there are poor Black kids on the streets of Harlem that could teach this lot something about being polite."

"I'm quite sure you're right about that. But tell me more about this gift you have."

"Gift? Sometimes it feels more like a curse. My mother had it and her mother before her, but it seems the mix of blood between her family and my father's has intensified everything to such a point that what you just saw can happen. I become a target for negative energies that see me as a threat."

"Why a threat?"

"Because I can see them, recognize them for what they are, and I also know how to deal with them." Coralie looked around the room. "Pip knows a little of my – shall we say abilities? Not much though. I haven't felt inclined to talk to him in the way I'm speaking to you now, so he doesn't have a clue the real reason I wanted to come here. I merely said I was curious to meet the Mordenhyrsts. I had read an article about them in one of those society magazines and there was a photograph of Mordenhyrst Hall. Something about the sight of it got to me. I had a feeling about this place even before I set my foot to the ground and I had to come here and see for myself. Boy, was I right. This house has more than its fair share of negative energy and it is quite capable of physical manifestation. Have you seen anything strange since you've been here?"

I didn't hesitate. I told her about the first night and about the strange marks on the wall of the Mauve Room. Her expression grew more concerned as I described each event.

"So, what do you think caused it?" I asked.

"Something that doesn't want you here. Something that sees you as a threat."

I nodded over to Cecilia, who was on the far side of the room, with her back to me. "You mean...?"

"Possibly, or something much older and stronger."

"Are we talking about a person here or...something else?" I hadn't a clue what to call it.

"I don't know yet but.... Watch out, we have company."

"Here you are, Coralie," Cecilia said. "All safely delivered to you in one piece." She unwound herself from Pip's arm.

"Oh, Lia," Pip said. "You are such a terrible tease. You know perfectly well that Coralie and I are simply friends, aren't we, Coralie?"

"Indeed we are, Pip. Just good friends."

Coralie never let her gaze wander from Cecilia's face. It was as if she was trying to penetrate that too-perfect veneer. Whatever she was doing, she had certainly caught Simon's sister off guard.

Cecilia looked around. "Oh Fleur, I must ask you something. About Ascot." In a cloud of expensive perfume, she was off.

Pip stood awkwardly for a moment. "I can see you two ladies are getting along splendidly so I'll leave you to your conversation, but may I get you some more drinks?"

"That would be fine, Pip," Coralie said.

"Yes, please," I added.

Pip seemed relieved to have an excuse to absent himself.

"Great martini," Coralie said, draining her glass. "Dry, just as I like it."

"Simon mixes them. The bartender at Claridge's gave him the recipe."

"I shall have to acquire it myself."

"I'm sure Simon will take that as a compliment, coming from an American."

"Maybe he will at that."

I wondered why she sounded doubtful. Surely, she didn't mean that Simon would treat her any differently because of her color? But how would I know? Thinking back, I couldn't ever remember meeting a Black woman before, but now that I had, it made no difference to me. I liked her. We had something in common, as she herself had said. Neither of us quite fitted in with the company we were keeping. I felt a wave of gratitude that fate had brought us together. At least now I would have someone I could talk to. As long as she didn't decide to return to the States anytime soon.

Our drinks replenished, we chatted some more until Buckingham entered to declare that dinner was served. We paired up. Or at least, everyone else did. Cecilia cornered Simon, Fitz took Fleur's arm, Lilo went with Candice, Billy with Dorcas and Pip partnered Coralie, leaving Percy and me bringing up the rear.

"She won't let him go, you know," Percy whispered to me. "Not ever."

Before I could ask her what she meant by that remark we were going into dinner and separated. Cecilia sat at one end of the table and Simon at the other. I was positioned on Cecilia's left-hand side, too far to exchange any pleasantries with my fiancé and, as Coralie was seated to his right, I couldn't speak to her either. Next to me, Pip was far more interested in gossiping to Fleur. No one took the slightest bit of notice of me, and it didn't matter. I had nothing to say to these people.

After dinner, Cecilia and Simon put the latest dance records on the gramophone and vigorous demonstrations of mixed degrees of prowess at the Charleston and Black Bottom ensued. Coralie was even persuaded to join in, to rapturous applause.

Percy was at her most vocal, following a lavish quantity of wine at dinner. "I say, Coralie, have you ever thought of taking that up professionally? I'm sure you'd give Josephine Baker a run for her money at the Folies Bergère. Do you know her, by the way?"

"No, I don't."

"Oh, I thought your paths might have crossed."

"Sadly, they haven't. Have *you* met her?"

Percy looked as if she had smacked her. "Me? Gracious no. Where would I meet a burlesque dancer, for heaven's sake?"

"I have no idea. I haven't met any either."

Conversation stopped, stone dead. The two women were like cats, each trying to outstare the other. I knew who my money was on. I won my bet. Percy changed the subject.

"How about another record, Simon? I fancy another Charleston."

Simon obliged.

Coralie came to sit by me. "You're not a fan of dancing then?"

"I'm not very good at it. Two left feet, I'm afraid. I had lessons when I was younger. I learned the waltz, foxtrot and all those other dances that no one ever does these days. I tried the Charleston but kept falling over or tripping over my feet."

"I could teach you, if you want. Your fiancé seems to enjoy taking to the dance floor."

I watched him executing some nifty moves with Cecilia while Fleur and Percy cantered around the room in increasingly unsteady undulations. Pip cheered from the sidelines and Lilo appeared to have nodded off on a chair.

"I may take you up on that offer, Coralie. Thank you."

She reached into her evening purse and withdrew a small piece of white card. "Here's my address and telephone number in London."

I glanced at it. "Belgravia. You're not far from where I'm staying with my aunt."

"Excellent. You shall come for coffee when you get back. When will that be?"

"As soon as I can extricate myself from here," I said, surprising myself at the vehemence with which I uttered those words. To have Coralie, who clearly possessed some psychic ability, confirm that all was not well here merely served to bring all my fears bubbling up once more to the surface. The big question was, of course, if I felt like this now, could I really go through with my impending marriage? Merely doing it to spite Cecilia was hardly a good enough reason to decide the destiny of my future life.

I had some serious thinking to do.

"Coralie." Cecilia's voice broke into my thoughts. She advanced toward us, wafting tobacco smoke from a bejeweled cigarette holder. She completely ignored my presence and addressed herself to my companion. "Pip here tells us you can see into the future. He says you're an absolute Ducky's quack with tarot cards."

Her sarcastic tone was clearly not lost on Coralie. Between us, she clenched her hand into a tight fist before releasing it and splaying taut fingers. It was as if she was channeling all her pent-up anger into that one gesture.

What was Cecilia up to? Surely she could see that Coralie possessed real powers. I knew at that moment that those powers could do great harm if released, yet my future sister-in-law continued to stare at her, her lips in a mocking half-smile.

Everyone had stopped talking. All eyes were fixed on the two women.

"A 'Ducky's quack'? Does he now?" Coralie glared at the hapless Pip, who looked as if he wished the ground would open and transport him away from his embarrassment. "Actually, the cards I use are not tarot. Their origins are far older. The pack itself is at least eleven hundred years old."

The whole party exclaimed their amazement at this, me included.

"And you can read the future with them?" Percy said. "It's all rubbish, isn't it? The stuff of fairgrounds and gypsies."

Coralie's stare must have chilled Percy, because she shivered and moved away.

"An ancestor of mine died for possessing the cards," Coralie said, ignoring the effect she had on Percy. "She was accused of witchcraft.

Clothilde Gasparyan was burned at the stake, but they never found the cards. By the time the first faggot was lit, they and her daughter were many miles away from Connecticut."

Coralie certainly knew how to hold an audience's attention. Finally, Cecilia spoke. "I think Coralie should give us a demonstration of her powers. Do you have the cards with you?"

Coralie shook her head. "I never carry them around with me. They are in a safe place."

"Here or in New Orleans?" Fleur asked.

"I never reveal the whereabouts of the cards. Knowledge is power."

"But you can tell us, surely?" Cecilia said.

"Not if she doesn't want to, Lia," Simon said as he gave an almost imperceptible shake of his head.

But Cecilia was not to be thwarted. "It doesn't matter anyway because Pip says you can do all sorts of things." I couldn't believe what she was doing. Cecilia was mocking Coralie. Goading her. She turned to her friends. "She can see colors around you and tell you what sort of person you really are."

Lilo let out an exaggerated giggle. "Whatever would I want to know that for? I know what sort of person I am."

"As do we all, darling." Percy, who appeared to have recovered her composure, blew out a cloud of smoke.

Her twin laughed. "You are a card, Percy."

"Thank you, darling."

What made me open my mouth, I will never know, but I did. "I think Coralie should decide for herself what she wants to do and not be pressured by any of us. She's not a performing seal, for heaven's sake."

Cecilia looked down at me. "I don't remember asking for *your* opinion, Grace. I'm quite sure Coralie can speak for herself. Can't you, Coralie?" Once again, Cecilia blanked me out.

Coralie stood, her face expressionless. "Thank you for an... interesting evening, Cecilia. Right now, I'm feeling rather tired and I'm going to retire for the night. Good night, one and all."

"Shame," Cecilia said. "Still, there's always tomorrow. Maybe you can show us one of your party tricks then."

Coralie stopped at the door. She spun round on her heel. "Cecilia, whatever knowledge or wisdom I possess, it is most assuredly not born of any party trick. When I look at you, I see a lost soul. More than that, I see a soul whose existence is in danger. There is a black aura around you and it's growing closer, cloaking itself ever tighter around you to stop any light getting in. Soon your soul won't be able to breathe because of it. It will wither and die. As will you."

A stunned atmosphere hung heavy in the room. Coralie left, closing the door firmly behind her. Her footsteps faded on the marble floor.

Simon broke the silence. "Well, that was some exit, wasn't it? I wonder how long it took her to rehearse that little piece."

It broke the ice and they all laughed; Pip and Lilo a little nervously, and Cecilia's laughter was brittle, a smile extending no further than the corners of her mouth. It seemed I alone failed to see the humor in Simon's words. Once again, he had disappointed me. This whole evening was supposed to be a celebration of us and, I had assumed, our engagement, but not once had that been mentioned. Simon showed no sign of rectifying that either. Was this really the same man I had fallen in love with?

CHAPTER FOUR

I came down at nine-thirty to find Cecilia had already breakfasted and was out riding with Pip and Lilo. Through the window, I saw Coralie taking a walk around the garden, where early roses were already in bloom. I was alone in the dining room with Simon, who was tucking into a breakfast of eggs, bacon and deviled kidneys. The rest of the house party, judging by the set places, hadn't yet emerged.

Picking lid after lid off the array of silver chafing dishes, I inhaled the delicious aromas, but nothing would unclench my stomach enough to entice me to eat. Joseph brought fresh toast and I settled for a slice of that along with a cup of strong coffee.

"Not hungry?" Simon indicated my meager fare.

I shook my head. "I was thinking I would go back to London."

Simon paused, his fork halfway to his mouth. He replaced it on the plate. "What's brought that on?"

He needed to ask? I bit my tongue. "Wasn't yesterday supposed to be our engagement party? No mention was made of it."

"Ah, yes. Well Cecilia felt...I mean, we both felt that as Papa had needed to return to France and your father couldn't be with us—"

"I wasn't aware my father had even been invited."

"We thought that he would feel out of place with our friends. Not his sort of people."

I slammed my hand down so hard on the table that the plates rattled. "Oh, come on, Simon. I'm not nearly as stupid and vacuous as some of your fancy friends."

"That's hardly polite, Grace."

"Polite? Don't lecture me about being polite. Your sister and her...*chums*...are some of the rudest people I have ever had the misfortune to encounter. In fact, you yourself have complained about their shallowness and ignorance, or perhaps you've forgotten that? And don't pretend you have anything to do with the decisions made around here because I won't believe you. Mordenhyrst Hall has one mistress and that is your sister. In all but name, Mordenhyrst Hall is hers to rule over like some old-fashioned dictator."

Simon threw his napkin on the table. "You're going too far, Grace."

"Too far? I have barely started." My heart was racing and my anger was at full gallop. I knew I had to rein it in fast or I would say something I should regret later. I took a series of deep breaths, aware of Simon staring at me as if he had never really seen me before.

When I finally trusted myself to speak, I carried on, keeping my voice low. "I think it's obvious to all of us that I don't belong here. Your sister has done her utmost to drive me out, her friends look down their aristocratic noses at me, and the only person who has shown me any consideration is someone who also feels unwelcome at Mordenhyrst Hall. Coralie."

"That's hardly fair, Grace. You haven't given us a chance yet. I see no evidence you have made any effort to get along with Lia, or any of the others for that matter. Last night, you and Coralie set up your own little clique and spent the entire evening in a *téte-à-téte*. I wanted to come and have a chat with you, get you up for a Charleston, but you blocked me out completely."

Had we been at the same party? "The reason Coralie and I spent so much time together was because everyone else ignored us. That is, until they wanted Coralie to perform for them. Their behavior towards her was nothing less than insulting. I found myself cringing at some of their crass comments. Especially that Fitz, and as for Persephone—"

"There's nothing wrong with Percy. She can go a little far sometimes, as can Lia, but she's harmless. If you tried to get along with them, I'm sure they would welcome you with open arms. After all, when we're married, they will be your friends too."

"I doubt that."

Simon pushed his plate away and lit a cigarette. Joseph immediately removed the half-eaten breakfast. After the footman had departed, Simon leaned forward. "You doubt what? That they will be your friends or that we will be married?"

I inhaled deeply. "Both."

He sat bolt upright as if I'd shot him but recovered himself before speaking. "When were you planning on telling me?"

"I didn't. Plan it, I mean. Simon, can't you see how different you are here? I've said it before. It's as if this house exerts some kind of force on you. Coralie can sense something here too. She told me last night."

"That's a load of mumbo jumbo. It's all the rage down in the Deep South of America, I believe. Voodoo and spells, black magic, that sort of nonsense."

"She was being entirely serious."

"And you bought into it?"

"It's not a question of buying into it. She was honest and sincere. Take what she said about Cecilia's aura—"

"Her *what*?"

"Aura. The colors around her. You heard what she said as she left the room. There's a blackness all around your sister. It hangs there like a shroud."

Simon threw back his chair and stood so abruptly, it toppled over. The footman returned and immediately started to set it upright. "That'll be all, Joseph."

Still the footman tried to do his job. Simon's voice rose. "I said, that'll be *all*."

Joseph let the chair fall back. "Very good, My Lord." He hurried out.

"Grace, if you feel like this then perhaps you *should* go back to your aunt. Maybe even back to Yorkshire. Perhaps some time apart will do us good."

"You're going to stay on here?"

"Yes. For a week or so."

"And carry on traveling all the way to London and back three or four times a week?"

"Why not?"

I pushed my chair back from the table. "Fine. I'll pack my bags and be out of here on Monday when everyone else leaves. I'll telephone my aunt and warn her."

Simon ran his hand through his hair. At that moment, he looked uncomfortable rather than angry, almost as if he wished he could take his words back. When he spoke, his tone was conciliatory. "Grace, I'd rather you didn't leave with everyone else. Flapping tongues and all that. Why not wait until the end of the week? Give us all one more chance...." His face brightened up. "I'll tell you what, how about we drive into the village this morning? I'll introduce you to some of the locals."

I hesitated. For a second or two the old Simon had returned, hot on the trail of the Mordenhyrst Hall version, who had knocked the chair over. Could I make this Simon stay? A rush of the old feelings came flooding over me and I nodded before I was aware of what I was doing.

Simon smiled, looking genuinely relieved. "That's settled then. Let's see if we can't make you change your mind about us here at the old Hall."

There was no sign of Coralie as we drove off in Simon's Alvis. The sun was shining, and it was warm for early June, so Simon put the top down. The light breeze caressed my face. Nothing like fresh spring air to put things into perspective and restore the spirit. Had I overreacted to Cecilia's hostility? Surely what Simon and I had found in each other was worth giving another try....

As it was Sunday and the morning church service had ended earlier, the village was quiet. Simon parked outside the pub, where we encountered Mrs. Chesterton. She scowled at me. Or was it at both of us? As soon as Simon spoke to her, she focused on him alone and her sour expression was replaced with a smile, so I had my answer there.

"Mrs. Chesterton," Simon said. "I would like to introduce you to my fiancée, Miss Grace Sutcliffe. Grace, this is Mrs. Chesterton, I don't think this village would operate without her, would it?"

The middle-aged woman actually blushed. "Oh, I wouldn't go that far, Your Lordship," she said, still avoiding eye contact with me.

"Nonsense. You're far too modest. Mrs. Chesterton organizes all the rotas for the church, she's head of the Mother's Union, the local Women's Institute, Sunday School, Secretary of the Parish Council…. Is there anything you're not involved with, Mrs. C?"

"I do leave the Boy Scouts to their Akela, Your Lordship. I am not one for little boys grubbing about all over the place."

"Indeed, Mrs. C. I was one of those grubby boys once, Grace. Wouldn't think so to look at me now, would you?"

I laughed with him, and it felt good, but Mrs. Chesterton's insistence on pretending I didn't exist was beginning to grate and I was glad that Simon decided it was time to move on and commandeer someone else. This time, he happened on the rector, who was emerging from the rectory. Once again, he made the introductions. This time I was welcomed.

"A pleasure to meet you," the rector said, shaking my hand. "I believe I caught a glimpse of you a week or so ago. You were in the Mordenhyrst Arms with Lady Cecilia."

"That's right. I was. Mrs. Chesterton was regaling you with quite a lot of news, I think."

The rector smiled. "That's a polite way of putting it, my dear. She is a very hard worker though, and perhaps a little lonely. Her only daughter emigrated to Australia after the war, you know. She hasn't seen her since. Well, it's such a long way, isn't it?"

I nodded.

The rector took out his pocket watch. "Oh, dear me, I'm late again. Parochial Church Council meeting. It started ten minutes ago."

"Really?" Simon said. "We just saw Mrs. C and she didn't seem to be in any hurry."

The rector shook his watch and held it to his ear. "Stopped. I forgot to wind it yesterday." He looked up at the clock on the church steeple. "It looks like I may actually be on time for once. Cheerio, Your Lordship, Miss Sutcliffe." He raised his Panama hat to both of us and scurried away as fast as his sixty-plus-year-old legs would carry him.

"Come on," Simon said, grabbing my hand. "Let's go over to the pub. It's opening time and I could do with a pint of Sykes's best bitter. It'll wash the taste of having to be polite to Mrs. Chesterton out of my mouth."

I held back. "I'm not sure I would be terribly welcome."

"Why's that?"

"When I came here with Cecilia, we left without paying."

Simon laughed. "She's a minx. Always doing things like that. Don't worry. I'll square it with Sykes. He's a nice old chap."

I found it hard to accept Simon could be so flippant where a man's livelihood was involved. Of course, I was just as guilty. I hadn't offered to pay either.

"That should settle it, Sykes, old man. Sorry about the confusion. My sister can be a little absent-minded at times. Here's a little extra for your trouble."

"Thank you, Your Lordship. Much obliged."

I piped up. "I'm sorry too, Mr. Sykes. It was only after we left that I realized the mistake."

"No harm done, miss. Now, what can I get you both?"

"Lemonade for me please," I said and sat down at the same table Cecilia and I had occupied previously. I peered out at the village square. A couple of men dressed in brown corduroy trousers and flat caps were making their way across to the pub. A neatly dressed mother pushed a pram, and a couple of older women neighbors stood at their respective front gates chatting with one another. A horse and cart trundled past, followed by a couple of cars and a young man on a bicycle. A typical day in a typical English village.

But if that were the case, why did I have a feeling like icy fingers crawling up my spine? I shivered and turned to Simon, who placed our drinks on the table and sat opposite.

"Bottoms up," he said, clinking his glass of flat beer against my tumbler of lemonade.

"Cheers," I said.

We took a few swigs of our drinks. The cold sensation was getting worse. I forced myself to concentrate on Simon. "You've lived here in Cortney Abbas all your life, haven't you?"

He set his glass down. "I was born here. At the Hall. In the Mauve Room actually. Dr. Stratton delivered me. Slightly awkward birth. Typical of me, of course. Cecilia had popped out like a cork from a bottle but in my case it was more that I resisted being born. At least that's what Mama used to say."

"Didn't you think that was an odd way to describe it? Your birth, I mean."

"No, I mean, I suppose I grew up hearing that expression, so I never thought anything of it. What do you find odd about it?"

"You were close to your mother, weren't you?"

Simon looked down at the table. "I loved her very much."

"And she loved you too, so it seems to me that she might have used a more...I don't know...humorous...or pleasant way of describing your birth, even if it was difficult."

Simon looked up again and his expression had darkened. "I've never given it any thought and, to be frank, I don't wish to talk about it. Can we change the subject, please?"

"I'm sorry, I didn't mean to upset you."

He pasted a smile on his face. I wondered if he knew how fake it looked. "You didn't upset me. I simply prefer not to think about it, that's all." He pushed his drink aside. "Look, will you be all right here for a few minutes? There's something I need to attend to. Nothing for you to concern yourself with, but as I'm here, I'd like to get it sorted out. I won't be more than ten minutes or so."

I nodded and Simon left.

The farm laborers were the only two other customers. They stood at the bar, supping their ale and tucking into cheese sandwiches, made with slices of white bread as thick as doorstops.

I drained my glass of lemonade and Mr. Sykes approached me. "Shall I get you another one?"

"Yes please, Mr. Sykes, and then, I wondered if I could ask you something."

"Certainly, miss." He left and returned a couple of minutes later with another brimming tumbler of lemonade.

"Thank you. Please join me." I indicated Simon's vacant seat.

The landlord hesitated for a moment as if unsure whether it was appropriate of him to sit in my presence. Deciding it was, he sat down.

"What can I help you with, miss?"

I was aware of two pairs of eyes watching us from the bar. Well, let them. I had nothing to hide and had every right to be interested in the village that was supposedly to be my new home. "I know your family has lived here for generations, Mr. Sykes, and you know pretty much everything that goes on in Cortney Abbas, but are you aware of anything…." The two pairs of eyes seemed to bore into my head. The men stood on the periphery of my vision, but they might as well have been directly in front of me. The icy fingers gripped my spine harder.

"Am I aware of what, miss?"

"Is there any history of…I mean, does anyone practice anything…." *Get a grip, Grace.* I searched for a word and the only one that came to mind was the one I uttered. "Unchristian?"

One of the men banged down his pewter mug on the bar. The landlord shot the laborers a warning glance, then resumed the pleasant smile he seemed to have reserved for me.

"Unchristian? I'm not sure as I know what you mean by that, miss. I'm sure many in the village turn up to church on Sundays and make their peace with God but, as for the rest of the week, well, we're all human, aren't we? Uncharitable thoughts, the odd unkind deed. There's not a lot of thieving goes on. I'd say, on the whole, we're pretty much like any other village."

But you're not, and you know it. Right now, though, I hadn't any proof of anything other than suspicion in people's eyes when they looked at me. I tried again. "There's been a fair amount of adultery, I believe."

A guffaw came from the bar and one of the men spoke. "If you want to find the culprit there, you'd better look close to home. The Absent Earl has put his mark on many a young girl around here, and not always with her consent neither."

"That's enough, Stan," the landlord said.

"She's the one who brought it up."

"He's right," I said. "I did. And I am aware of the earl's reputation."

The laborer was lubricated with a couple of pints, and it had loosened his tongue. "That's why he spends so much time away from here, down in that South of France, as far away as he can get."

Mr. Sykes stood. "All right, you two, sup up and be on your way. I reckon you've both had enough ale for one day."

Amid grumbling, the men downed the rest of their pints and left, slamming coins on the bar. Their hobnailed boots clattered against the stone flags.

"Sorry, miss, bit of a sore subject. Stan's sister is one who had a son out of wedlock. Twenty years old he is now. Fine strapping lad, but no doubting who his father is."

"I shouldn't have brought it up," I said. "It's just that…I feel as if people here would prefer if I went away. I can't really explain it any better than that."

"Don't worry about them, miss. It's because they don't know you. Give them time. Show them you want to be a part of things. Once you and Lord Simon are married, get yourself involved in village life. That'll make them warm to you."

"Unless I upset Mrs. Chesterton and she thinks I'm taking over."

"Oh, don't mind about Hilda Chesterton. Everyone falls out with her at some point. Shame really, because I remember her when she was young. Pretty little thing. She had the most beautiful blue eyes and she turned many a young man's head, I can tell you." He looked wistful.

"Even yours, Mr. Sykes?"

The landlord laughed. "Aye, even mine. I won't deny it. Then she married Harry Chesterton. Took everyone by surprise, that did. The local gossips had a field day of course. All eyes were on her waistline for months. The old biddies were counting on their fingers.... Well, of course, she wasn't in the family way. Not for another couple of years. Then poor old Harry died and that's when she changed. Almost overnight. She dressed different, did her hair in that severe bun, started wearing those unattractive spectacles.... But all that was one thing. It was her entire personality. As if she were a different person. All the sparkle and radiance went out of her. Like someone had snuffed out a candle. Pfft."

"And her daughter emigrated."

"That's right. Went to live in Melbourne. Got married, I believe. Don't know if she had any children. Hilda never talks about her. I think there was some bad blood between them before the girl left. Anyway, don't you worry about her, and don't worry about the village folk either. We're not a bad bunch on the whole, just don't like change. And anyone coming in from the outside – especially if they're going to live up at the Hall – well, that represents change that could affect all our lives. We've seen them come and seen them go too. Some good, some not so good."

"Like the Absent Earl."

"That's not for me to say, miss."

The door opened and Simon was back. Mr. Sykes returned to his place behind the bar. "I'll refresh your pint, Your Lordship."

"Thank you, Sykes."

"Well now, Grace, has Sykes been filling you in on all the village gossip then?"

I smiled. "Some of it. One or two of Mrs. Chesterton's best kept secrets."

"And she has a few of those, doesn't she, Sykes?"

The landlord looked awkward as he served Simon's ale.

Having established that I was happy with my lemonade, Simon

rejoined me. He downed half a pint in one go. "I needed that. Parched as a desert in a drought."

"Did you get your business done?"

"What? Oh yes. Needed a quick word with our local accountant. I was lucky. You normally have to make an appointment to see old Jackass. Sorry, I mean Mr. Jackson. Lia and I always called him Jackass for reasons which will become clear the first time you ever hear him laugh. Sounds exactly like a donkey. Anyway, I got straight in. There are certain advantages that go with the title." He grinned broadly.

"It's unusual for an accountant to work on a Sunday, isn't it? No money worries, I hope."

"Oh no, nothing like that. We use a firm in London for matters relating to the bank but I wanted to move some of my personal investments about. Might as well make sure the money works as hard as it can and, for all his eccentricities, Jackass is a sound fellow. Knows his stuff and always loyal to the family. That's why he agreed to see me today."

"What shall we do this afternoon?" I asked.

"Back to the Hall. We've missed lunch but I've no doubt Sykes can rustle us up a couple of sandwiches here if you like."

Ham sandwiches duly ordered, Sykes disappeared out to the back. I shifted in my seat.

"Uncomfortable? We can move if you like. It's like the grave in here today. Usually it's bustling at this time."

"Yes, I thought that was a bit odd. Apart from those two earlier, no one has set foot in here since we arrived."

"Just one of those days, I expect."

A couple of women passed close by outside. They averted their eyes when they saw me looking at them, but I knew they had been staring at me and, as they carried on walking, I also knew I was the topic of their conversation. Was it, as Sykes had insisted, just suspicion of an outsider? Or was it, as the almost crippling iciness in my spine was telling me, something more specific than that? Since my last visit, with Cecilia, something had gone round the village. I was sure of it. These weren't the suspicious looks I got last time. This was much more serious and personal. Maybe I was being paranoid but, at that moment, I felt certain someone was spreading false information about me to ruin my reputation in this village, and I could only think of one person who hated me enough to do that.

Cecilia.

Back at the Hall, Coralie was pouring tea in the drawing room. Simon greeted her and then excused himself. "I would love to join you both, but I have a report to prepare, and it must be ready for me to take to London tomorrow. Enjoy your tea."

He gave me an affectionate peck on the cheek and squeezed my hand. For a second, I felt happy, but then I remembered the looks from those villagers and my good mood evaporated.

After Simon had left us, I went to sit near Coralie and accepted her offer of a cup of tea. She rang for one of the servants.

"Sorry I missed you this morning," she said.

The door opened and Buckingham appeared. As soon as he saw who had summoned him, his lips set in a thin line. Coralie ignored the expression. "Please bring us another cup and saucer, Buckingham," Coralie said, her back ramrod straight.

The butler said nothing, inclined his head as slightly as custom would allow, and left us.

Coralie raised her eyebrows. "I'll just bet he's biting his tongue right now." We both laughed.

Buckingham returned, said nothing, and placed the cup and saucer in front of Coralie. "Thank you," Coralie said.

Once again, the merest hint of acknowledgement before the butler strode out of the room.

With the door now firmly closed, Coralie poured herself tea, sat back and addressed me. "I hear you and Simon went to the village. How did that go?"

"The landlord was friendly, and the rector. As for the rest...."

"Did you sense anything when you were there? Anything peculiar. Out of place perhaps?"

I nodded. "I got the impression someone had been spreading stories about me. What those stories were about I have no idea, but I'm guessing they emanated from this place and that the instigator was Cecilia."

"That's interesting. What makes you say that?"

"Her whole attitude towards me. I don't think she would stop at anything to rid herself of my presence here and if she can enlist the help of others in the process, so much the better."

Coralie sipped her tea, deep in thought. "You see, I didn't actually mean that sort of thing." She set her cup and saucer down and leaned forward. "When Pip and I drove here, we came through the village. Even before we arrived there, I had a bad feeling, a sense that all was not well. It's something I've only experienced once before in my life and on that occasion, the result was.... Let's just say that the result was fatal. People died. Others disappeared and have never been heard from since."

"When did that happen? Was it here or in America?"

"In Louisiana. Once again, a small community was involved. A village where everyone knew each other, and a lot of interbreeding had gone on over generations. Most of the inhabitants were descended from slaves. All believed in black magic and voodoo – their own particular brand, of course. Everything centered on an old woman called Beersheba Atkins. She was blind, but when the spirit took her, she could see as clearly as you and me. She could see auras and speak in tongues. Ancient Sumerian was her specialty. It took a professor from New York to decipher what she said, and no one could explain how she knew the language. She had never moved more than a mile or so from where she was born, eighty, maybe ninety years earlier, the daughter of the man who owned the land and a slave girl who took his fancy. The professor diligently took down every word Beersheba said when she went into one of her trances. As always, the whole village was gathered together to hear her."

"But they wouldn't have understood what she said unless he had been there."

"You would think that, wouldn't you? But that wasn't the case. When she would speak, everyone knew what she said even though they didn't understand a word of the language she was using. The problem arose when the professor decided to translate out loud. He was an expert in dead languages, but he hadn't the first idea of the dark world of the ancient spirits. As soon as the villagers heard Beersheba's words in English, they turned on each other. The professor fled and was never seen or heard of again. That night, twelve of the villagers were hacked, mauled and bitten to death. Six disappeared and it's rumored that one or maybe even all of those were eaten in some frenzied cannibalistic mayhem. Through it all, Beersheba sat, transfixed, mumbling to herself, oblivious to the carnage around her. Hiding in the thick vegetation mere yards away, a little girl watched her, her eyes never leaving the face of the old woman...."

In an instant, I knew. "That little girl. She was you, wasn't she?"

Coralie nodded. "I don't recall the terrible slaughter. Maybe my mind blocked it out, or maybe Beersheba took away the memory, because she suddenly fixed her gaze right at me and I knew that, despite the effective camouflage and her own affliction, she knew I was there. Something passed between us that night. I felt her presence enter my body and it has never left even all these years later, and long after Beersheba passed into the next world. That's why I can see and feel things others are oblivious to. It's also how I sense a kindred spirit even though they may be unaware of their own capabilities. I don't always understand at first. Beersheba shows me images and they're hard to comprehend sometimes...." Her voice faltered and I was aware that her attention had been drawn to something over by the fireplace. It was only a moment's distraction before she looked back at me. "You don't realize it yet, but you have the gift, Grace. Or you may grow to think of it as a curse."

I stared at her. "But I can't see auras, or speak in tongues, and I certainly can't sense things the way you do."

"Can't you? You merely have to open your mind. Currently I sense a barrier, like a closed and locked door in your mind. All you have to do is unlock it and you will see all that I see."

"But do I want to? You said I might learn to regard it as a curse."

"That's true, but to keep it closed is to deny yourself the chance to influence the outcome. To continue in your ignorance is not only a waste of your talents but also a dereliction of duty to others. Your gift can help protect others. Sometimes from their own actions."

"I'm not sure I understand any of this. I also don't understand what your story has to do with Cortney Abbas. I mean, it's a quaint English village tucked away in a secluded corner of the countryside thousands of miles from the swamps of Louisiana."

"Evil crosses all boundaries. It adapts to fit. You don't need a Beersheba to channel spirits here, merely a soul as black as that which attacked those villagers twenty years ago."

"But was Beersheba on the side of good or evil?"

"Would the answer were as simple as that. You know your Bible? Lucifer, the most beloved of God's angels, His 'morning star' cast out of Heaven? Satan, to give him his other name, wasn't always evil. He was anointed as a cherub. Truly one of God's chosen. But he transgressed. He sinned so badly, first with being prideful, then violent and corrupt. The blameless one had become sin personified. But he hadn't started out that way. So it is with evil spirits. And it works in both directions. Perfect good can become perfect bad, and vice versa."

"So, you're saying Beersheba was both good *and* evil?"

"Exactly."

"And you have both sides in you."

"Don't we all?"

"So, how do we know who...or what...to fight? Kill?"

"Welcome to my world, Grace. I never said it would be easy."

I drained my tea.

CHAPTER FIVE

Fleur exhaled a cloud of smoke from a particularly foul-smelling Turkish cigarette. "Oh, come on, Coralie. Be a sport."

"I think not," Coralie said.

We were all gathered in the drawing room after a particularly delicious meal of roast beef with all the trimmings. Feeling mellow after a couple of glasses of vintage Margaux followed by two generous cognacs poured by Simon, I leaned back on the comfortable settee and nestled in the cushions.

"Yes, come on, Coralie," Simon said, puffing his after-dinner cigar. "Who knows when we'll have an opportunity to do this again? You're all off home tomorrow."

Encouraging noises came from the others.

Coralie chewed her lip – the first time I had ever seen her anything but poised and sure of herself. She seemed to be fighting her own internal battle, but Percy wasn't going to let her off. "Look, we know you haven't got your cards or whatever they are, darling, but surely you can give us a demonstration of this power of yours. Tell our fortunes or something."

Coralie stopped chewing her lip. Her expression changed from indecision to anger as she stood abruptly. "All right, if you want it that way, so be it. Don't blame me if you don't like the consequences."

Pip clapped his hands like an excited sixteen-year-old girl. "Good-oh. Well done, old girl."

Coralie flashed him a look and he let his hands drop into his lap. He crossed his legs in an awkward fashion as if she had been about to punch him in a delicate part of his anatomy.

I had no idea what she intended to do, but a feeling of dread began to creep up my body from my toes. By the time she caught my eye, it was halfway up my back. The look she gave me was curious. Part sympathy, part triumph. It was the latter emotion that troubled me most.

All eyes were fixed on her. The nagging sensation grew stronger inside me. I tasted a strange burnt flavor as if I had eaten some scorched dry toast. My mouth dried and I reached for my brandy glass. Empty. I couldn't interrupt so I would just have to keep swallowing in an effort not to choke.

As I watched, the air around Coralie seemed to darken and coalesce. I could make out nothing tangible, only curls and swirls like charcoal smoke. Was I seeing my first aura? If so, I wished it were a lighter color. I glanced at the others. I could see nothing materializing around them and, by their steady gaze, they didn't seem to have noticed anything untoward. Coralie's lips moved and bile shot up into my throat. I swallowed it down hard, the sour taste mingling with the burnt flavor and making me gag uncontrollably. Cecilia glanced my way and issued a loud shushing noise. Simon touched my hand and passed me a glass of water he had poured from the jug next to him. I nodded my thanks, unable to speak for fear of vomiting.

I relished the cool fresh water as it dissipated the vile taste in my mouth. My stomach continued to heave and churn, and the more Coralie muttered her indistinct words, the worse it became, until I felt as if I were standing on a boat as it pitched and tossed in a stormy sea.

Coralie's eyes flashed open to a collective gasp from her audience. She began to chant.

"What language is that?" Simon whispered to me.

I shook my head. In the chair next to us, Lilo leaned forward. "Is that Ancient Greek?"

"Doesn't sound like it," Simon replied, earning another 'shush' from Cecilia.

Coralie's words grew louder, more frenetic. The aura around her darkened until I could barely make her out. I closed my eyes but that only made the pitching and tossing sensation worse. I opened them, and I couldn't see her at all. Only a thick blackness hovered in the air where she had been.

I finally trusted myself to speak. "Where did she go?" I asked Simon.

He looked at me as if I had uttered the most ridiculous question ever posed. "What do you mean? Coralie's right there." He pointed at the cloud, then glanced at Lilo, who shook his head and raised his eyebrows.

Coralie's words flowed through me. I could understand them within my mind even though I hadn't a clue about the language she was using. They came to me more as a sense of what she was saying rather than actual words and phrases. She warned of something in the village that was fighting for control. It wanted release. It wanted life. Most worrying of all, it seemed I was the one who had to stop it.

With the suddenness of a light being switched off, Coralie stopped speaking. The dread left me. I looked across at my new friend, sitting calmly in her chair. No cloud, no aura.

The guests seemed perplexed. Cecilia was the first to speak. "Well, I don't know what to make of that. Thank you, Coralie. Most... unusual."

"What was that language?" Pip asked.

Coralie looked across at me and gave a slight smile. "A language I do not speak. In fact, one that hasn't been spoken in centuries. Sumerian."

"Well, I must say, you do speak it awfully well," Pip said.

"And how would you know that, Pip, old bean?" Percy asked, coming over and ruffling his hair. "You can't speak the language. She might have been spouting gibberish for all you know."

"But she wasn't," I heard myself say, only to wish I hadn't. All eyes turned to me. "What I mean is, I understood the meaning behind her words, so they couldn't have been gibberish, could they?"

Cecilia waved her cigarette holder around. "I had no idea you'd studied classical languages, Grace. I didn't think there was much call for that sort of thing in Yorkshire."

"*Lia*," Simon warned.

Cecilia feigned innocence. "Merely making an observation, brother dear."

"I'm not sure that there is," I said. "Nor do I speak any, but somehow I caught the gist of Coralie's words. I'm surprised none of the rest of you did."

The others exchanged glances. "You seem to be on your own there," Fleur said, patting her hair. "Maybe it's Coralie's accent. Perhaps you're better attuned to it than we are."

I stared at her, more in pity than anger. So much physical beauty wasted on such a lamentable soul. She smiled her pretty smile and I saw the darkness around her while Lilo smothered a giggle behind a cough.

Dorcas Merryman stared open-mouthed like a floundering goldfish, while to her right, Billy and Candice exchanged glances as if relishing the night's entertainment. Fitz puffed smoke from his cigar while casually trailing a stray finger down Fleur's bare arm.

Simon broke the awkward silence. "How about more drinks, everyone?"

Fleur and Percy immediately drained theirs and Simon circulated with the brandy decanter. I had lost the taste for it and declined, preferring to stick with the glass of water that had refreshed my palate. I turned my attention away from Coralie as Simon rejoined me and started chatting about something I was paying little or no heed to. I merely nodded and hoped it was in the right place as my mind raced with new revelations. That I had some sort of gift of second sight, there seemed little doubt. As to how and why it should have been triggered this evening, I had no clue. Unless it was something to do with Coralie. I glanced over to where she had been sitting. Her chair was empty. She was nowhere in the room. I interrupted Simon mid-flow. "Have you seen Coralie?"

"She was over...." He pointed to where she had been. "She must have slipped out for a moment."

"Will you excuse me, Simon?" I stood and crossed the room.

Out in the hall, no one was about. Maybe she had gone to her room. I knew it was in the same wing as mine but wasn't sure exactly which one. I hurried up the stairs and moved down the hallway, knocking and trying door handles. Some were locked. Outside the Mauve Room, I listened, pressing my ear hard against the door, my hand on the handle. I knew no one was supposed to be in there, but from inside, I could swear I heard heavy breathing. Then, to my disbelief, I felt pressure on the handle as if someone on the other side were turning it. Stifling a cry, I hurried along. I glanced back. The door remained shut.

Two doors from my room, I knocked and heard a familiar voice. "Who is it?"

"Hello, Coralie. It's Grace. I wanted to make sure you were all right."

There was a pause. "Come in, Grace."

On opening the door, I found Coralie changed and ready for bed. She wore an elegant peach negligee that flowed down to her ankles. Devoid of makeup, her face looked fresh and young. She smiled as she saw me. "Come in and sit a spell. I'd appreciate your company."

I sat at the dressing table, while she relaxed on a chaise longue. She ran her hand over her short black hair. She sighed. "Those people downstairs. I find their presence so draining."

"Me too," I said. "I hope I never become as shallow as they are."

"You won't. Trust me. It takes generations of breeding to become as inconsequential as any one of them. And to think, my pa wants me to marry one of them. If he only knew...."

"So, what are you going to do?"

"Go back to the States probably. I hate to let my father down, but I cannot spend the rest of my life tied to a creature like that."

"They're not all as bad as Pip and Lilo. Actually, those two aren't that bad. I think the war had a lot to do with it. They were all so young and idealistic. Going off to fight the war to end all wars only to find themselves knee deep in a muddy quagmire amid the rats, death, stinking gangrene and ordure. That's what my brother said anyway. A week later, he was killed."

"In France?"

"Yes. One of millions of decent, good boys deprived of a life by the greed and poor judgment of a bunch of old men who treated them like their tin soldiers."

"It's still raw, isn't it?"

I nodded. "I don't talk about it often. My father won't mention it. He blames himself for encouraging Will to enlist so early. Everyone has told him it wasn't his fault, but he still blames himself. Now, if ever the subject of the war comes up, he gets up and leaves the room."

Coralie closed her eyes.

"I'm sorry. You must be tired. I'll leave you to it."

Coralie opened her eyes. "No, it's quite all right. Like I said, I would appreciate your company. I need to talk to you about Simon."

"Simon?"

"Simon and Cecilia, actually."

Once again, that creeping dread feeling I had experienced downstairs started in the lower half of my body. "What about them?"

"You know perhaps that there is a strong bond between them?"

"I know they're very close. But Will and I were too."

"No, this goes much farther than the bond between a brother and sister. Farther even than a bond between twins, such as Fleur and Percy might have. It's as if Simon and Cecilia are two halves of a whole. I only realized it today. It's as if one cannot exist without the other."

I shuddered. "That doesn't sound...healthy."

"I'm so sorry, Grace. I know you don't want to hear this, but I sense it isn't the shock it might have been. Your own inner light is forming. I knew when I came out of my trance downstairs that something had changed. You can see auras now, can't you?"

I hesitated. "Not for everyone. I think it only happens when there's a big shift. It happened when you went…under…if that's the right word. And I saw blackness around you, like a cloud. Only for a short while. Until things calmed down, I suppose."

"That's the way of it at first. You've taken your first steps. From now on, you'll see more and more, and your senses will sharpen. I don't know what's going on here at Mordenhyrst Hall. I know you love Simon and I believe he loves you, but how Cecilia fits into the equation is the part that eludes me, except for this…bond…they have. I urge you to tread warily. There's something I'm not getting. Something I don't understand. Probably a whole lot. But it's all tied in with this house and the village somehow, and you are an intrinsic part of it."

I thought back to that feeling I'd had, that somehow, I was meant to stop some kind of dark and menacing force. "Are you saying this house is evil?"

Coralie shook her head. "I really don't know. I'm sorry. The visions aren't clear. But you can tell me one thing."

"What?"

"Why would I keep seeing birds out of the corner of my eye? Not just any birds. Birds of prey. Falcons, I think. I haven't seen one for years and now I'm seeing them everywhere around Mordenhyrst Hall. Only they're not real. Beersheba is showing them to me."

"That's why you were staring at the fireplace a few minutes ago. The falcon is part of the Mordenhyrst crest. Some legend. An old feud involving a rival and their pet falcons who fought a battle to the death. It resulted in the loser issuing a curse on the Mordenhyrsts. And there's something else. I've been seeing them too. In the Mauve Room and even outside, through the window at least. Falcons and Mordenhyrst Hall seem inextricably linked."

"That would go some way to explaining it. It may even explain why I'm here in the first place."

"What do you mean?"

"I mean that I have only ever seen falcons when Beersheba has put them in my mind. That first night when I was a child. And ever since I arrived here."

CHAPTER SIX

I poured myself a large brandy and tried to understand what Coralie was saying.

"You believe you were *destined* to come here?" I proffered her the decanter, but she declined with a shake of her head.

"Sounds crazy, doesn't it? Maybe it is. Maybe *I'm* crazy. You wouldn't be the first to think so. But, honey, all I can tell you is that your love for Simon will come at an expensive price. You need to be prepared for that. This house…." She gazed around her and shivered.

"I've seen and heard things I can't explain here, and I know others have too," I said. "But for all I know, someone has been playing tricks to try to frighten me. Cecilia would be my first bet."

Coralie inhaled deeply. "If only it were that simple."

"So, you believe this place is haunted, then."

Coralie nodded. "But not in the way you might think. Forget any of those ghost stories you may have read curled up in front of a winter's fire. These ghosts will not manifest themselves as demons or ethereal spirits wandering aimlessly through the grounds. These are no Gray Ladies or headless earls, with maybe one exception – Simon's late mother. No, these ghosts are the manipulators of the mind and soul. Think less about a wandering wraith searching for peace and more about a parasite looking for a host."

"I've heard about people being possessed by the devil."

Coralie laughed, but there was no mirth in it. "Yes, and there's truth in that. Not in this case. As I've told you. Nothing is simply black and white. That is the truth I learned from Beersheba. That is the truth you'll have to learn."

"Why have I been chosen? Before I met you, I was plain Grace Sutcliffe from Yorkshire. Engaged to a viscount admittedly, but in the past few days so much has changed."

"I can't tell you why. In my case I have always known there was something within me. It runs in the family. Remember my ancestor, Clothilde Gasparyan, who I mentioned on my first evening here? On my mother's side, the gift has persisted down the generations, through the female line. Beersheba merely enhanced it and made it more than it would have been. In your case, I had nothing to do with it. I merely sensed that which was within you. I think maybe your realization helped to bring it to the surface. As for being plain Grace Sutcliffe from Yorkshire.... You do yourself an injustice. You're a beautiful young woman. It's hardly surprising you caught the attention of a viscount. What will you do now, Grace?"

"I told Simon I wasn't happy here, but I promised to stay the week. I did tell him I wanted to leave with the rest of you, but he's worried about the gossip that people like Fleur and Percy would generate. He asked me to stay a little longer and try to acclimatize myself here. Now you've told me what you believe, I really don't know what to do." I toyed with the idea of telling Coralie what I most feared, that I was somehow meant to stop the rot that had infested Mordenhyrst Hall and all that dwelt in it. I told myself I didn't know her well enough. That I could be wrong. That I *wanted* to be wrong. I caught her looking at me with a curious expression on her face, as if she would read my thoughts but didn't know what lay behind them.

"Let your inner spirit guide you," she said. She looked exhausted, her eyes fluttering as she forced them to remain open.

I stood. "Thank you so much, Coralie."

She managed a weary smile. "I can't think what for. All I've done is cause you hard decisions."

"No, you haven't. I needed to know what you had to tell me. I'll leave you to rest now."

This time she didn't detain me. "Promise me you'll visit me in London when you get back."

"I promise."

I wished her good night and made my way back downstairs. When I opened the drawing room door, all conversation stopped. So, once again I'd been the topic. Simon made it even worse by his exaggerated greeting, kissing me warmly on the lips, taking my hand and leading me to sit beside him.

Fleur, Fitz and Percy chatted to Pip and Lilo. Billy and Candice were trying not to look bored while Dorcas regaled them with one of her interminable stories about a recent Girl Guide camp she had supervised, or whatever it was Guide Captains did. Cecilia smoked and cast angry glances at me when she thought I wasn't looking. I wanted to tell them what a seedy, inconsequential lot of morons I thought they were, but found I couldn't be bothered to waste my energy, so I ignored their snide looks, fake smiles, and supercilious glances.

Simon squeezed my hand. "You haven't been listening to a word I've said, have you?" He didn't sound angry, only perplexed. "What is it, Grace? Is it something I've done?"

I took a deep breath. "Nothing has changed since yesterday. I don't feel comfortable or accepted here and I don't just mean the Hall, it's the village as well."

"I thought we'd been over that. They don't like change, or new people at the Hall. They'll soon get used to you."

"The thing is, Simon, I have to ask myself whether *I* want to get used to *them*. Right now. I'm not sure I do. I'll keep my promise and stay until Friday but then I'm going to return to London, and we'll see." I could feel Cecilia's eyes boring into me from across the room.

Simon released my hand and glanced over my shoulder. Did he and his sister have the power of communicating telepathically? After what Coralie had told me I felt it quite possible.

He returned his attention to me. "Very well, Grace. If that's what you want."

"I'm sorry, Simon, but I think it's for the best. Maybe in a little while, we'll get back on track."

"A little hard to do if we're not seeing each other…although…. I've told Lia I'll stay on until the end of the month. That's three weeks away. Why don't we meet up on the day I officially move back to Mayfair? We could have dinner at Claridge's."

The urge to politely decline was strong, but equally forceful was the desire to say 'yes'. I settled for, "Let's think about it and decide later." Neither side of me was satisfied but it was a workable compromise.

I retired to my room soon after and discovered Nell turning down my bed. Despite my best intentions, I had been unable to dissuade her from leaving me to my own devices at bedtime.

"You're early, miss," she said. "Did you enjoy the party?"

I glanced at my watch. A little after midnight. Not exactly early in my book. "It was…different," I said. "But I'm feeling tired so I thought I would leave them to their reminiscences."

"Do you need me for anything else tonight, miss?"

"No, thank you, Nell. Good night."

"Good night, miss."

She left and I locked the door after her. My bed was, as always, perfectly turned down. My nightdress lay ready for me. From outside, I heard muffled giggles, the owner of which could have been Fleur or Candice. Percy wasn't, I had noticed, a giggler. If she laughed, it was at full belt. Presently, a door slammed a little way along from me.

As I removed my makeup, I heard more giggles. This time they were followed by the none-too-gentle closing of two doors. Then came the rasping of another door opening, moments before I heard scurrying footsteps approach and pass my door. Yet another door opened and closed. At least one person, or most probably more than one, wouldn't be sleeping in their own room tonight.

I stood and started to make my way across the room to my bed when a noise stopped me. I stared at the source of it.

My door handle squeaked a little as it turned this way and that. I held my breath. It stopped. I listened for footsteps moving away but there were none. A sliver of light from the corridor was visible under the door. If someone were standing out there, surely there would be a break in that light where they stood. I had a perfect view of the entire width of the door. The line of light remained unbroken. I listened. No footsteps. The corridor was quiet.

I told myself I had nothing to fear from these people. Even if there was someone standing outside my door, maybe to one side where their presence would be undetected, it would be someone I had met during the course of this weekend, or Simon. But, after our words earlier, I doubted he would come to me. After all, he'd had plenty of opportunity when there were far fewer people in this house, and he hadn't taken it.

I grasped the handle and turned the key, pulling the door open a crack as I did so. Outside, the corridor was as I suspected. Empty. I looked up and down. No one. A few muffled giggles. Nothing else.

I was about to close the door when I heard it. The distinctive sound of a woman sobbing. It started up from nowhere and I couldn't begin to guess who was weeping their heart out somewhere nearby. My first thought was Coralie. I paused long enough to grab my dressing gown and plant my slippers on my feet and then slipped out of my room, closing my door behind me. The sobbing seemed louder now. I made my way along, pausing at each door to listen. Each time, I came up with a blank, but still the sobbing followed me. It seemed to be everywhere and nowhere all at once. I paused extra long outside Coralie's room but heard nothing at all coming from inside. From the room next to hers, the obvious sounds of a couple indulging their lust for each other penetrated through the door. I hesitated at the Mauve Room, dreading that it would come from inside there. Fortunately, all was quiet, and I moved on.

As I reached Simon's room, I hesitated, hoping and praying he was on his own, relieved when I pressed my ear close and heard silence.

I came back to where I started and made to open my door. I gasped. The sobbing was coming from inside.

Trembling, my mouth dry, I turned the handle. The door opened. The sobbing stopped. My room was in total darkness, even though I knew I had left the main light and bedside lamp on.

With shaking fingers, I reached for the switch.

The ceiling light flashed on, and I blinked. For one second, I could have sworn I saw a face. The face of an old woman. I told myself it was my imagination. My eyes playing tricks on me as the sudden brightness cut through the blackness. I continued to tell myself this as I tossed my dressing gown aside, climbed into bed and I heard, once again, a woman sobbing.

I lay on my side, closed my eyes and prayed the sound would go away, but it didn't, and my eyes refused to stay shut. Whatever it was, however bad, I had to see.

A ball of light glowed in the far corner of the room. I couldn't pretend it was my eyes or some kind of wakeful dream. I drew my knees up under my chin. My breath came in shallow bursts as the light swirled in front of me, alternating from a muted yellow to a white so bright it made my eyes water. I wanted to call out for help but, if I did so, whatever this was would know I was there. Maybe, just maybe, if I stayed silent and unmoving, it would go away. I prayed harder than I had ever prayed in my life, but the light only grew in size and intensity until I could make out a distinct shape and a scene.

A woman, dark-skinned, elderly, her eyes reflected in a small fire in front of her. Her lips moved but I heard no sound from them. She passed her hands over the fire, so close to the flames she must surely burn herself, but she did not flinch. Another figure appeared – a young woman who kept looking back over her shoulder and then around as if she had no idea where she was or why she was there. The light wavered and waned and cast deep shadows around her, partially obscuring her. The old woman passed her hands over the fire once more and she was alone. She picked up a stick...no, a bone. A human bone. I was sure of it. A long thigh bone, bleached white through age or treatment. Still the woman's lips moved.

She caught sight of me and pointed the bone in my direction. The light flashed. I screamed. The vision blinked out.

I was aware of a furious hammering at my door. Someone rattled the knob. I snapped on the bedside lamp, threw on my dressing gown and unlocked the door.

"Oh, thank God." Simon took me in his arms. "What on earth happened?"

"I...I had a nightmare," I said. "'I'm sorry. I screamed in my sleep and didn't realize I'd actually done so. I didn't mean to worry anyone."

A few doors had opened, and one or two guests had come along to see what the cause of the commotion was. As soon as they saw it was me, they wandered back again, some rather unsteadily, others with a trace of annoyance at being disturbed. Only Coralie lingered. She gave me a questioning look, but I nodded and pasted a smile on my face. She didn't move. I got the impression that if Simon hadn't been there, she would have come to look after me.

Simon came in with me, tying his dressing gown closer around him. He left the door open.

"Now, suppose you tell me what actually happened."

I sat down on the bed while he took the stool in front of the dressing table. Always the soul of propriety – at least when he was around me.

"This will sound bizarre but...well, you asked so I'll tell you." I relayed all that had happened, including the sobbing and the inexplicable vision.

When I had finished, he spoke. "And you're certain you weren't asleep."

I shook my head.

"The old woman you saw.... Have you seen her before?"

Again, I shook my head. "She seemed not to belong here. But the younger woman.... She didn't belong *there*."

"Would you know either of them again if you saw them?"

"Possibly. The younger woman almost certainly."

Simon stood and went over to a chest of drawers I hadn't explored. He opened the top drawer and took out a photo frame, which he brought over to me. "Did she look anything like this?"

I took one look and gasped. It was as if I was seeing the vision again, down to the last detail. The tall, slender woman in the fashionable late-Victorian silk dress – wasp-waisted, her dark hair drawn back – was the image of the vision I had seen. "Who is she?"

Simon sighed and stroked the face that stared out at us, a half-smile playing at her lips. "She *was* Elise Valois. My late mother."

I grasped his hand. "I'm so sorry."

He looked at me. "This was taken on her birthday, just a week before she...died." He took the picture back and returned it to its drawer.

"Why not leave it out? It's such a lovely picture."

He shook his head. "Makes me too sad. You may have noticed, there are no photographs of her on view. Plenty existed. When she died, Papa ordered every one of them to be destroyed. He found them too painful to look at. A sort of superstition, I suppose. Some people believe the camera captures a little bit of your soul in every photograph. Maybe he feared that...." Simon shrugged. "I managed to keep this one, but I hid it here so he wouldn't find it. There's only one portrait, too. My father commissioned it to be painted shortly after they were married, so I suppose it holds a special place in his heart. You may have seen him staring at it. He does that a lot, but only that picture. She had discovered she was pregnant with Lia, and Papa said she had such a glow about her, he needed an artist to capture it in oil. He chose John Singer Sargent. Mama was painted a number of times. Artists loved her. More than one remarked on the translucence of her skin. They loved to capture her, especially with sunlight caressing her face...." He paused and a tear trickled down his cheek. He wiped it away with his finger. "After she...died, Papa had all the other portraits taken down and stored. Only that first one remains on view."

"But where are they now?"

Simon shrugged. "To tell you the truth I haven't even thought of them for years, but I should imagine they're tucked away in the attic, under a dust sheet."

"What a waste. Why doesn't he present them to the National Portrait Gallery? Much better than having them molder away, gathering dust."

"Maybe one day. Some things are best not discussed. These days, we never talk about Mama in front of Papa."

"I thought theirs was a love match."

"It was." Simon averted his gaze. "When Mama died, Papa felt betrayed. He felt if she truly loved him, she would have stayed with him."

"Even though she knew he was serially unfaithful to her?"

Simon shot me an angry glance. "Your middle-class morals don't really apply here, do they, Grace?" He stood and strode to the door. "I'm glad it was nothing serious and that you're unharmed by your experience here tonight. I hope you have a good night's sleep. Good night."

He left before I managed to utter one word.

CHAPTER SEVEN

Mordenhyrst Hall seemed so quiet and still without the other guests, even if I didn't appreciate their company, with the exception of Coralie. In fact, by the end of Monday, I missed her far more than I thought possible of an acquaintance I had only met for the first time two days earlier. Being alone in the house with Cecilia didn't help. Oh, there might have been an army of servants beavering away, keeping the great Hall running smoothly, but they went about their business quietly, mostly out of sight.

Simon left early on Monday for London. The chauffeur drove him and Coralie to the station to catch the mid-morning train. All the others had left without saying goodbye to me – rude behavior that would have earned me a stern rebuke from my father had I done it. I couldn't resist remarking on it to Cecilia when our paths crossed at lunch.

"I didn't realize they'd gone," I said.

She paused in eating her poached salmon. "Really?"

"I thought they might have said goodbye."

"Why would you think that?"

My ire rose. Wasn't it obvious? I shook my head and carried on eating. We didn't speak again. Lunch eaten, Cecilia rose and left the table and the room without a word or a backward glance.

Left to my own devices, I decided on a whim to take a trip down to the village. I rang for Buckingham, and he duly arrived, looking as if he had a nasty smell under his nose.

"Please, would you ask the chauffeur to take me into the village? I wish to do a little exploring."

He blinked a couple of times. "I will check with Lady Cecilia, miss."

Once again, anger begged for release from my pent-up mind, but he continued. "I don't know what plans Lady Cecilia might have made for the afternoon. It could be she needs the car herself. She probably wouldn't have anticipated that you might request it."

He had a point. "Very well, Buckingham. Please do that and let me know what she says."

"Very good, miss." He closed the door.

As I waited, I stared out of the window at the rolling countryside beyond the immediate gardens. Everywhere, in all directions, as far as the eye could see, belonged to the Mordenhyrsts. By fair means and foul, they had acquired thousands of acres of land. But at what cost? I wondered how many people had been trampled over in their greed.

Finally, after about fifteen minutes, the door opened and Buckingham strode in. "Lady Cecilia says you may have the car as long as it is returned safely by five o'clock this afternoon."

"The car? Am I also to have the services of the chauffeur?"

"Lady Cecilia said that will not be possible. She needs Morgan to drive her to a party in Oxford and his services will be required until early tomorrow morning. She has, therefore, already allowed him time off this afternoon to rest. Shall I ask him to bring the car round now, miss?"

Cecilia knew she had got me. She knew I couldn't drive. At that moment, I resolved to learn at the earliest opportunity. But one thing I *could* do was ride. I had been up on the back of a pony almost before I could walk. "I've changed my mind," I said, with as much haughtiness as I could muster. "Have one of the grooms bring...." I searched for the name of a horse I had heard Simon mention as being the most docile. After all, it had been a few months since I had taken my mare, Morning Star, galloping across the moors.

"Dulcie. I'll take Dulcie for a ride into the village instead. It's a beautiful day and it will be good to be back in the saddle. I presume Lady Cecilia doesn't require the horses today as she has her party to prepare for?"

He couldn't have missed the sarcasm. My voice dripped with it. He kept his expression deadpan. "I'm sure that will be quite in order, miss. I'll have the groom bring her round. When would you like to leave?"

"As soon as I've changed. Please ask Nell to come up to my room."

"Yes, miss."

I knew, of course, that he would go immediately to Cecilia and tell her of my new plan. Well, let him. For now, I had foiled her. It felt good.

"Lovely riding boots, miss." Nell helped me pull them on. "Such soft leather."

"Thank you, Nell. Spanish. My father bought them for me as a birthday present a couple of years ago. My others were beginning to show their age. Sadly, with me spending so much time in London, these have had far fewer outings."

"It'll be nice for you to get out and about, rather than staying around this house all the time."

"It will indeed, Nell." I thought for a moment, while Nell fixed my hat with an assortment of pins.

"We don't want it flying off in the wind," she said.

"We don't," I agreed. "Nell, I want to ask you something."

"Yes, miss?"

"You've known the family here all your life, haven't you?"

"Yes, miss."

"So, if there were anything…untoward…you would know about it?"

She paused and a frown settled on her face. "I'm not sure what you mean, miss."

"I mean I know the rumors about the Absent Earl's…exploits with the village girls but I'm talking about something more serious. Something that could involve Lady Cecilia and the viscount."

Nell shifted her gaze away from my reflection in the mirror. She positioned herself behind me so that part of her face was concealed behind my riding hat. "I don't know what you mean, miss."

"I think you do, Nell, and I really need you to tell me."

I sat riveted to the mirror. Behind Nell swirls of color mingled and entwined. Pale blues and lilacs grew darker, seemingly attacked and overwhelmed by darker hues of purple and gray.

"Oh, Nell. It's in you too, isn't it?"

Nell stepped back and became enshrouded by the dark and menacing aura.

"I…don't understand…what's in me? Nothing's in me. You're frightening me, miss."

Of course I was. If anyone had spoken to me as I had spoken to her just now, I would have been frightened too. She wasn't the best educated and my words must have sounded bewildering to a young woman who had been doubtless brought up to be God-fearing.

"I'm sorry, Nell. I didn't mean to scare you. It's just that I don't feel accepted in this house and I'm trying to find out why. I thought it was because of my place in society and I still think that has a lot to do with it, but seeing the viscount with his sister…. It's different to my relationship with my late brother. Very different. It…bothers me."

As I spoke, the colors around Nell began to settle and fade. The charcoal lightened to a dusky lilac as her face emerged. She was no longer frowning but I knew I was right. Whatever spirit or force Coralie had detected in Cecilia and Simon was also present in Nell. It was strange that Coralie hadn't detected it, but maybe that was because she had barely been in contact with her. But if it was within Nell, then how many others in the village?

Riding sidesaddle after years of wearing jodhpurs and sitting astride my beloved Morning Star felt uncomfortable. I had ridden this way many times earlier in my life before women began to discard the cumbersome skirts and awkward posture for the altogether freer and more natural feeling of sitting astride their mounts. I had brought my jodhpurs with me, but high society still frowned on ladies in trousers, especially when seated on horseback, so, back to the old-fashioned ways it had to be. I couldn't afford another *faux pas*, especially as I was going to be mixing with people holding traditional and fixed opinions.

Dulcie was a pretty, dark chestnut mare with kind eyes and a gentle temperament. I introduced myself to her as I always did, much to the bemusement of the groom. I ignored him and spoke gently to Dulcie, before stepping back a few feet. Still talking gently to her, I extended my hand toward her nose, letting her smell me. She inclined her head and that gave me the signal to start petting her. I advanced a few steps, and proceeded to stroke her nose, scratch her shoulder and pat her. All the while, the groom stood, holding her bridle. Slowly, a smile twitched his lips and then extended outward.

"You know your horses, miss," he said.

"I thought every rider knew this. You don't just leap on a strange horse and expect them to like it. It's the equine equivalent of meeting someone for the first time and sweeping them up in your arms."

He laughed and Dulcie appeared to agree, judging by the way she nodded her head.

"You won't have no problems with this one," the groom said. "There's not an evil bone in Dulcie's body. Always been my favorite, she has. It's odd though. Everyone loves her and she loves everyone, except she won't have no truck with Lord Simon or Lady Cecilia."

"What about the earl? Does she like him?"

"I don't know, miss. He never rides these days. Can't remember the last time he came down to the stables. Probably before Dulcie here was born. Her mother was Her Ladyship's…that's Lady Cecilia's mother's…favorite. They used to ride off everywhere together. It was awful when Her Ladyship passed on. Cornflower, Dulcie's mother, died a few months later. Vet said he could find no physical cause. He said it was as if she had died of a broken heart."

"That's so sad. You say the viscount and Dulcie don't get on?"

"Indeed no, miss. Dulcie kicks out whenever she sees him. She crashes around. Takes me ages to calm her."

"Yet, Lord Simon told me she was the most docile of all the horses."

"And he's right, miss. She is. Just not with him or Lady Cecilia."

I considered this for a moment. All my life I had trusted horses. They had an innate intelligence and could spot a bad character a mile off. They could also sense when something wasn't right. Or didn't quite fit. Once again, warning bells clanged in my mind.

"Well...I'm sorry, I don't know your name."

"Harper, miss."

"Well, Harper, I think Dulcie and I have the measure of each other now. It's time for us to enjoy our ride."

He moved over to my side, bent down and cupped his hands. I would need help getting into position and a good strong lift was required. Harper, it turned out, was expert and I was soon arranging my legs and my skirt in the appropriate manner aboard Dulcie.

"Thank you, Harper," I said.

He smiled and nodded. "Enjoy your afternoon ride, miss."

"I'm sure I shall."

Proceeding at a walking pace down the drive toward the lane leading to Cortney Abbas, I felt sure I was being watched, probably from an upstairs window. Cecilia? I thought so. I smiled to myself.

Beneath me, Dulcie proceeded at a steady rhythm. We would not be galloping across fields together today but maybe another time. At least it got me away from that house. I had hoped Nell would be an ally. Now, with this afternoon's episode, I no longer felt I could trust her. And if I couldn't trust her, I had no allies at Mordenhyrst Hall. Worse than that, I had enemies. Probably more than I was even aware of at that moment.

I tied Dulcie up outside the pub, right next to a trough full of water that would quench her thirst. Riding crop in hand, I made my way inside.

This time, the bar was buzzing with its exclusively male customers enjoying pints of ale and thick crusty sandwiches. The conversation stopped when the first of them caught sight of me. Another taboo broken. Here I was, an unaccompanied woman, entering a male enclave. I could almost smell the testosterone and half expected I would begin to detect antagonistic auras. To my relief that didn't happen. I held my head high and strode up to the bar. The men parted like Moses and the Red Sea, but their eyes burned into me.

The landlord looked uncomfortable, as if he didn't know whether to ask me to leave or offer me a drink. I took the upper hand. "Mr. Sykes, please could you let me have a glass of lemonade?"

A few murmurs sounded around me. One man drained his beer mug and slammed it down on the bar. Two others quickly followed suit when they saw Mr. Sykes was going to comply with my request. I made my way to a vacant table and sat to await my drink. My heart pounded, louder and harder as each man finished his drink and stormed out of the bar.

By the time Mr. Sykes brought me my lemonade, three quarters of his lunchtime trade had left.

"I'm so sorry. I had no idea they would do that," I said.

Mr. Sykes gave me a wry smile. "Old habits die hard. A young lady such as yourself coming into a local pub on your own? Not very respectable. That's what they think anyway. The truth of it is they wouldn't like their wives to find out about it."

"So, it's not the men who resent my presence, but the women?"

"Bit of both, really. The wives wouldn't like it so that means the men have to leave. *They* don't like it because this is the only pub in the village."

"Oh dear. I have caused a dilemma, haven't I? Don't worry, I shall just drink this and leave."

"Not to worry, miss. They'll be back this evening after work."

"I really came because I was hoping you could fill me in on a little village history."

The landlord glanced over at his deserted bar, shrugged and wiped his hands on his apron. "May I?" He indicated the wooden chair opposite me.

"Of course."

He sat and put his hands flat on the table. "What do you want to know?"

"When I was here last with the viscount, we were discussing Mrs. Chesterton and a few other bits of information about the village, including the Absent Earl. I wondered if I could ask you some more about it."

The landlord shifted his weight. He seemed uneasy. I pressed on. "I know the earl has had his way with a number of the local girls over the years, but were his ancestors like that?"

"Oh yes, miss. They took it as their right, see. *Droit du seigneur* they called it back in the olden days. Only, some of them earls liked the traditions of the olden times a bit too much to let them go even when time and customs had moved on. This village has always been set in its ways and that's how the Mordenhyrsts like it. As long as they don't have to abide by those rules themselves, of course. Lady Cecilia for one. She and those fast London friends of hers. They've caused more than one rumpus around here. These silly games of theirs. Scavenger hunts they call them. One of them ended up in front of a magistrate for stealing the local constable's bicycle. She didn't seem to understand that what she'd done was wrong. She said what would she do with a battered old bobby's bicycle when she had her Rolls? Well, the magistrate didn't take kindly to that, and she received a hefty fine, which her father paid, or so I understand. Probably with cash from his back pocket."

I could sense the seething anger behind Sykes's words and empathized with him. "Her name wouldn't have been Montague-Tarleton, would it? Persephone or Fleur?"

"That's the one. Persephone, only she corrected the magistrate and told him he should be calling her Percy. He settled for Miss Montague-Tarleton. She brought her friends with her, including Lady Cecilia, and they all roared their support from the gallery, until the magistrate had them cleared out. Then they came back here and celebrated with cocktails. You may recall Lady Cecilia mentioning it when she first brought you here?"

"Oh, so that was the occasion. Celebrating what though?"

"From what I could gather, they were celebrating that she didn't have to pay the fine herself, that she had her father twisted around her little finger so he could deny her nothing, and that she wasn't 'banged up in jail' as she put it. I'm sorry, miss, I really shouldn't be talking about my betters like this."

"But they're not your betters, Mr. Sykes. Not when they behave so appallingly."

"It's always been like it though. Poor Hilda...." He shook his head and tears formed in his eyes.

"I'm so sorry, Mr. Sykes. What happened to Mrs. Chesterton? I mean, apart from what you already told me."

He took a ragged breath and passed his hand over his face. "I don't know anything officially. I mean, she never said anything to me.... When her husband died, I told you she changed into someone I barely recognized. I wasn't the only one who noticed either. It was the talk of the village for quite a while, especially as the changes was so sudden. Then someone from up at the Hall got a little drunk one evening and started talking about the current earl's father and how he had taken a shine to Hilda. Now, the old earl was in his eighties at the time, virtually housebound. Bedridden some of the time. Hilda was working up at the Hall. She was governess to Lady Cecilia, who was only a child. It seemed to be working out all right. She was grieving her husband of course, but at that time everyone reckoned she was pulling round quite well. The viscount was only a toddler really so he couldn't know anything that was going on.

"Anyway, this one evening, the chap I'm talking about supped a few pints and it loosened his tongue. He seemed in a bit of a state. Said he had heard screams coming from the old earl's room. He rushed to investigate but as he started down the corridor, the door opened and Hilda came out, clutching at her blouse. As she ran past, Gordon saw her clothes were torn, her hair was all awry and her face was white. The next thing, the old earl appeared in the corridor, standing upright, not a sign of any gout, no stick or anything. Then he started walking towards Gordon. That put the willies up him and he turned and ran after Hilda, but she'd already gone. The cook said she almost flew through the kitchen, wrenched the door open and was off. I went and knocked on the door of her cottage and her little girl, as she was then, said her mother was a bit poorly and couldn't come to talk to me.

"Well, this went on for a week. Different people kept going round to see her but always got the same reply. The child looked healthy, clean and fed so there weren't too many concerns about her welfare. But then, one day, about a week later, the rector called around and Hilda opened the door herself, looking as she does now. He got the shock of his life."

"I'll bet he did."

"You see, her hair had gone gray as well. Lovely head of fair hair she had. Now it was iron gray and tied back in that severe bun of hers. Like I said though, it wasn't just her appearance. Everything about her had changed. The little girl and she didn't seem to get on so well either. Poor child was discouraged from bringing any friends home to play in the garden. Seems as soon as she could, she escaped. Couldn't get away fast enough, or far enough."

"So, you believe the old earl tried to rape Mrs. Chesterton."

"Oh no, miss, I don't believe he *tried* to. I believe he succeeded. You see, about six months later, people had started to notice that, while her dress was still severe, her skirts had become more... voluminous I think the word is. Some said she was putting on weight. Others though, and they were mainly women, said she was in the family way. No one felt they had to look too far to find the father."

"What happened to the baby? I assume there was one."

"We don't know for sure because, once again, Hilda dropped out of sight. Only for a few days, but not long after she reappeared, the skirts became slimmer again. Now whether she lost the baby or had it early and it died, or maybe there was never one in the first place, I don't know. No one does."

"Except Mrs. Chesterton."

"Exactly. And she isn't telling. Gordon left the village soon after. Don't know where he went. It's a good few years ago now. The old earl died, and we were blessed with the current one."

He sounded anything but blessed.

"Why does the Absent Earl spend so much time away?"

"It started when Her Ladyship died. Most people say it's guilt. Some are a bit more fanciful. I really couldn't say."

But I felt he could say, if he wanted to.

If he dared to.

The door opened and a couple of farm laborers entered, chatting. They stopped as soon as they saw me.

"Don't worry," I said, draining my glass. "I only popped in to have a word with Mr. Sykes. I'll be off now, thank you," I said to the landlord and handed him sufficient coins to pay for my drink plus a little extra for his trouble.

"You're welcome, miss. Where's your horse?"

"Oh, Dulcie's tied up outside."

He looked at me quizzically. From where he was standing, he could see out of the window.

"There's no horse out there."

"*What?*" I spun round. Sure enough, Dulcie was nowhere to be seen.

The two men sniggered behind me as I charged out of the pub, with Mr. Sykes hard on my heels.

We looked up and down the lane and across the square. Wherever Dulcie was, she wasn't here.

"Hey lads," Mr. Sykes said. "Did you see a chestnut mare on your way here?"

The two men shook their heads. "No."

Panic overtook me. Dulcie was a valuable animal. How would I ever explain that I had managed to lose her? Cecilia would have a field day at my expense. Simon…I dreaded to think what his reaction would be.

"Well, as I see it, there's only one thing for it," the landlord said. "I'll get my horse and cart and we'll take a trip down the lanes. She can't have gone far. She's not the type. Must have gone off with someone she knows. Maybe someone from the Hall saw her here and thought she had been taken by mistake. She's probably back up there munching on her oats, waiting for you."

"That's very kind of you, Mr. Sykes. But I can't take you away from your business. You have customers."

"Oh, they'll be all right. Jack? Tom? Look after the bar, will you. I'm trusting you now."

The young men grinned and touched their caps to him. "Aye, Mr. Sykes," Jack said, "you can rely on us. No drinks on the house till you get back."

"That's it, boys. Won't be long."

I waited for the landlord to hitch up his horse and cart and we set off in pursuit of Dulcie. The closer we got to the Hall, the more certain I became that whoever had taken her had done so deliberately. "Could someone have kidnapped her, do you think?"

"Dulcie? I shouldn't think so. Lovely mare but not one you would breed from, and she isn't a hunter. No, I think it's an innocent mistake."

I knew it was essential he keep his eyes on the road ahead, but still I wished I could see the expression on his face as he uttered those words.

My heart sank lower and lower as Mr. Sykes's horse clip-clopped ever closer to Mordenhyrst Hall and there was still no sign of Dulcie.

The gates were ahead of us. Mr. Sykes steered his horse and cart through them and up to the stables. Harper emerged from behind the stable block and to my great relief he was leading Dulcie.

As fast as my cumbersome riding skirt would allow, I scrambled off the cart ahead of Mr. Sykes, who had come round to help me. I raced up to the horse and threw my arms around her. She nuzzled my neck, and her brown eyes gave me a look of surprised sympathy.

"She came back on her own a few minutes since, miss," Harper said. "Gave me a proper fright, she did. I've checked her over and there's no sign of any injury. Then I got to thinking what might have happened to you."

I laughed. Typical that he would think of the horse before the human. "I'm so glad she's all right. I tied her up securely outside the pub but somehow she got away."

Harper exchanged a look with Mr. Sykes.

I looked from one to another. "What is it, Harper? Mr. Sykes?"

"It's just that...." Harper seemed uncomfortable. "Dulcie isn't one to go off like that. Even if you hadn't tied her up, chances are she would have stayed there until you came out again."

"So.... Are you saying someone deliberately untied her and led her away while I was talking to Mr. Sykes?"

"I never saw anyone, you understand," Harper said. "Dulcie came in here by herself, and I did look, because I was expecting you to be right behind her. I'm as sure as I can be she came back by herself."

Mr. Sykes cleared his throat. "The important thing is no one was harmed and Dulcie's back, safe and sound. Now I must be getting back before those two young reprobates drink me out of house and home."

"Thank you for all your help, Mr. Sykes," I said as he climbed back onto his cart and took the reins.

"Don't mention it, miss. Goodbye for now."

I watched him go. Next to me, Dulcie whinnied.

"She knows you have some sugar for her," Harper said.

"And she shall have it." I reached in my pocket and pulled out a few sugar cubes, which she accepted eagerly. I stroked her nose. "If only you could talk, Dulcie."

Back in my room, I started to pack. Nell came in and was clearly taken aback to see me folding clothes and laying them in a suitcase.

"Oh miss, I didn't know you were going so soon. I'll do that for you."

I hesitated. But it was her job after all. I stepped back and sat down by the dressing table.

"You do that very well, Nell. Much better than I do."

Nell gave a slight smile. "It's my job, miss. I wouldn't be much good if I couldn't fold a pretty frock so that it didn't arrive looking like a dog's dinner, would I?"

"I suppose not, Nell."

"Are you going back to London, miss?"

"Yes. Back to my aunt's."

"But you'll be back here soon, won't you?"

"I really don't know. I have a lot to consider. I may return to Yorkshire, to my family home. We'll see."

Nell paused in the act of folding my nightdress. "I suppose I shall have to go back to being a parlor maid again then."

"Not necessarily. You could always apply for a position elsewhere. Besides, it would probably do you good to get away from Cortney Abbas. See a bit of the world while you're still young enough to enjoy it. I'm thinking of doing the same." I hadn't, but now I mentioned it, perhaps a trip to some of Europe's capital cities would be fun. As for a traveling companion…maybe I could persuade Coralie to join me. I would certainly look her up when I got back to Belgravia.

"I couldn't come and work for you, could I, miss?"

"If I had my own home, I would be happy to employ you. But at this moment, I don't, I'm afraid." But would I employ her? The strange thing was I believed I would, as long as she was away from this place and everyone in it.

Nell resumed packing. "What's Yorkshire like, miss?"

"God's own country," I said wistfully. I closed my eyes and images of the moors I grew up on sprang into my mind. I heard the bird calls, the whistling wind, and saw the rolling heavy clouds shrouding the looming bleak Pennines in an enveloping, damp mist. Purple heather and ling, vivid yellow gorse, rich, dark peat and the ever-present earthy smell and sound of bubbling brooks and streams threading their way across the marshy landscape that had not altered in millennia. How to describe all that to a young woman who had barely set foot outside Cortney Abbas in the green and gently rolling Wiltshire countryside?

"Suffice it to say, Nell, Yorkshire is the largest county in England and its beauty is not to be found anywhere else in the country. It's moody and magnificent. Have you ever read *Wuthering Heights* by Emily Brontë?"

"Can't say I have, miss. I'm not a good reader. So, Yorkshire's not like round here then?"

I smiled. "No, Nell. It's about as far as you can get from being like here."

She frowned. "I don't know if I should like it."

The door opened before I could answer her. Cecilia burst in, her face a deep shade of angry red. "Leave us, Nell," she said. The girl scurried out of the room. "What do you think you were doing?" she demanded, noting the suitcase.

"What do you mean?"

"Taking Dulcie down to the village. Who gave you permission to do that?"

"Buckingham was aware of it. When I told him I had decided to ride there rather than take the car."

"And since when has a servant been empowered to grant your requests?"

"I didn't think I needed to ask, quite frankly."

"You're not the lady of this house yet, Grace. And the rate you're carrying on you never will be."

"You mean if you have anything to do with it."

"Don't be absurd. Simon makes his own decisions."

"Influenced by you."

"Now you're being ridiculous and childish."

"Am I really? I don't think so. This isn't about me taking Dulcie out, is it? It's about you not wanting to relinquish any of your control over your brother to someone you consider unworthy of him."

"Not just him. You're not worthy of any of us. You don't fit here, Grace. Isn't that obvious? Go back to Yorkshire and stay there. Leave those of us who were born to it alone."

"What I do and don't do is nothing to do with you, Cecilia."

"I can see you're going anyway." She indicated the suitcase.

"I am returning to London a little earlier than planned, that's all."

"Does Simon know?"

"Not yet."

"Very well, I'll leave you to it. Bon voyage."

She swept out of my room and Nell returned. "Lady Cecilia's ever so cross," she said.

"Isn't she?" I said. "I expect she'll get over it. The moment I've gone."

My packing was nearly complete when there was a tap on the door. Nell answered. The housekeeper came in. "There's a telephone call for you, miss. Lord Simon."

"Thank you, Mrs. Bennett."

I left the room and followed Mrs. Bennett down to the drawing room. I picked up the telephone. "Hello, Simon?"

The line crackled and hissed like frying bacon.

"Grace? It's a terrible line, I'm afraid. Listen. Lia's telephoned me, in a frightful flap about you taking one of the horses without telling her and she told me you're thinking of returning to London straightaway. Is that true?"

"Yes. Things are simply not working out down here, and it's getting worse all the time. I wanted to go out and requested the car and chauffeur, but Cecilia had other plans, so I took Dulcie for a ride into the village, and she found her way back to the Hall by herself. There was no harm done. Cecilia has been totally unreasonable, and I've had enough. I'm sorry, Simon, but I'm catching the early morning train."

"Back to your aunt's?"

"Yes. I shall place a call to her after I've spoken to you."

"I wouldn't bother. There's no one there. The flat is shut up for the rest of the summer."

"What? But she knew I wasn't staying at Mordenhyrst Hall long."

"I have no idea why her plans changed, but you try telephoning there if you don't believe me. You won't get any answer. I called yesterday and spoke to a servant who was closing everything up before she went to join her."

"Where have they gone?"

"To Yorkshire, to stay with your father for a few weeks. The weather's been so good up there for a change."

I said nothing. With my plan thwarted, I needed an alternative.

Simon spoke. "So, you see, you need to stay there. I'll be back later tomorrow, and we can chat then."

"'Bye Simon," I said.

"'Bye, dar—" I cut him off.

Two minutes later I dashed up to my room, retrieved my purse, and took it back down with me. Nell called after me, "Is everything all right, miss?"

"Fine, thank you," I called back.

In the drawing room, I rummaged in my purse, found Coralie's calling card, picked up the telephone and called the operator. A few minutes later, I got her on the line. She sounded pleased to hear from me and we exchanged the usual pleasantries.

"So, you want to come and stay with me," she said.

"How did you know that?"

"It transmitted itself down the wire," she said, a smile in her voice. "That and the over-effusive way you told me you were fine, meaning, of course, that you were anything but."

"It's that obvious, is it?"

"Let's put it this way, don't audition for any leading roles until you've perfected your acting skills a bit more."

I sighed. "My aunt's away and I have to get out of here. Cecilia's impossible and any relationship I had with Simon is pretty much dead in the water. He's not the man I knew even as recently as a couple of weeks ago and I don't see how I'm ever going to get back what we had." Saying it out loud like that made it seem so final. My eyes filled with tears and spilled over my lashes, forming tiny rivulets as they coursed down my cheeks.

Coralie's voice soothed me. "Of course you can stay with me, as long as you wish. And you're right. You must get out of there as soon as possible. One more thing…. This is crucial. Don't take anything with you out of the house. Only take what you brought. I cannot stress this enough. Only take what you brought with you."

"I hear you, Coralie. I'll do that. It's so kind of you to put me up."

"You're sounding like a waif and stray. I'm delighted to help. It'll be fun having someone else around. Especially someone who, like me, doesn't fit the mold. We'll shake 'em up a bit. How about it?"

I laughed. Already I felt better. A fresh start. It was what I needed. In a way I was grateful to my aunt. Whatever whim had caused her to up sticks and go up to Yorkshire had turned out well. My new friend and I were going to have some fun.

CHAPTER EIGHT

Coralie's flat may have only been a quarter of a mile from Aunt Penelope's, but it couldn't have been more different. In place of my aunt's late-Victorian fussiness and clutter that required every surface to be crammed to the rafters with framed photographs, vases of flowers, plants, stuffed birds and walls heaving with heavily framed pictures of idyllic landscapes, Coralie had designed her apartment with the newly fashionable exuberantly contrasting colors and patterns that were fast becoming all the rage in smart society. Everything was geometrically shaped, from mirrors in different shades of glass to plain white walls adorned with extraordinary pictures of stylized modern men and women. Over a fireplace in the drawing room hung an enormous painting of a young woman at the wheel of a sports car. I looked for a signature.

"Tamara de Lempicka," Coralie said as her maid brought us tall glasses of homemade lemonade. I must have looked blank. "She's quite the thing in New York now, but she comes from Poland I believe and spent some time in Paris. I picked this one up last month at a gallery in Mayfair. I have the feeling it was a good investment. She kind of draws you in with that sultry expression, doesn't she?"

Personally, I thought she looked half asleep, or drunk, but didn't like to say so. I had to admit though, it wasn't a painting you could ignore.

Coralie laughed. "You hate it, don't you?"

"I don't *hate* it. I'm not very good with art. Especially modern art."

"Don't worry. You'll get the hang of it. Or maybe not. Either way, it's not important. Thank you, Nancy." The maid nodded and left.

Coralie motioned me to sit, and I lowered myself onto a chair shaped like three sides of a box, with narrow steel legs. It was surprisingly comfortable, with its deep, dark blue leather seat cushion. I took a long drink, relishing the way the chunks of ice clinked in the glass. The sprigs of mint added extra flavor. "This is so refreshing," I said as I set the glass down.

"I seem to have become acclimatized to your English weather. I'm sure if I had just arrived here, I would find it quite pleasantly cool after the humidity I'm used to at this time of the year, but I must say, even *I'm* finding this heat oppressive."

"London can be like that in summer. I think it's all the tall buildings. You feel hemmed in, and I think it keeps the heat in too. Like a greenhouse. In Yorkshire I would go up on the moors on a hot day. There's always a breeze to keep you cool."

"I think I had better take a look at these moors of yours myself." Coralie laughed lightly, wafting an exquisitely decorated Japanese fan. Then, abruptly, she snapped the fan shut and laid it down next to her drink. "Okay, Grace, to business. What happened at Mordenhyrst Hall after I left?"

That directness of hers was one of the qualities I admired about Coralie. During the next quarter of an hour, I told her about my visit to the village, what the landlord of the pub had told me, and about Dulcie. I finished with my last argument with Cecilia. Through it all, Coralie said nothing. She listened intently, encouraging me to continue when I faltered, sure that she must be thoroughly bored by now. When I finished my narrative, she took a deep breath.

"How have you been sleeping? Any dreams?"

"Most nights, pretty well, with one glaring exception. Otherwise, I fall asleep easily enough and don't remember any dreams when I wake up."

"And the glaring exception?"

I repeated my experience of Sunday night.

Coralie's face remained impassive throughout. Only when I had finished my account did she speak. "The old woman you saw, can you describe her to me? Did she have skin my color?"

I nodded. "She wore a sort of bandanna around her head, a brightly colored dress and her face was deeply wrinkled. She may even have been the oldest woman I have ever laid eyes on. There was a timelessness about her."

Coralie nodded. "And she held a femur…a thigh bone. Human?"

"I think so. It looked like one anyway. If I had to guess I would say she was making some kind of incantation, only I couldn't hear any words." A thought occurred to me. "Do you think you know who she is?"

"I can't be sure. But my presence in that house at that time may have caused her to manifest there. You say the young woman didn't seem to belong in that vision."

"It was something about her expression. She was looking around as if she didn't recognize anything. She seemed lost, whereas the other woman was in control of her surroundings. Who is she, Coralie?"

"From what you describe, you may have been visited by the spirit of Beersheba Atkins."

"Beersheba? You mean the woman who passed on her knowledge to you?"

"The one and the same. Grace, I'd like to try something with you if you don't mind."

"Try something?"

"Yes. You open your mind to me, and I receive your thoughts. It might help me understand more of what's going on here."

"And you think this will help?"

"It can't hurt."

Coralie gazed at me intently. I hardly knew this woman, and after everything that had been happening, I didn't know who to trust, but there was something calming and reassuring about her. Right now, she seemed the only one who had the slightest notion of how to deal with whatever I had become mixed up in. I took a deep breath. "What do you need me to do?"

"Nothing. Just sit back and relax, close your eyes and let yourself drift."

I settled myself deeper into the chair, which seemed to contour itself to the shape of my back, providing relaxed yet firm support.

Coralie's voice drifted toward me like gentle waves breaking on a sandy beach. Her voice softened, became one with the imagined waves, until all I could hear was their slight shushing.

I lay on the soft, white sand, the sun caressing my skin, the calmest of breezes wafting around me. And then I wasn't alone. I opened my eyes and Simon smiled down at me. He kissed my nose and stroked my cheek. I closed my eyes again and drifted deeper....

When I opened my eyes, the beach was gone. Simon was gone. I was alone. I felt chilled and shivery in the cold half-light. The air was fetid, tainted by something long dead, or meat left to go rotten. I hugged myself, trying to get warm, and momentarily closed my eyes. When I opened them again, I thought I'd gone blind. Blackness enveloped me. I couldn't even see my own hand stretched out in front of me.

"Simon! Coralie!" My cries echoed around me as if I were surrounded by a wall of some kind. I reached out all around me but could feel nothing. Only black emptiness.

Wake up. You must wake up.

The voice in my head grew louder, took form. I tried to stand but fell back. There was nothing under me. Somehow, I was suspended above the ground. I had no way of knowing how high. All around me, I heard the beating of invisible wings as if a flock of enormous birds were carrying me along with them. I looked down again. Far below me, and receding fast, were green swathes of grassland. Above me I saw nothing, but in that moment, I knew. The wings belonged to a bird that had me in its grasp. I could feel nothing, no pain of talons gripping my skin, but a slight pressure on my shoulders told me it had a firm hold on me. Blackness now filled my sight. Then, something distracted me.

Ahead of me, a pinprick of light had appeared. So faint at first I thought I had imagined it, but it grew brighter, like a small candle. A voice came with it – a tiny whisper I could barely make out, but which grew stronger every second. It came closer...closer.

Coralie's voice. "Grace, come back to me. Come back to me."
I squeezed my eyes shut and felt a tap on my cheek. I opened my
eyes and stared into Coralie's concerned face. "You had me worried
there for a second," she said, and smiled. "How are you feeling?"
I sat forward and my head swam and buzzed as I tried to orientate
myself. My shoulders ached. "I don't know. I had the oddest...dream,
I suppose you'd call it. First it was lovely, I was lying on the most
beautiful beach in the world and Simon was there, and he was as he
used to be. Then it all changed, and I was...I don't know where.
Something had me in its grasp, it was carrying me high above ground.
A huge bird I couldn't see.... Then there was a chink of light and...
here I am."

Coralie stood back and returned to her own chair. "I saw what
you saw. Down to the last detail, I should imagine. Let me see
your shoulders."

I eased my dress down over my right shoulder and winced.

Coralie beckoned me to the mirror. "See for yourself."

I stared in frozen disbelief at the claw marks. Something had dug
right in, piercing the skin.

Coralie rang for her maid, who appeared within seconds. "Bring
the medical kit. Miss Sutcliffe has been hurt."

Nancy nodded and dashed off.

"I don't understand," I said, my teeth chattering with nerves.
"How could this happen? I never left this room, did I? Yet it was all
so real. What does it mean?"

"I wish I could give you a definitive answer, but I can't. You're
right about one thing though. You physically never left this room.
All I have now is guesswork, and if I were to share that with
you...well, it could be dangerous. If I'm wrong, it could be more
than dangerous."

"*More* than dangerous?"

Coralie nodded. "Possibly fatal. Though, at this moment, I don't
know for whom."

"So...I'm in danger?"

"You could be, but you're here now. You should be safe, but as for Simon.... I can't make it out. He could be in great danger, but I simply don't know for sure. It could even be that you are the only one who can help him but, again, I may be way off."

Nancy returned and ministered to my cuts and grazes. She bathed and then doused them in some kind of antiseptic which stung and made my eyes water. Then she applied gauze dressings and I rearranged my dress.

"Thank you, Nancy," I said. She smiled, collected her supplies, and left us.

Coralie stood and went over to a bureau in the corner of the room. She opened it and removed a small black bag which she brought over to a small card table. "Come over here, Grace. I need to show you something."

I did as she requested. She loosened the drawstring on the velvet bag and scattered the contents. They consisted of small, gleaming white stones of varying shapes and sizes but none larger than a marble. She murmured an incantation I couldn't understand and gathered the stones back together into a pile which she then scooped up and replaced in the bag. She mouthed something else and released the stones once more. They clattered and bounced more vigorously than before, finally coming to rest in a recognizable star shape. I watched, fascinated as the stones took on different hues, glittering like cracked ice in shades of purple, red, orange, yellow, blue and pink. Two grew darker until they resembled the sort of jet Victorian ladies would wear in their mourning jewelry.

"I've never seen stones do that before," I said.

Coralie smiled. "You've never seen *stones* like these before. They are exceedingly rare. These have been handed down for generations in my family. I'm not even entirely sure where they came from, possibly from Clothilde Gasparyan herself, but whatever their origins, they always tell the truth."

"And what are they telling you, right now?"

"Some good things. Some bad. Many things couched in imagery I shall need to work on. But one thing at least is undeniable."

"What's that?"

She fixed her gaze on my eyes. "You are indeed going to marry Simon Mordenhyrst."

CHAPTER NINE

I could barely breathe when she uttered those words. Finally, my mouth dry, I managed to respond. "I can't get my head round this. I mean, after all that's happened.... Surely he and I aren't meant to be together."

Coralie looked back at the stones. "Nevertheless, it's all there. Remember I said I thought he might need your help. I still don't know if that's right, but there is no doubting you are to marry."

"Which part of this...arrangement...tells you that? Is it the black stones?"

"No. You see, Grace, reading these stones is not a matter of saying, 'that purple stone over there represents this or that event.' It's much more complicated than that. It's an overall picture broken into shards of detail and this picture tells me you are destined to go ahead and marry Simon. Sooner rather than later as well. Certainly before the year is out."

"What else do you see there?"

My friend returned her attention to the stones. Maybe it was my imagination, but they didn't seem to be glittering as brightly as they had. "The energy is waning," Coralie said. "Something is interfering with this." She put her hand to the side of her head and winced. "Such pain." She staggered away from the table. I put a steadying arm around her while she stumbled toward her chair. I helped her ease herself down onto it.

I waited for her to recover. Once she had lowered her hand and seemed to be breathing normally again, I spoke. "What happened just then?"

She raised her eyes to me, and I gasped. Both eyes were bloodshot so badly I could barely see any white in either one. "Don't worry. I know what I look like right now, but it will pass. I'll sit here quietly and sip some lemonade."

"Here, have the rest of mine." I set my half-empty glass next to hers and she accepted it with a slight smile.

"Has anything like this happened before?" I asked.

"Only once," Coralie said. She still seemed to be having great difficulty speaking. I didn't ask her any more questions. I stole a glance over at the table and my skin prickled. Every stone had turned black. A dull, lifeless black that put me in mind of my awful vision earlier on. I desperately wanted to know what Coralie could tell me, but her eyes had closed, and she looked as if she had fallen asleep.

As quietly as possible, I stood and went over to the table.

The stones sat in their star shape, dead and drained of all power. Seeing them like that convinced me they were capable of generating a fair amount of energy when charged up by whatever it was Coralie did. Right now, they looked as alive as a pebble on a beach. What would happen if I touched one? It couldn't do any harm. Not as they were now. I reached out and was about to pick one up.

"No, Grace. Stop."

Coralie was on her feet, her eyes still red but less terrifying. She put her arm out to me. "Don't ever touch one of those. Promise me."

"I'm sorry, I was just going to see what it felt like."

"Please move away from that table and sit down."

Only when I had done so did Coralie once more sink down into her chair. "Those are not ordinary stones, Grace. You must understand that. Their power is great and can be misused, even innocently. Don't ever touch them. Do you understand?"

I nodded. "I'm so sorry. I didn't mean any harm."

"I know you didn't. I shall put them away when I've recovered myself." Coralie gasped as a wave of pain seemed to hit her. "My head is splitting. It's been a long time since I felt anything as powerful as this."

She fingered the right side of her face, and, to my horror, I could see why. "Your cheek's badly swollen."

"I thought so. My eye's closing up too."

"It looks as if someone actually punched you. Is it always like that?"

Coralie attempted a smile but winced from the effort. "No, thankfully. Ring for Nancy, would you? I'd like to bathe my face in iced water."

"I thought steak was good for swollen eye injuries?"

"Old wives' tale. You merely ruin a good steak. No, I need a bowl of iced water and some cloths. Nancy knows that."

I pressed the bell and went to help Coralie. By now the whites of her eyes were back to normal, but her right eyelid was purpling and closing fast. "Nancy will think I beat you." I wasn't joking either. How else should Coralie's injury be explained?

"Don't worry about that. Nancy's been with me for a few years. She's seen more than one inexplicable injury on me."

Nancy flinched the moment she set eyes on her mistress, but she said nothing and went off to fetch the water.

She returned with a bowl of water in which floated a large quantity of ice cubes and immediately set about wrapping some in a cloth she had soaked in the freezing water. She handed it to Coralie, who clamped it to the right side of her face. "Thank you, Nancy, I can take it from here."

"If you're sure, Miss Coralie."

"I am."

The maid cast me a quick glance and I couldn't tell if it was accusatory or merely concern for her employer. She left us.

Coralie kept the ice firmly planted on the injured side of her head. Once again, I waited until she felt sufficiently recovered to continue.

"I have to tell you, Grace. I have seen many strange things and been in many dark places in my life, but I have never come across anything to match this. There is evil in Cortney Abbas that goes back to a time long before men walked there. It infests the place and everything in it. What the stones revealed only bears out what I suspected and feared. It is not a place where anyone should live. It's a place where everything should be razed to the ground, burned and destroyed. The very soil should be dug up and taken away, disposed of somewhere that will never be found. If it were possible, a force field should be sent up around that place so that no one ever breaches its boundaries. I repeat, never have I ever encountered such a force for evil."

I struggled with the impact of her words. "And yet you tell me I shall marry Simon, which means I shall be mistress of Mordenhyrst Hall and live in that place."

"That's the part I cannot understand...unless you persuade him to leave Mordenhyrst and Cortney Abbas."

"One of his friends, well, one of Cecilia's friends if I'm being accurate, warned me that Simon would never leave Cecilia. That she would never let him go."

Coralie removed the ice pack and laid it down on the table next to her. "Who said that?"

"Percy, I think. Yes. It was when we went in to dinner on Saturday. She just came out with it and never elaborated."

Coralie picked up the ice pack and reapplied it to her face. The swelling showed no sign of abating.

"Is there anything I can get for you, Coralie?" I asked. "It must hurt a lot."

"It will pass, honey. Don't worry. But thank you for caring."

I hesitated, then asked the question uppermost in my mind. "What do you think Percy meant?"

"I can only guess. Have you noticed anything strange about Simon and Cecilia's relationship?"

"Only that he seems to defer to her judgment in most things. I don't get a look in when she's around. Oh, don't get me wrong, I understand. With their mother dying so young and Cecilia having to grow up too soon, she's assumed more of a parental role than a sibling one...." I stopped. Coralie's frown and the way she was shaking her head spoke volumes. "You don't mean that at all, do you? You mean.... No. No, I've seen nothing like that. Has someone said anything?"

Coralie once again laid the ice pack down. "No. I just got to wondering, that's all. They only really had each other growing up."

"But I don't believe anything...of that nature...took place between them."

"I expect you're right. Grace, I want to do something you may find worrisome, but given the situation we're in I need your cooperation. Will you help me?"

The feeling of dread, which had clutched at me with Coralie's earlier words, tightened its grip. Whatever it was she wanted to do would hardly be a pleasant game of cards. But what choice did I have? "What do you want me to do?"

"Contact Beersheba."

I felt as if someone had winded me.

"It's the only way, Grace. I need to know why she manifested herself to you at Mordenhyrst Hall while I was under the same roof. This is the only way I have a chance at getting the answer. Will you help?"

I took a deep breath. "What does it involve?"

Coralie went over to a bureau and unclasped a long chain from around her neck, revealing a small key, which she now inserted into the lock. Once the lock opened, she extracted a small box and took it over to the card table, around which were four matching chairs.

"Come and sit with me here," she said, and I did as she requested. She opened the box, releasing a strange aroma of mixed herbs and spices, but I couldn't make out any individual scents I recognized.

"These are ancient and rare herbs," she said. "I have no idea how old or even where they originate. I only know this box, like the stones and the cards I spoke about, has been handed down through my mother's family going back many generations. We shall need only a tiny amount of the powder for our purposes. Now, please would you ring for Nancy, and bring me an ashtray and my lighter."

I nodded and did as I was instructed. I could tell Nancy had witnessed such a scene before, judging by the calm manner in which she came straight over to the table and sat down. She gave me a shy half-smile.

Coralie sprinkled maybe a quarter teaspoon of the herbs into the ashtray. She passed her hands over the herbs, while she murmured words in that archaic language that this time I couldn't understand. Nancy joined in, also reciting the same unfamiliar words. Before my eyes, a halo of light appeared around both of them. Initially pale blue, it seemed to traverse the entire spectrum of light, finally settling on a vivid scarlet. I didn't dare interrupt Coralie and Nancy in their task but couldn't help wondering if my aura was the same as theirs.

I lost all sense of time passing, my only sensations being of a strange lightness followed by an equally powerful heaviness, as if someone was pressing a weight down on my head, which now ached with the sensation. I had suffered with migraines in the past and this was becoming uncomfortably like one. I pressed my hands to my temples.

Coralie struck a match and dropped it into the ashtray. She closed her eyes and her lips moved, forming words that grew into a chant, echoed by Nancy. Instantly, the herbs smoked, sending out a pungent, heady vapor that made my head swim and set me coughing. The herbs smoldered, the vapor turned to deep gray smoke while Coralie and Nancy's auras slid from red to charcoal to black, where they lingered before lightening and returning to red, but an intense red, so bright it hurt my eyes.

Coralie opened her eyes and I flinched from the ferocity of her gaze. Her irises had changed from deep brown to piercing blue. I glanced at Nancy. Hers were the same. The women's murmuring became a chant and grew louder, more urgent. I moved my hands to cover my face against their penetrating stares, which stabbed at me, sending daggers of pain through my body.

"Look, Grace," Coralie said, her usually soft, mellow voice harsh and insistent. "Turn and look behind you. Turn and do not be afraid."

I didn't want to. That voice, could it be Coralie? Had something else possessed her body? I looked from Coralie to Nancy, and it was like staring at a mirror image.

"Turn, Grace. Look and see."

Reluctantly, I edged my way round in my seat. Behind me, a few feet away, a scene was unfolding. Some kind of campfire, similar to what I had witnessed in my room that Sunday night, glowed faintly, growing stronger by the second. A shadowy dark figure in a brightly colored dress poked at the fire with the long white bone she had used to point at me. Her features formed into those of an old woman – the same woman I had seen before. To one side of her, something emerged out of the undergrowth. Not the scared young woman who had been Elise Mordenhyrst, but a small child. The old woman stopped poking the fire and met the enquiring eyes of the little girl. Instinctively I knew this was a reenactment of the night Coralie had witnessed the terrible massacre of her village. In this vision, there was no shouting, no dead bodies, only an ancient woman and an impressionable child. The woman made a gathering-in gesture with her hands and arms and the little girl took hesitant steps forward.

When she was within the woman's grasp, she appeared to half-faint. The woman caught her before she fell into the fire, burning herself in the process. I could see the skin on her lower leg blister and scorch. The hem of her dress smoked and seemed about to catch fire, but she managed to deposit the child on the ground next to her and throw clumps of earth over the fabric in time.

The child recovered, sat up and opened her eyes, apparently none the worse for her ordeal. She fixed her steady gaze on me. The old woman pointed the bone at Coralie, who slumped in her chair.

I jumped up to help her.

"*Leave her!*" Nancy cried. "Sit down and don't move."

I did so, alternating my gaze between the vision and Coralie, whose aura had faded to a muted shade of gray. I had no way of knowing whether that was a good or bad sign.

All around us, the air grew stifling. The lingering stench of the herbs, which still smoldered in the ashtray, combined with something emanating from the vision itself, made me nauseous.

Coralie suddenly sat bolt upright, eyes wide and staring, hands outstretched and her body rigid. I glanced at the vision and cried out. The old woman was no longer there. She was in the room with us. I felt her pass behind me and touch my wounded shoulders. The claw-like hands gripped tighter until I gritted my teeth to stop myself from crying out in pain. The woman bent closer to my ear and her breath stank of death and decay. She murmured something I couldn't understand. I squeezed my eyes shut and prayed to God she would go away. She didn't. But this time, when she spoke, I understood her.

"I have no communion with thy spirits." The voice was cracked, dry, hollow and rang in my head rather than my ears.

The old woman moved on to Nancy. The clawed hands settled on her shoulders as they had on mine. The murmur in her ears, exactly the same. Did Nancy hear the same words? But surely those words to me were uttered because I was praying. Imploring a spirit for help that she did not want around her.

When the old woman reached Coralie, my friend's body relaxed. The ghost of a smile appeared on her face. She opened her eyes, and they were normal again. Her aura went from gray to red in an instant. No clawed hands settled on her shoulders. Instead, she received a loving embrace and returned it warmly. The sight of the corpse-like woman – whose once brightly colored dress now hung on her more like a faded shroud – holding Coralie in a maternal embrace revolted me. How could she bear it? For an instant, she seemed to transform. Her arms became like wings, and in my mind, I saw a great falcon poised and ready to take flight. In a second the illusion was gone, and the room returned to normal. The herbs had burned away and only their smell remained. My headache vanished.

"Was that Beersheba?" I asked, knowing the answer. "And I swear I saw a falcon."

Coralie nodded. "You did and so did I. It is as I thought. Mordenhyrst Hall, Cortney Abbas and all that resides there is cursed. That is why Beersheba came to you rather than me. You and I are in this together, but you, Grace, *you* are the one around whom everything will revolve. You've been chosen."

"Chosen?"

"We can never know the reason for the riddles the universe presents us with. All we can do is accept our fate and do what has to be done. In your case, this means that you must return to Mordenhyrst Hall. Something momentous is about to happen there and you are to be at the heart of it. You must return to Mordenhyrst Hall, and you must marry Simon Mordenhyrst."

CHAPTER TEN

Panic set in, infesting every nerve in my body. My hands trembled and I shook from head to foot. All I had just witnessed...and now this. "But...but I don't understand. I have no special powers. I...I can't do it. I...." Tears took over and I wept.

Nancy stood, came over to me and handed me a handkerchief. I accepted it gratefully and she pulled me to her, cradling my head while I sobbed my heart out. Nothing made any sense. I had been simple Grace Sutcliffe, living a normal, if somewhat predictable and uneventful life in Yorkshire. I had craved a bit of excitement. That was all. How could I have been so stupid and thoughtless? If only I could turn back time and go back to my simple, boring world.

When I had cried myself dry, Nancy let me go with a pat on my hand and a sympathetic smile. She had abandoned all pretense of being a simple servant. Her role in Coralie's life was far more significant than that.

For now though, she switched back to doing her employer's bidding when Coralie requested brandy and sodas for her and me.

"Come and sit over here," Coralie said to me. "You've had quite a barrage of shocks. You need time to absorb everything."

I welcomed the comfortable cocoon of the easy chair. Nancy reappeared with drinks, ice clinking in the glasses. She added a splash of soda to each and presented them to us on a silver tray. I took a sip of mine and exploded in a fit of coughing, but the burning turned to a comforting warmth, and I took another swig with no ill effect. Gradually, a mellow calm overtook the panic as my muscles relaxed.

Coralie's voice washed over me. "You'll need strength, Grace. I'll help all I can, but you must channel your inner being. I know you have the power. It lies dormant within you, waiting for your summons. Lie back and close your eyes. Be calm, be still. No one can hurt you. No one can harm you in any way. Listen to my voice.... Let your body float...."

I lay in a sea of calm and peace. Around me, only gentle sounds of nature. Soft birdsong, the humming of bees.... Deeper and deeper I floated.... Warm waves caressed my body and licked my face. I tried to raise my arm, but it seemed too far away to respond to my mental command. It was as if I was *in* my body but not *of* it. It should have mattered. It didn't. Soon, the humming of the bees faded with the birdsong. Only the soft kiss of the water penetrated the perfect stillness. I saw colors, not substances. Pale lilacs, soft peaches, muted pinks, greens and blues. The water around me reflected the colors. I was at peace. A perfect peace I had never experienced. And I never wanted it to end.

Time meant nothing. Space was infinite. Wherever this was didn't matter, except....

The beating of giant wings surrounded me. Once again, I felt the sensation of being raised and transported overland. I repeated my earlier motions of staring down, where, once again, the grassland appeared far, far below. Above me, only blackness. This time there was no pinprick of light ahead. A stab of fear and then....

"No!" My voice scythed through the air. For one split second, it was as if a veil had lowered from my eyes. As far as I could see, in every direction except downward, a sea of flying creatures like giant falcons but with features that did not belong in my world. The wings of the one that held me in its grasp beat rhythmically. It emitted a loud and raucous caw, echoed by its fellows.

The vision ceased as abruptly as it had begun, and I was back in the tranquility of that calm sea. I was once again at peace. Stronger. Rejuvenated.

Everything made sense now. Of course. I hadn't gone anywhere except deep within myself. I had touched my inner spirit, communed with it. Here was my place of safety. My retreat where no one could harm me.

The colors danced before me and around me. When I concentrated, I could lift my arm, but it seemed far away. Not really a part of me. It too reflected the colors around me.

Far away in the distance a voice murmured softly. It was calling to me, willing me to go toward its source. I wanted to remain there but knew I must obey. All I had to do was will myself forward and, when I did so, the voice grew louder, and I recognized Coralie's honeyed tones. I couldn't speak, but in my mind I said, "I want to stay."

"It's time to return, Grace. You have much to do. Much to accomplish."

The separation felt strained, as if I was tugging on a piece of elastic that kept yanking me back, but Coralie's voice urged me on. I pulled...

...and woke, slumped on the chair. It was like emerging from a delicious long sleep. "How long was I out for?"

"About ten minutes."

"It felt much longer."

"Time has no meaning where you were."

"I know. I felt that. I slipped inside myself somehow, didn't I?"

Coralie smiled and nodded. "You're learning fast, Grace."

The door opened and a flustered Nancy entered. "There's a telephone call for Miss Sutcliffe. It's Viscount Mordenhyrst."

"Thank you, Nancy," Coralie said.

She looked as if she wanted to say more but decided against it and left us.

Coralie picked up the receiver. "Hello, Simon. Coralie here. I'll pass you over to Grace."

She handed the candlestick telephone and its receiver to me and mouthed, "He sounds upset."

"Simon? What's happened?"

"Oh Grace, thank God." He sounded as if he were desperately trying to fend off sobs. "It's Papa. There's been an accident. He's dead, Grace. My father's dead. Please, I need you, please would you come back to Mordenhyrst?"

"Oh, Simon, I'm so sorry. What happened? Can you talk about it?"

"He...he was on his yacht. Eglantine said he had been a bit out of sorts for a day or two. Since he got back there apparently. She returned early from her cruise and found him lying drunk in the bedroom. She left him to sleep it off and a few hours later he joined her for dinner, apparently sober and his usual self. The next day the same thing happened and the day after that. He wouldn't talk about it. Finally, he seemed to pull himself together and they spent a few pleasant days but then last night...." His voice broke. "Last night they had dinner for a few guests. Everyone went to bed. Papa said he would join Eglantine soon and she went off to their room. The next thing, she heard an almighty splash and the crew shouting that there was a man overboard. They anchored the yacht, lowered a lifeboat, used what searchlights they could, but it was pitch black out there. This morning, the coast guard found him. Dead."

"That's terrible. I'm so sorry."

"Will you come? I don't think I realized fully until today how much you mean to me. Please let's try again. Things will be different this time, I swear."

"Just give me a moment, Simon, I need to think."

I covered the mouthpiece with my hand and relayed the essentials to Coralie.

"You know what you have to do, Grace. You must go."

"I'd feel easier if you were there."

"That would look extremely odd, don't you think? I can join you all later. And you can always call me or send me a cable if you need to."

That made sense. I nodded and uncovered the receiver. "I'll catch the mid-morning train from Waterloo. Can you send someone to meet me at the station?"

His relief was almost palpable. "Thank you, Grace. You have no idea what that means to me."

"I'll see you tomorrow."

"I love you, Grace."

I replaced the receiver without replying. My mind was whirling. "I'll need to hurry," I said, pushing aside the nagging voice that was urging me to ignore Simon's call for help.

Nancy responded immediately to Coralie's summons. "Miss Sutcliffe has had an urgent request to return to Mordenhyrst Hall, Nancy. As a result, she will only be staying one night and leaving tomorrow morning. At what time, Grace?"

"Nine a.m. to be on the safe side."

"Please would you pack her bags accordingly? She'll need a cab to Waterloo Station in the morning."

Nancy left us.

"I'm way out of my depth here," I said. "I have no idea what I'm supposed to do when I get there."

Coralie put a comforting hand on my arm. "Remember one thing. The hierarchy has changed. Simon is now Earl Mordenhyrst and you are his intended. Once you formalize things, and marry, you will hold seniority over Cecilia."

"She won't like that."

"She can like it or not. That's her prerogative, but she can do nothing about it."

"I wish I was as certain as you are on that point."

"My certainty comes from my belief in you. You have the inner strength to fight her whenever you need. Remember that. Don't let her get the upper hand again."

"All I can do is try."

"Oh, you can do far more than that. Believe me."

The door opened and Nancy hurried in. She was holding something, and her hands trembled.

"Whatever is it, Nancy?" Coralie asked.

Nancy thrust out her hand. "I was packing Miss Sutcliffe's bag and this.... This was in it."

Coralie took the object off her and showed it to me. A bird's claw. No, not a mere claw, this was a talon. It must have belonged to a bird of prey. I recoiled.

Coralie examined it. "It could be a falcon's. Did you pack your own bag when you left Mordenhyrst Hall, Grace?"

I shook my head. "Nell helped." We looked at each other.

"It was tucked away in a front pocket of the bag," Nancy said. "I never opened that when I unpacked. I'm so sorry."

"There's nothing you could have done, Nancy," Coralie said. "It was meant to be there. Don't worry any more about it."

"What do we do with it?" I asked, hoping against hope whatever it was didn't involve me touching it.

"We take it to the river and throw it in. It will go from there into the sea and the power of the water will cleanse it. That and a few wise words. Put it in a linen bag, Nancy. We'll go down to the river at midnight. Just the three of us."

"Yes, Miss Coralie." Nancy reluctantly took back the claw and left us.

"What does it mean?" I asked. "Why would Nell put it there?"

"Maybe she didn't. Perhaps someone else did. It would have been easy enough, wouldn't it? For someone determined enough to open the front pocket and slip it in unnoticed."

She was right, of course. I had hardly mounted a guard over my bag. Once again, my naivety had let me down. Would I never learn? Is this what my future at Mordenhyrst Hall was destined to look like? If so, why was I even going back there? But it was as Coralie had said. This was my destiny. My latest visions had sealed that. Coralie seemed to read my thoughts.

"It's understandable you would want to put as much distance as possible between yourself and Cortney Abbas right now, but you know as well as I do, the die is cast. You could escape all the way to the Arctic, and it would still find you and bring you back. Believe me, nothing would give me greater pleasure than to get myself down to Southampton and onto the next liner bound for New York, but I know it's my destiny to stay with you. The odds of the two of us ever meeting were stacked against it, but our fate was drawn long before we were even born."

"Did Beersheba tell you that?"

Coralie nodded. "Just as her fate was sealed and Clothilde Gasparyan's generations earlier. We are all the product of predestination. The genesis of ours lies farther back in history than anyone has ever imagined."

I sank lower in my chair while tears fell softly down my cheeks.

★   ★   ★

At midnight, the river mist cast an eerie silver sheen as we made our way along one of the many bridges that crossed the Thames.

Coralie stopped around halfway across. "This is the place." A solitary car passed us as we did our best to pretend we were three ordinary women out for a late-night stroll. The driver and his male passenger cast a quick glance at us as they passed and we watched as the mist enveloped them and they faded into the distance. Below us, the river flowed as it had for thousands of years, oblivious to the three pairs of eyes that now gazed down into its dark depths.

"Now, Nancy," Coralie said.

Nancy opened her capacious leather bag and withdrew the canvas wrapping enveloping the bird's claw. Nancy had attached a lead weight firmly to it so it would drag the package down into the water. Coralie raised it high as she and Nancy chanted words of some ancient invocation. When they were finished, Coralie drew her arm back and flung the tightly wrapped small bundle far out over the river. It seemed to hover in the still air before dropping like a swooping bird of prey onto the surface. Within a couple of seconds, it sank.

"It's gone," Coralie said. "The river has taken it and will hold it captive."

"Are you sure?" I asked. "It won't wash up somewhere? Bodies do. It's always happening. People who drown accidentally or on purpose are always turning up, sometimes weeks or months later, miles downstream."

"Not this. We've seen the last of that."

"What would have happened if Nancy hadn't found it when she did?"

Coralie shook her head. "It would depend on the curse that was put on that claw. Nothing good though and that's for sure."

Nancy cried out. "Look. Over there!"

She was pointing downriver. At one point, the mist had coalesced into the shape of a large bird with flapping wings. It hovered for a moment before taking off and soaring high into the sky. Ghostly white in the moonlight, it flapped its wings and flew away from us, out of sight.

"What does it mean?" I asked.

Coralie was frowning. "The river has rejected the spirit, or it has cleansed and released it. I'm not sure. I'm really not sure."

"So, it's a good sign?" I asked.

"We can only hope, Grace."

Next to me, Nancy shivered.

CHAPTER ELEVEN

Mordenhyrst Hall was in mourning. Mirrors were draped in black, curtains drawn, staff wore black armbands and Simon in his black suit looked tired, his eyes red-rimmed.

He greeted me at the main entrance and kissed me warmly on the cheek. Before, that would have made me so happy and set my heart racing. Now, I didn't know how I felt. There were too many emotions churning around inside me.

Inside, Cecilia held court in the drawing room, surrounded by pungent-smelling white lilies. The sickly sweet scent was so strong it made me gag. 'Death flowers' my mother used to call them. I wished Cecilia would open a window and let some of the stench out, but here, as everywhere else, the drapes were tightly drawn.

"Grace. How…nice…to see you again." Cecilia touched her scarlet lips with the small black silk handkerchief she was otherwise wafting around. Swathed in severest black, she appeared every inch the grieving daughter, until you looked in her eyes. That's where the real Cecilia dwelt. Not one iota of genuine human emotion emanated from them. Her coldness was all I saw, and it sent a chill through me.

"I'm sorry about your father," I said, knowing it was expected.

Once again, she performed the insincere wave of the handkerchief which, this time, barely touched her eyes.

"Have a drink, Grace," Simon said. "I'm afraid we've been hitting the brandy a little hard today."

"Only to be expected in the circumstances," I said, as warmly as I could.

Simon poured me a drink before topping up his and Cecilia's

glasses. "You'll be in the room you occupied last time. Nell will look after you again. She'll be pleased to see you."

"Thank you, Simon." I accepted the drink and sat down, taking care to position myself well back as if I owned the chair and not perched on the edge like some hovering bird. It had the effect of sending a much-needed surge of self-confidence through my veins. As for Nell resuming her duties as my personal maid...well, let's just see how she behaved. I would be watching her closely.

I took a sip of my drink and set the glass down on a small table next to me. "What can I help with? There's always so much to do on these occasions, isn't there?"

Cecilia gave me a cold stare. "It's all in hand. They're flying Papa's body back in a few days. There has to be a postmortem of course, but there's really no doubt as to cause of death. He had been drinking on and off for days and he stood too close to the edge. A wave came, jolted the yacht and...."

"Yes," I said. "Such a tragic accident."

"If you believe that," Simon said, his voice bitter.

I hadn't expected this. "But surely there can't be any doubt?"

Simon examined his hand as if it had suddenly taken on a newfound importance. "A deckhand reported seeing a large bird soaring overhead. A gyrfalcon, he said. Only there shouldn't have been any gyrfalcons anywhere near there. They're Arctic birds mainly. Of course, where Papa was concerned, anything was possible."

"*Simon!*"

"Oh, what's the point in fooling ourselves, Lia? Papa was rotten to the core. He killed our mother, did shady deals with crooks, and had a string of mistresses even when Mama was still alive."

Cecilia stubbed out her cigarette, unwrapped herself from the chaise longue, stood and strode over to the window, where she stared out.

I broke the awkward silence. "You think someone *murdered* him?"

Simon nodded, then appeared to correct himself. "Someone...or something. You could never be sure with Papa."

Cecilia spun round. "That's enough, Simon. You know we don't talk about such things in front of strangers."

"Grace is hardly a stranger. Granted, we've had our problems, but if she's willing to give us another try, nothing would give me greater pleasure than to place a ring on her finger and make her my wife. The next Countess Mordenhyrst."

Was it my imagination or did Cecilia actually wince? She certainly blinked hard and repeatedly.

"I'll leave you to your touching reunion. I have a funeral to plan." Cecilia swept out of the room, and her heels clicked across the marble hall floor.

Simon closed the door. "I'm sorry about my sister. It's hit her pretty hard. Well, both of us actually, but…well…you know daughters and their fathers. I expect you feel the same about yours."

I refrained from saying that any similarity between Acton Sutcliffe and the late Earl of Mordenhyrst was purely a matter of biology. Suddenly I missed my father with a gnawing ache. I longed to hear his matter-of-fact voice and resolved to bring him down here to Mordenhyrst as soon as I was in a position to do so, although quite what he would make of all that had happened, I couldn't imagine. I had no idea how I was ever going to explain it to him. I knew if I tried, he would insist I leave Mordenhyrst Hall immediately and forever. He would have no truck with Coralie's pronouncement that it would do no good.

I switched my mind back to the matter in hand. "Do you know when the funeral will take place?"

"Probably sometime late next week, or the week after. Papa will be buried in the family vault in the parish church, as are all the Mordenhyrsts going back to the sixteenth century. Then I suppose it will really hit home. Not that it hasn't already. Word's getting around as well. Before you arrived, there's been a steady stream of villagers coming round to the servants' entrance with flowers, cards and letters. I expect it's still going on. I asked Buckingham to manage it. Can't get my head around all this love my father's being shown. He didn't seem to get much of it when he was alive." He gave a slight rueful smile. "Oh, Grace, thank you so much for being here."

Despite all my misgivings about him, he looked so lost, I couldn't help but feel a wave of sympathy. I went over to him and put my arms tentatively around his waist. He responded by holding me so tight I could barely breathe.

"I'm sorry. I didn't mean to squeeze so hard but.... Grace, can we try again? Will you be my wife?"

What could I say? This wasn't the way it had been before, but nothing would ever be like that again. I nodded. "Yes, I will, Simon. But things will have to change. Cecilia...."

"I know. Look, she'll have to come to terms with it and if she won't, well, she'll have to live elsewhere. Goodness knows we own enough land and property around here."

Now was not the time to mention that if she refused to change, I would insist she not only move out of Mordenhyrst but that she live as far away from Cortney Abbas as was humanly possible.

★   ★   ★

Cecilia and I kept our distance from each other in the days leading up to the funeral. The authorities released the earl's body, and, in due course, a gleaming black hearse delivered an impressive mahogany casket containing his mortal remains. The earl was to lie in the drawing room so that villagers and other more illustrious personages might come and pay their last respects. Privately I wondered why this was necessary. It did seem somewhat archaic and feudal, but Simon said it was the way the Mordenhyrsts had always done it going back centuries.

"I suppose no one has ever thought to change. Feel free to do whatever you like with me after I'm gone," he said, with a mischievous wink.

That one simple gesture reassured me, even if only a little. A subtle change seemed to have come over Simon since I had arrived. It was as if his father's death had freed him in some way. Maybe it had. Cecilia, on the other hand, seemed withdrawn and preoccupied. Each day saw a decrease in her snide comments and sly remarks. More than once I caught her having a silent weep, and had withdrawn to give her some privacy. For all her faults, she had loved her father.

Of Eglantine there was no sign.

"Good riddance," Simon said. "Filthy little gold digger. Can't see what Papa saw in her."

"I'm quite sure you're the only heterosexual male who can't," his sister said, in an increasingly rare attempt at humor.

"Well, yes, of course, apart from her obvious physical attributes, but did he really have to spend quite so much money on her? The furs alone cost enough to fuel the economy of an African country. Don't forget, I saw the bills. I swear, if he'd lived much longer, she would have emptied his bank account."

"Don't speak like that about him. He was our father, for God's sake!" Cecilia stormed out of the room. She was doing that a lot.

"She's taking it really hard, isn't she?" I asked.

Simon made a noise somewhere between a snort and a guffaw. "Don't be fooled, Grace. Despite what I said the other day, she hated his guts."

"*What?*"

"She blamed him for Mama's death just as much as I did. More so, maybe, because she was older and understood far more of what Mama was going through – what *he* was putting her through. Make no mistake about it, I doubt there is one person in the whole of Cortney Abbas who didn't breathe a sigh of relief when they heard the Absent Earl had perished. Oh yes, they come, call, leave sympathy cards and flowers, but it's out of respect for the position rather than the man. I would also like to think that maybe they're hopeful I will usher in a new and more acceptable era. At least they know they don't have to lock up their daughters anymore."

Once again, he gave a smile. I was still reeling from the revelation that Cecilia had harbored such negative feelings about the man I thought she adored.

"You know we would normally have an open casket, don't you?"

I shook my head. I had always thought such practices gruesome. As a young child, I had been forced by my parents to file past my grandfather's open casket at his funeral.

"Say goodbye to your granddad," my mother urged and lifted me so I could look down on his waxy, makeup-enhanced dead face. At any moment, I was sure his eyes would spring open. I remember howling my head off in terror and having to be rushed out of church by my embarrassed nanny. I had nightmares about it for weeks after.

Simon lit a cigarette and blew out a cloud of smoke. "I saw his body, you know. I had to make a formal identification before they would release it to me." He shuddered. "There was no question of an open casket."

"I thought he had only been in the water a relatively short time."

"He had, but how long do you think it takes for the fish to find a free and sumptuous feast floating around? They had made rather a mess of him. His face…. Anyway, enough of that gruesomeness. After the funeral, how about you and I go up to London and buy you that engagement ring that should be gracing your finger? Then we can make the announcement in *The Times, Tatler* and all the usual society pages. We'll organize a sitting for you with a professional photographer. Maybe Cecil Beaton. I think Pip is acquainted with him. Of course, everyone wants Beaton these days, so he's impossible to book, but I'm sure Pip could wangle something. Oh, and why not invite your father down here? Our last meeting didn't go too well, and I really would like to try again, and gain his blessing. What do you say?"

"I…I…." My mouth had dried up and I could barely speak. Simon had set off like a steam train with no brakes on a steep downward gradient. A whirlwind of conflicting emotions crashed through my brain. I knew that marrying Simon was my destiny and during the past few days I had begun to warm to him again. But the rush of love I used to feel whenever I laid eyes on him seemed well and truly doused. Could I really marry a man who didn't arouse passion in me? Yet Coralie had told me I must, and my newly awakened inner spirit only served to reinforce that conviction. If only I could be clearer as to why I had been chosen in this way, I might have felt better about it. But, on the other hand…. I began to feel like some kind of sacrificial lamb and, for some reason, a painting by William Holman Hunt came to mind. I had seen *The Scapegoat* at an exhibition somewhere. That poor creature – standing alone in a barren landscape, portrayed by the artist as having taken on the sins of the world – deeply affected me at the time. There was something so sad and fatalistic about the goat's expression.

In that second, my inner voice spoke. If I carried on this way, I would end up feeling sorry for myself. I was no scapegoat and I wasn't about to offer myself up as a sacrifice either. *You're Acton Sutcliffe's daughter. Get on with it, girl.*

Simon was waiting. The longer I delayed, the more anxious his expression grew. I had to say something, so I said the first thing that sprang to mind. "Of course. That will be…lovely. I'll call Father this evening."

"You could invite him to the funeral if you like."

Had he really suggested that?

"No, I don't think that would be appropriate, but a few days next week, if he's not too busy, should be fine."

"That's settled then. Let's have a martini. I'm parched."

★   ★   ★

"Simon is formally going to ask you again for my hand in marriage, Father. He's hoping you might see him in a more favorable light this time."

An exhalation of breath hissed down the telephone. "Is he now? And what do you feel about this young man? I thought you two weren't as friendly as you had been. I worry for you, Grace. You haven't been born to all that high society folderol. Just come back to Yorkshire. Come home where you belong."

"No, Father. I've made my mind up. I want to marry Simon and this time it's going to stick. I really want your approval. Please, come down to Mordenhyrst Hall and get to know him properly. I'm sure you'll revise your opinion."

"I very much doubt that, daughter, but…oh, very well, I'll come down to Mordenhyrst Hall for a few days. Tuesday. I'll let you know which train I'll be on."

Simon was thrilled when I told him. Naturally, I edited our conversation. He didn't need to know right now that he would have an uphill struggle to win my father's approval.

"I'll look forward to getting to know him better."

"What about Cecilia?"

Simon shrugged. "She can do as she pleases. She will anyway. She's told me she's planning to go back to Mayfair the day after the funeral, so we'll be spared her presence, probably for the duration of your father's visit. Oh yes, Lia has all sorts of plans for the summer."

"She's a very social person."

Simon laughed. "I probably shouldn't say this as she is my sister and I do love her, but she can be the shallowest, most selfish person I have ever known. Look how she's behaved towards you."

"But you defended her to me. You told me I wasn't trying hard enough."

"I know. And I'm sorry." Simon put his arms around me. "Am I forgiven?"

We kissed and, for the first time in ages, I responded. A tiny spark of desire flickered inside me. It wasn't much but maybe it would grow, given time.

That night I awoke to the certainty that something had disturbed my sleep. I lay in the darkness, listening for any sound, however small. It was a still night and no wind howled or rattled the panes. I was about to close my eyes and try to get back to sleep when I heard footsteps running outside my door. By the light, short steps I guessed they belonged to a woman. On this corridor that meant Cecilia.

I got out of bed and pulled my dressing gown around me.

Outside my door, all was still. Only the gas mantels gave off a slight hissing sound as they illuminated the corridor with their flickering, dim light. Shadows moved where the light failed to penetrate.

The footsteps had been running toward the staircase and I made my way there, pausing at the top of the wide, sweeping flight that descended into the softly lit hallway.

I listened intently as I took my first tentative steps downward. Then a distinctive noise reached my ears. It came from the drawing room. The sound of a woman sobbing.

The sight that greeted me when I opened the door both horrified and fascinated me.

Cecilia, dressed in a flowing white negligee, was leaning over the open coffin of her father. Hearing me, she turned her tear-stained face toward me.

"Get out. You don't belong here."

I remembered what Simon had said but this wasn't the reaction or behavior of a woman who hated her father. Ignoring her command, I approached her. She clung to the sides of the coffin, shielding her father's body from my sight. Tears coursed down her face.

"Cecilia, I'm so sorry. It must hurt so badly. I—"

"You have no idea. No idea at all. Now get out and leave us alone."

I put out my hand to her. "I want to help."

With a defiant look on her face, she moved to one side, let go of the coffin, and I automatically glanced down. I reeled back in horror.

"His *face.*" There was no face. Nothing recognizably human at any rate. The nose was gone, lips chewed, flaps of skin hanging loose on his cheeks. Incongruously, someone had dressed him in a dark suit and laid his…hands…across his chest. The fingers were black, nails green and grown over-long so that what remained gave the impression of claws.

If I hadn't known that was the late Earl Mordenhyrst, I would have sworn it was some kind of reptile.

I tore my eyes away and looked back at Cecilia. Her expression horrified me even more than what I had just witnessed.

She was laughing.

Pain ripped through my skull and blackness descended.

CHAPTER TWELVE

The next thing I knew I opened my eyes and blinked rapidly at the bright light. Sitting on the bed beside me, Simon held my hand. "Thank God. You've been out for ages. I don't know how long because I found you on the floor in the hall. Buckingham woke me to tell me you had had some kind of accident. Between us we managed to get you upstairs and Nell put you to bed. What happened, Grace? Did you fall down the stairs?"

My head throbbed mercilessly, and I put my hand to my forehead. Someone had wrapped a bandage around it.

"Nell did that. You've got an egg-shaped lump on top of your head. I suppose you must have struck something when you fell. Dr. Mortimer will be along shortly to check you over and make sure there's nothing serious to worry about."

My brain felt like porridge. I struggled to remember what had happened. Gradually the memory drifted back. "I was in the drawing room. I'd heard Cecilia crying and when I went in, she was bending over your father's open coffin. She seemed...demented."

Simon's expression changed from concern to confusion. "Demented?"

"She started laughing and then...then someone hit me from behind and I blacked out. They must have dragged me into the hall."

"But who would do such a thing?"

"I have no idea." For a moment I suspected Simon, but he was either innocent or giving a performance worthy of the great Douglas Fairbanks himself. I dismissed my fears.

He stroked my forehead, and his hand was soothing. "I think you need to sleep now. You've had a major trauma. Maybe concussion has set in. We'll know more when the doctor examines you."

I managed a smile, but a new fear hit me. "Where's Cecilia?"

"Still asleep I should imagine. It's only a little after seven."

"I think whoever did this to me did so with her blessing," I said, my voice little more than a whisper.

"Hush now, rest. We'll talk about all this later."

"Be careful of Cecilia, Simon. I don't trust her. There's something badly wrong there."

"Rest now. Leave Cecilia to me. Don't worry."

Within seconds I had drifted off to sleep, waking only when the doctor arrived. He held up some of his fingers and I correctly identified that there were three of them. He took my pulse and ran the full gamut of usual checks before declaring me shaken, sore, bruised but otherwise unharmed and predicted to make a swift, full recovery. He complimented Nell on her bandaging skills, and she blushed as she rewound the bandage, ready to reapply it to my aching head.

The doctor closed his bag with a resounding click. "You'll be very sore for a couple of days, but the swelling will soon go down. Just take it easy. Stay in bed today, and tomorrow take a little light exercise. Nothing too taxing."

"Thank you, doctor," I said. He was a kindly, middle-aged man with a neatly trimmed moustache and a shock of gray hair. I was also grateful because his order to stay in bed meant I would be spared the horrors of the earl's funeral due to take place that afternoon.

I fell asleep again after the doctor left and woke when Nell arrived with a bowl of consommé. "Mrs. Hawkins put a little sherry in it. She thought it might pep you up."

"Thanks, Nell." She helped prop me up against the pillows and set up the bed table. As she placed the soup bowl down, I could smell the sherry. One taste told me the cook had indeed been generous. Pep me up? Get me plastered more like. Still, I appreciated the gesture and soon emptied my bowl.

"Finished already, miss?" Nell removed the bowl. "You must have been hungry. Do you want anything else? Mrs. Hawkins said she's happy to make anything you fancy."

"Tell Mrs. Hawkins I'm most grateful for her delicious soup and for her kind offer. I think I just need a little sleep now." I didn't tell her the room was starting to spin.

Nell made sure I was lying comfortably before she left me to rest. I came to a few times. The first time I became aware of footsteps and voices outside my room. A quick, bleary glance at my bedside clock told me it was a quarter of an hour before the funeral was due to begin. Sure enough, a minute or so later, it all went quiet. Once again, I drifted off.

The next time I awoke, I heard voices. I guessed they belonged to the party returning from the earl's last send-off. I made out Cecilia's clipped tones but couldn't tell what she was saying. She certainly didn't sound like the wretched, insane creature I had witnessed the previous night. I also heard Simon, but once again, his words were lost to me.

The door opened quietly, and he entered. Seeing me awake, he advanced toward the bed, smiling. "How are you feeling?"

I grimaced. "Head feels like someone's crawled inside me with a sledgehammer, but apart from that...."

"Poor you. Is there anything I can get for you?"

"A glass of water would be welcome and some more aspirin."

"I'll ring for Nell."

"How did the funeral go?"

Simon pulled a face. "About as well as these things are capable of going. The rector said a lot of nice things. So nice I began to wonder who he was talking about. Cecilia held up well. All shrouded in black of course, with a black veil so you couldn't see the tears, or lack of them. The entire village showed up and the church was packed. All in all, he got a better send-off than he deserved. It was interesting looking around the congregation and seeing so many familiar faces. Familiar because every time I look in the mirror, I see traits of so many of them staring back at me."

I was spared the difficulty of coming up with a suitable response by Nell's arrival. Simon requested water and aspirin for me, and she duly departed to get it.

I had to ask. "Simon, you told me Cecilia hated her father, so why did she behave the way she did last night? Is she ill?"

"As far as I'm aware she's not ill in the slightest. She was fine today. Her usual self. A little quieter perhaps. I told her what you said happened and she drew a complete blank. She swore she was never downstairs last night so you couldn't possibly have seen her."

"If it wasn't her, it was her twin sister."

Nell came back with a carafe of water, a glass and a couple of pills, and I thanked her.

Simon waited for her to leave before responding. "How was she dressed last night?"

"Cecilia? She was wearing a white negligee. It was long and quite voluminous. Why do you ask?"

"No particular reason. A thought occurred to me but it's too absurd. Besides.... No, quite impossible."

"What is?"

"That you saw Mama's ghost."

I took a long drink of water. Could I have seen a ghost? "But she wasn't...I don't know. She wasn't ghostly. Not transparent or anything."

"And her hair? Was it in Cecilia's style, or was it long?"

I struggled to recall. I forced the image of the laughing woman back into my brain. I saw her. White, flowing nightdress, an almost demonic grin, the voice...all had been Cecilia's. But her hair? I tried to picture it long and flowing over her shoulders. That image didn't work but neither did the short bob in which Simon's sister habitually wore her hair. The harder I tried, the more confused the memory became.

"Right now, all I can tell you is that she had dark hair, but I can't remember if it was long or short. Maybe it will come back to me when all the swelling has gone down."

"Probably. Maybe you'll remember it wasn't even her at all. She really does deny being there, Grace. I have just tackled her again about it and she was adamant."

"As adamant as I am that it *was* her?" I asked.

Simon looked away before returning his attention to me. "Grace, I know my sister well and I know she is capable of a lot of things, many of which I heartily disapprove of, but I'll say one thing for her. She's no liar. It simply wouldn't occur to her."

"Neither am I, Simon."

But could I honestly say that now? I, who was planning to marry Simon under false pretenses. I put my hand to my head and Simon took the hint. "You're tired and I shouldn't be bothering you like this. I'll leave you to sleep and come up and see you again later."

"I'd like that." He kissed my forehead and I settled myself back down. This time sleep took longer to claim me. My head swam with questions. Why would Cecilia break the apparent habit of a lifetime and tell Simon an out-and-out lie? Maybe this was another scheme of hers to get rid of me. To force Simon to choose between her and his fiancée. If that was the case, I had no idea which one of us would emerge the winner.

I knew it was a dream because I felt an element of control in orchestrating it. Not that there weren't limits. I could choose whether or not to open the door in front of me. I chose to open it and it took me back into the drawing room. Cecilia was once again bending over the open casket.

When I called out to her, she turned. I had no control over what happened next. She flew at me, her eyes black hollows, teeth bared, skin flaking from bleached white bones. I shrank back, tried to find the door handle behind me. Failed. The creature hovered, arms outstretched toward me. It spoke.

"You'll never have him. He'll never leave me. I know what you plan to do. You and the witch. You won't succeed. You'll fail and he'll be mine forever."

I put my hands up to shield my face. "This is not real. It's not happening."

It...no, *she*...came closer. I could smell her disgusting, rotten breath. I dared not look as sharp nails raked my hands. "You're not real! You don't exist. This is a bad dream. Nothing but a dream. I shall wake up. Wake up *now*!"

I shot up in bed, panting, then just as quickly fell back again as the pain lanced through my head. It seemed as if the thing from my nightmare hadn't left the room. I could still smell it.

My fingers smarted and I examined them. Scratches oozed blood. I had to wash my hands before infection set in. I tried to get out of bed and nearly passed out. I rang for Nell instead.

When she saw me, her face blanched. "Oh, miss, whatever have you done? Your poor hands."

"Please, Nell. Please help me to the bathroom."

She did so. I used the toilet, managing to balance myself while Nell waited outside the door. Then she helped bathe my stinging hands. The bleeding had stopped, and the scratches weren't deep. Once we had them cleaned up, there was little to see.

"How did this happen, miss?" Nell asked as she patted my hands dry.

"I have no idea, Nell. Something scratched my hands in a horrible nightmare I had. When I woke up, they were like this."

She shook her head. "It's a mystery and no mistake." She steered me back to bed and I was shocked at how wobbly I was. I hobbled like an old woman of ninety. I sank down on the bed and let Nell tuck me in once more.

"Shall I bring you something to eat, miss?"

"I couldn't face anything."

"Maybe a nice cup of tea then?"

It did sound enticing. "That will be lovely, thanks, Nell." If only she wouldn't keep avoiding my eyes.

The tea served to soothe and refresh me, but once again, I needed sleep. This time, mercifully, no infernal creature came to haunt my dreams.

★   ★   ★

Three days later, and apart from a rapidly shrinking lump on my head, I was back to normal. My current version of it anyway. Cecilia was in London and our paths hadn't crossed since that night I increasingly believed to be the most vivid of nightmares. Still, a tiny, lingering uncertainty prevented me from offering a fulsome apology to my future sister-in-law.

My father arrived, sporting a walking cane and looking a little flustered. "Not the best railway journey I can remember," he grumbled when I asked him how his trip had been. "First Class isn't what it used to be." He caught me looking at the cane. "This?" He waggled it. "Old age, lass. It comes to us all one day."

"Mr. Sutcliffe," Simon said, hand outstretched to greet him. "A pleasure to see you again, sir."

Father shook his hand. "My condolences on your loss," he said, as if the words were alien to him. This wasn't like my father. He seemed awkward and ill at ease, and his discomfiture seemed to be growing as he moved farther into the house, through the hall and into the drawing room. He kept glancing behind him as if expecting someone to be there.

"What is it, Father?" I asked as we sat down.

My father shot Simon a quick glance and cleared his throat. He sat with the unfamiliar silver-topped cane between his knees, both hands perched atop it. "Nothing, my dear. Nothing." He shot another quick glance at Simon, who seemed oblivious to the rapidly cooling atmosphere.

I didn't pursue it. Whatever was troubling my father was not for Simon's ears. At least not yet. It would keep. For now.

Buckingham arrived with a tray of whisky, soda and glasses.

Drinks poured, Simon proposed a toast. "To happy days," he said.

"Happy days," I repeated. I couldn't make out what my father said.

"Now," said Simon, resting his drink on a side table, "I suppose we ought to be doing this in private, but as you know, sir, I asked for your daughter's hand in marriage some weeks ago. A lot has happened in that time and, naturally, Grace has had some doubts. After all, it's not as if we have known each other all that long."

"Indeed, you haven't," my father said.

"Yes…. Well, the thing is, sir, she and I have worked things out, haven't we, Grace?"

I nodded, aware of my father's eyes boring into me, examining my face for any trace of uncertainty, or maybe even of coercion. But the truth was that these past few days had seen Simon and me grow closer together. Cecilia's departure had helped leaps and bounds and left me with no doubt that she could have no active role in our lives together in the future. I had to make the best of things with Simon and, if we could find some kind of happiness with each other, surely that was preferable to the constant need to glance over my shoulder to see what Cecilia was getting up to.

"I think we have worked things out rather well," I said, earning a beaming smile from Simon. "We know each other much better now, Father."

"And you're sure this is what you want?"

I concentrated hard on looking him straight in the eyes when I spoke my next words. "Yes, Father. I'm sure."

Simon stood. "Mr. Sutcliffe, I would like to ask you formally for your daughter's hand in marriage. I promise to be a good and faithful husband, to provide for her in the manner to which she is entitled to be accustomed and to, at all times, treat her with kindness, courtesy and respect."

"Do you now?" Father breathed heavily and gripped his cane. "I can't say I don't have my reservations. I spoke my mind the first time round, and you know what they are, Grace. I have spoken to you about them enough. This difference in class. It bothers me. It would bother your dear mother if she were still alive, God rest her soul."

"I understand, Father. I really do. I know you only want what's best for me but, honestly, I love Simon." As I said it, I knew that, once again, I actually meant it. A warm glow poured over me. "I love Simon and want to be his wife."

My father tightened his grip on his cane. "But do you have any idea what you're taking on? You're not just marrying this young man, you're wedding his family, this mansion, even the village by all accounts. You're marrying into an entire dynasty."

Put like that, it did sound daunting, but I still had Coralie's words ringing in my ears. The one thing I could never talk to Father or Simon about. The dark secret this village hid within its very core. I pushed the unwelcome intrusive thoughts to the back of my mind. I would have to deal with all of that soon enough. At least I knew I had my inner spirit to call on. And Coralie with all her dark powers.

"I know, Father. Really, I do. I'm getting out to the village more so that people become used to seeing me." Only the previous day I had been driven down to the church and had a long chat with the rector about wedding arrangements. There had been some talk about a big London society wedding, but I was relieved to find that Simon didn't want that any more than I did, and we had the excuse of his father's recent death. We were still supposedly in official mourning although, apart from somber clothing, I saw little evidence of any grieving.

Then there was Mr. Sykes. He and I were getting along famously. I no longer caused him problems by entering his establishment unescorted. With the warm summer weather, I chose to take a glass of lemonade outside while I sat and watched the world of Cortney Abbas drift by. Not that there was all that much to see, apart from the laborers at lunchtime, and after they finished work, there were just the usual locals. As I tended to make my trips in the afternoon, I mostly only saw them. And Mrs. Chesterton, of course. She still avoided me as if I had contracted some nasty disease. I remembered what Mr. Sykes had told me about her tragic earlier life and resolved to be charitable. I smiled at her if our eyes met and tried to ignore the scowl, the vigorous shake of her head and increased speed of her gait.

Simon refreshed our drinks. My father, never a great drinker, nevertheless took a healthy swig. "I suppose I have little choice in the matter. You're both over twenty-one and don't need my consent anyway. But does it all have to be so rushed? Is there some reason you have to marry so quickly? Something you've not told me?" He looked pointedly at my waistline.

"No, Father, nothing like that," I said.

"It's just that we don't want to wait," Simon said, clasping my hand. "And there is really no need. Neither of us want a big wedding and Mordenhyrst Hall needs a new mistress...to ensure continuity." He didn't need to say it. Right now, he wanted Cecilia out of our lives as much as I did. That one sentence said it all. While she remained at Mordenhyrst Hall, she was in charge. Everyone deferred to her as they had since her mother died. The sooner the staff and the village got used to the new order, the better.

My father continued to frown and the knuckles gripping the cane were white with tension.

"Father," I said. "It would mean so much to me – to both of us – if you would give us not just your consent, but your blessing."

I knew I had put him in an impossible situation, but I couldn't help it. I meant every word. I really needed Father's blessing to give me added strength because, much as I was now reconciled to marry Simon, I was under no illusions that the following weeks, months and years were going to be anything other than challenging, if Coralie was right.

Father said nothing. He stared down at the Indian silk rug beneath his feet. When he looked up, he had tears in his eyes. I felt ashamed. Never in my entire life had I ever seen my father shed a tear. Not even when my mother was killed when they had gone on a holiday to Switzerland, and she had decided to try her hand at skiing. Father had demurred and his decision had saved his life. The avalanche that killed her also ended the lives of six other people, all more experienced skiers than Mother. He was devastated by her loss, but I never saw one tear, not even at her funeral. Now, though, his eyes were red-rimmed and watery. I wanted to reach out to him, to hug him, but that was never an option. Father was not the hugging type. To him, and so many of his generation, such displays of emotion were not appropriate.

Finally, he spoke. His voice cracked at first, but he managed. "Very well…. If it's truly what you want, I'll not stop thee. You both have my blessing. I hope…I hope you'll have a long and happy life together."

"Oh, thank you, Father."

Simon came over to me, knelt and clasped my hand. He gave the back of it a gentle kiss before standing and turning to my father, who seemed to have aged in the past few minutes. "Thank you, sir. I won't let you down."

"You had better not, young man. You had better not."

Simon's smile froze on his face. It was not hard to see why. The way my father had just spoken made his words sound like a threat. Simon quickly recovered his composure. "Well now, I think this calls for a celebration and there's only one thing to do when you celebrate. Drink champagne. I'll ring for Buckingham."

"Not for me." My father struggled to his feet. He straightened, the effort showing in his face. "I'm off to lie down for a couple of hours. That journey tired me out. I've brought my man, Stoker, with me. He'll sort me out ready for dinner."

With that, he limped out of the room.

Simon still had his hand on the bell. "Champagne for you, Grace?"

I shook my head. "Maybe later. With dinner perhaps. Do you know what Mrs. Hawkins is preparing for us?"

"Haven't a clue. That reminds me. We may as well start as we mean to go on. And, as Cecilia isn't here, there's no time like the present. Well, tomorrow anyway. Once a week, Cecilia meets with Mrs. Hawkins, Mrs. Bennett and Buckingham, separately of course. Household accounts and such like with Mrs. Bennett and menus with Mrs. Hawkins. Then Buckingham for everything else, including, of course, the wine cellar. Ready to pick up the gauntlet?"

"Cecilia won't like it. We're not married yet."

"She's not here, is she? You are."

"How do you think the staff will feel? I mean, they're used to dealing with a Mordenhyrst."

"You're almost one. You've got the ring. Well, an engagement ring anyway. You can start wearing that now. I'll get the official announcements under way and have a word with Pip about Beaton. How about wearing your ring for the first time this evening?"

A couple of hours later, dressed for dinner in a gorgeous dark green silk gown, I gazed at the exquisite emerald set in a yellow gold band studded with diamonds which fitted my finger to perfection. Simon had wanted me to have a diamond solitaire, but emerald was my birthstone, so we finally compromised. I would have my choice, but it would be graced by his preferred jewels.

Father gave it a dutiful if perfunctory glance and muttered something that sounded like, "Very nice."

"It was my choice, Father. I know Mother always loved emeralds and I was born in May."

"Of course."

His tone told me the subject was closed.

Dinner turned out to be turbot, served with a delicious champagne sauce. The Pol Roger Simon chose complimented it perfectly.

Buckingham served coffee and liqueurs in the drawing room. Before he left, Simon spoke to him. "Please ask Mrs. Bennett to bring the household accounts up to Miss Sutcliffe tomorrow, will you, Buckingham? What time is best for you, Grace?"

I swallowed hard. Not that I wasn't used to running a house. I had run my father's since my mother's untimely passing. But this was a whole new ball game. Buckingham was waiting. Simon was waiting. My father did his best to pretend none of this was happening.

"Eleven o'clock, please, Buckingham."

"Very good, miss, My Lord."

My heart beat faster. Simon lit a cigar. Father sipped his cognac.

The wheels were in motion. Tomorrow I would assume Cecilia's role. At least while she wasn't around to complain about it. In four weeks' time, I would be Lady Mordenhyrst.

My inner spirit quaked.

CHAPTER THIRTEEN

It went better than I anticipated. Mrs. Bennett was courteous and even managed a weak attempt at a smile. I still found her daunting though. When Mrs. Hawkins appeared and brought with her the broadest smile I had seen in a long while, my spirits lifted. Judging from her reaction toward me, I guessed she wasn't Cecilia's greatest fan. Not that she admitted it, but she seemed...well, relieved would not be inappropriate.

Her menu suggestions were faultless and sounded delicious. I complimented her on her choice of dishes during the time I had spent at Mordenhyrst Hall and she seemed quite taken aback. I had been used to rewarding good work with a 'thank you'. It seemed common courtesy, but evidently such an acknowledgment was pretty much unheard of around here.

"Thank you, miss. I must say, it's very nice to be appreciated."

"Not at all, Mrs. Hawkins. I especially enjoyed the beef consommé when I had my...accident. The addition of the sherry proved a real pick-me-up."

"There's some might say I can be a little generous with the sherry, but I think it does a body good when you're feeling out of sorts."

"Indeed it does."

Now we were getting along so famously, I felt at liberty to ask her a question. "You've been here a long time, haven't you?"

"Yes, miss. Nearly thirty years it is now. I started as a kitchen maid back in 1899. Dear me, the old queen was still on the throne."

"You must have seen a lot of comings and goings in that time."

Did I imagine it, or did a slight guard come up? Certainly, the smile wasn't quite as broad.

"I suppose I must have. Of course, being down in the kitchen I don't see as much as Mr. Buckingham or Mrs. Bennett, or even the parlor maids and footmen."

"Of course, I understand. But you must have heard lots of stories over the years."

"Yes, miss." Definitely wary now.

"To your knowledge then, has anything untoward ever taken place here?"

"Untoward, miss? I'm not sure I understand what you mean."

"Do you know of any occasions when inexplicable things have happened? I'm thinking especially of anything involving Lady Cecilia, or the present earl, and their mother."

I knew the instant the words came out that I should have held my peace until I had fully won her trust. What a fool I was.

Mrs. Hawkins shook her head so vigorously her hat came askew. She straightened it. "I don't know of any such thing, miss. Lady Mordenhyrst was the kindest, most charming person you could ever wish to meet. I was that upset when she was took. So young and so beautiful...." She reached in the pocket of her starched white apron for a clean handkerchief, dabbed at her eyes and blew her nose.

"I'm sorry, Mrs. Hawkins. I didn't mean to upset you."

The cook replaced her handkerchief in her pocket. "That's quite all right, miss. You had every right to ask. I'm sorry I couldn't oblige."

An interesting choice of words. Did she mean she was sorry she knew nothing, or that she was sorry she didn't feel she could talk about it? Whatever it was. Either way, I would get no more answers today and I didn't want our meeting to end on a difficult note. We had covered all the menus for the following week, so....

"I tell you what, would you make one of your excellent Charlotte Russes for dessert on Sunday? I'm sure my father would love it. He's quite a fan."

Mrs. Hawkins instantly perked up. She took out her pencil and crossed out our previous choice, replacing it with the desired Charlotte Russe. "Anything else, miss?"

"No, I think we've covered it all. Shall we make this our regular weekly meeting? Until Lady Cecilia returns, that is. Assuming she does return before the wedding."

"That will be most agreeable, miss."

The cook left and I breathed out, still cursing myself for my cack-handedness. I was self-remonstrating when my father came in to join me.

"Did you enjoy your walk, Father?"

He flashed a look that said he hadn't, then sat down. Once again, his walking cane was very much in evidence and he really looked as if he needed it.

I pointed at it. "How long have you needed that?"

"Oh, it's nothing. Just a bit of gout. Damned nuisance. I'll throw it away soon. Can't abide the thing. Makes me look like an old man. I went round to the stables. Your groom seems to know his horseflesh, I'll say that for him. Pretty good stable there too."

"Dulcie's my favorite."

"She would be. You always preferred mares, didn't you? Even as a child. Your first pony was a little chestnut. Do you remember her? Nutkin, wasn't it?"

I remembered the bright-eyed pony with the thrashing tail and jaunty gait. "Yes. I named her."

"Happy days," Father said. And they were.

"You seemed not to have enjoyed your walk when I asked you, but you had a nice time with Harper."

"He drove me in a carriage into the village. Strange place full of the most extraordinary people. Downright rude, most of 'em. I tipped my hat and said 'How do' to a sour-faced baggage in a straw hat and she tutted at me. *Tutted* at me and scurried away as if I'd made some improper suggestion."

I laughed. "That would have been Hilda Chesterton. Cut her a little slack, Father. She's not had the easiest of lives and has less than happy memories of working here at the Hall, if what I've heard is correct."

"Well, that's as may be, but the only civil person I came across was the rector and he seemed in a world of his own half the time. Kept saying something about the old earl's funeral. That something was amiss. Couldn't make it out. And another thing I found peculiar. Have you noticed how so many of the villagers look so similar? Reminds me of a trip I went on once to East Anglia. Stayed with an old friend of mine. I went for a ride across the Fens and there was a small town there. I forget the name of it, but every other person had the same vacant look, same coloring, same narrow-set eyes. Put the willies up me. I was glad to get back to Norwich. Told my old friend about it and he laughed. He said there was a lot of interbreeding in some of those villages and small towns. I reckon you've got the same problem here."

"Most people put that down to the feudal practices of Simon's father and his predecessors, but you needn't worry, Simon's not like that at all. I think the local people are very happy with the passing of the crown to the next generation."

Surely my father should have looked a little happier when I said that. As it was, his frown grew deeper. "Lass, I've been thinking," he said, always the precursor of something I wasn't going to like. "Happen I'll go back home for a while."

"But my wedding's next month."

"Aye, lass, if you're still determined to go through with it. Just remember you can call it off at any time. There'll always be a home for you at Caldwell Grange."

"Thank you, Father, but I'm going to marry Simon. My home will be here, and I will be Lady Mordenhyrst and be involved in all village events. Ours will be a benevolent time. The old earl and his ways are over."

"And that includes his daughter, does it? Seems from what I can gather that you'll have your work cut out there."

"And what have you heard?"

"Nothing substantial. Nowt you could throw a stick at anyroad. Nasty piece of work though. Penelope told me when she came to stay. Her spies are everywhere, as you know. Cecilia Mordenhyrst is not popular with the gentry, with the exception of those worthless idiots she calls her friends. Penny heard there were rumors something was badly wrong with her." He tapped his head. "And not just her either. It runs in the family."

"What does?"

"Some sort of insanity. Penny thinks it may have slipped by Simon as there's nothing particularly untoward doing the rounds about him, but as for *her*...."

"What exactly did Aunt Penelope tell you?"

"Court appearances, drugs, petty theft just for the hell of it, drunken orgies, unpaid gambling debts. You name it, she's up to it. She's only managed to escape prison because of her connections and title. Others she hangs around with haven't been so fortunate. One of her friends is even awaiting sentencing for murder. If he's convicted, he'll hang. Make no mistake about that. Does she care? Has she done anything to lift a finger to help him? No. Apparently this chap is besotted with her. He has told others he would lay down his life for her. Now it looks as if he is going to have to."

"But, Father, surely if he committed murder—"

"That's the point, Grace. The majority of people don't believe he did. Oh yes, someone died. A single gunshot, which they couldn't have inflicted themselves. The gun has never been found. The thing is, the young man who was shot operated some sort of illegal gambling den in Soho. Lady Cecilia and her friends were known to frequent this place. The seediest sort of establishment you could imagine. Anyway, most people believe the victim demanded Cecilia pay off her debt, which amounted to quite a hefty sum. He made the mistake of making his demands in public. Cecilia left immediately with her entourage scurrying after her like a load of clucking poultry. Next morning the chap was found dead and, although it was never reported, the caliber of the bullet indicated it was from a small pistol most usually carried by women. Police started their investigation, interviewed Cecilia and some of her lot, including the young man who has now been tried and convicted. He confessed and Cecilia went out to a party the very same night."

Why hadn't Simon told me any of this? "When did this happen?"

"It was fresh gossip when Penelope arrived. She couldn't wait to tell me. In fact, I got the impression that was why she had asked to come up to stay at such short notice. She's worried about you, Grace. We both are. Neither of us can understand why you want to attach yourself to such a family. Every way I turn, I hear and see more bad news about them. Today's walk round that village merely confirmed my worst suspicions. I fear for your safety here, lass. I really do. That woman will stop at nothing to get what she wants, and Penny is certain she doesn't want you around in her brother's life. It disrupts her power. She is the only lady of Mordenhyrst Hall as far as she's concerned."

It was a lot to take in. I resolved to talk to Simon about it as soon as he came back from a business meeting in London.

"Are you sure Aunt Penelope didn't get any of this wrong?"

Father struggled to his feet and limped over to me. He sat down on the settee next to me and took my hands in his. "Grace, you know I love thee. You're my only daughter and now my only child. I want only the best for thee. I want you to be happy with the right man. Simon isn't right for you. Your aunt's sources are impeccable. She's very friendly with Lady Constance Farrar's companion, a Miss Sewell. Lady Constance is friendly with practically the entire cast of *Debrett's Peerage*. The Mordenhyrsts have a besmirched reputation that goes back generations. It seems anyone who comes into contact with them ends up regretting it. Lady Elise Mordenhyrst was merely the latest in the line of earls' and viscounts' spouses to have committed suicide in suspicious circumstances."

"I shall be fine, absolutely fine, Father. You mustn't worry about me." If I kept on saying that, maybe I would grow to believe it.

"What sort of father would I be if I didn't?"

He treated me to one of his rare smiles but there was a twinge of pain in his eyes. "That gout playing you up today?"

"A little. Think that quack gave me the wrong pills. These damned things don't even take the edge off. I'll see him when I get back, give him a piece of my mind."

"I'm sure you will, Father."

That evening, I tackled Simon about what my father had told me. He frowned and poured himself a Scotch and soda. "It's a sad old business. Tommy Shadbolt was a good sort but there was always something... not quite right about him. He became obsessed with Lia to the point where she had to tell him she would have nothing further to do with him. Needless to say, their paths crossed from time to time and, one evening, things got a bit ugly."

"Someone demanded she pay back her gambling debt," I said.

Simon flashed me a look of surprise. "How did you...? Yes, something like that. Lia insisted she owed nothing and left, hotly pursued by both the owner of the club and Shadbolt. Lia swears she came straight home. Next day the club owner was found dead in his office, with one fatal shot to the head. Shadbolt's fingerprints were all over the place, on a brandy glass near the body, all sorts of places. No gun, but it was obvious he had done the deed."

"I believe they said the gun used was more typically owned by a woman."

"A lot of hearsay and nonsense. Lots of men own those guns. They're small and easy to carry around."

"So, you believe Cecilia's story then?"

"Of course. She's telling the truth. She unfailingly does. Shadbolt, sadly, is guilty. Out of his mind. But guilty nonetheless."

"They say he'll hang for it."

"Not necessarily. He may end up in an asylum for the criminally insane or some such place. Now, can we talk of pleasanter things? We're getting married in a few short weeks."

With that he took my hands in his. I looked deep in his eyes and wished I hadn't seen such sadness there.

★ ★ ★

Father left the following day and I blinked back the tears. He was clearly in pain, and I could only hope his doctor could prescribe something stronger. I didn't want him suffering at my wedding, or any other time, for that matter.

London beckoned for the final fitting of my wedding dress. The couturier tutted a little and spoke through a mouthful of pins. "If you lose any more weight between now and the wedding, the dress will hang like a sack on you. You must eat."

Despite Mrs. Hawkins' delicious cooking, I wasn't eating as much as I used to, but the combination of frantic wedding preparations and all the goings-on at Mordenhyrst Hall had meant I sometimes completely forgot. I resolved to try harder to remember.

I put aside the tragic story of Tommy Shadbolt as Simon and I continued to grow closer. Every day made me more certain that the rotten core of Cortney Abbas must have bypassed him. He couldn't have been more solicitous or tender, while still observing the proprieties. Sometimes I wished he would be a little less proper, especially when we were alone together, but he would always draw back. "I want to, Grace. I truly want to make you happy in every way, but I couldn't look your father in the eye if I overstepped the boundary before I made you my wife."

How could I argue? If I insisted, I would look like a cheap slut, or be as bad as Cecilia and her friends. I bit my lip and pleasured myself instead, imagining Simon caressing me...and much more. He entered my dreams at night in ways I wished he would enter in reality.

Soon, I told myself, soon....

And then Cecilia came back.

CHAPTER FOURTEEN

"Lia!" Simon jumped up to greet his sister, who swept into the drawing room and immediately reclaimed ownership of it.

"Sy, darling!" She waved her long cigarette holder around, releasing smoke that managed to envelop me in a cloud of Turkish tobacco.

I fought back the cough that tickled my throat. Only then did she appear to notice my existence. "Grace. Good to see you again."

The words might have conveyed that sentiment, but the cold eyes and taut lips failed to back them up.

"Cecilia," I said.

She ignored me again and switched her full attention back to her brother. She hooked her arm into his and walked him over to the settee, where they both sat. It was as if by that one gesture she had erected a stone wall between us. I refused to show any reaction. I merely sat where I was and watched them.

"You simply must tell me all your news, Sy. What have you been getting up to? Percy said she saw you in Boodles the other day, or was it last week? Can't remember. Anyway, she said you seemed to be getting along famously with that American actress. What was her name?"

"Tallulah Bankhead. We met at the Kit Kat Club. She was there with Cecil Beaton, Nancy Cunard and a whole host of others. I remember Fleur and Percy arrived late and they were still sober. The Jungman sisters ragged them about it and then proceeded to spike their drinks. Within an hour they were rip-roaring drunk and dancing on tables. Fleur got into a clinch with Tallulah, and they were asked to leave." He glanced over at me and winked.

I gave him a half-smile while wondering why he had never mentioned one word of this to me. But, of course, Cecilia would have guessed that, wouldn't she? Anything to make trouble between us. Well, just let her do her worst.

Cecilia unwound her legs, removed her cigarette from the holder and stubbed it out. She had decided to fix her attention on me. "So, Grace. Your father was down here, I believe."

"Yes."

"But he's returned to Yorkshire. Won't he be here for your wedding? I assume you are still getting married, Sy."

Simon nodded. "Of course. Everything's in full swing. Announcements have gone in *The Times* and everywhere else you could care to imagine. Cecil Beaton took some amazing photographs. You must have seen them. In *Tatler* perhaps? Or *The Illustrated London News*?"

"Can't say that I did. Must have missed those editions. London's been so busy this summer. So many parties."

"How very tiring for you," I said, and enjoyed her startled reaction.

She glared at me and turned her attention to Simon. "How many people are coming?"

"To our wedding? Around one hundred and fifty, judging by the acceptances."

"And how many of them are *your* people, Grace?"

She knew how to touch a nerve. Of course, there weren't many. Just my father, Aunt Penelope and a couple of cousins I hadn't seen in a decade or more. Most of the guests were from the aristocracy, including Cecilia and her coterie of cronies. But I had insisted on Coralie, and she would be arriving any day now, following a visit to Paris. I couldn't wait for her to get here. At least I would have *her* in my corner.

"As you know, I don't come from a large family," I said. "Nor do I have to invite people I would rather not spend time with. Simon doesn't have that luxury."

Cecilia crossed her legs. "People in positions of power rarely do. It's the price we pay, I suppose. The villagers will turn out in their best bib and tucker, no doubt. It'll provide an afternoon's entertainment for them."

"Indeed, it will," I said. "And I shall be delighted if they enjoy it as much as I intend to."

Simon laughed. "Ladies. If these remarks get any sharper, I shall have to ask you to put down your rapiers. Someone might get hurt."

"Really, Sy?" Cecilia curled her lip. "I rather think Grace is enjoying our little banter, aren't you, Grace?"

"Banter? I hadn't realized we were bantering. I was merely responding to your comments."

Cecilia gave a harsh, brittle laugh. "She's getting better at this," she said.

And so it went on. Every time we met, at mealtimes and in the evenings, the same back and forth, back and forth. But I wouldn't let her win.

★   ★   ★

"Coralie, you can't begin to know how pleased I am to see you. Father and Aunt Penelope are arriving tomorrow and—"

Coralie put up her hand. "Let's go somewhere we can talk."

I steered her out of the hall into the library where we sat in comfortable Chesterfield chairs, surrounded by walls of bookcases, crammed with volumes that gave off a comforting, timeless smell of age, paper and the old leather in which they were bound.

"What is it, Coralie?"

"Your aunt Penelope will be coming tomorrow but your father can't come. He's not well enough."

Tears sprang to my eyes. "Oh no. Whatever's happened?"

"He's been suffering from gout apparently?"

"Yes, his foot was paining him a lot when he was here."

"His doctor referred him to a specialist and the result is he needs an urgent operation, so he's in a hospital in Leeds. Your aunt asked me to tell you, so she didn't have to break the news over the telephone or wait until he clearly wasn't with her when she arrived."

"I'll have to call off the wedding. I can't get married if Father isn't here, and I want to be with him. If he has to have an operation this urgently it must be serious. I must go to him."

"*No.*" The vehemence of her exclamation took me aback. "Sorry, Grace, but your father was adamant he didn't want you to do that. Your aunt said he insisted you were not to come up to Yorkshire and you most definitely were not to call off your wedding."

That stopped me in my tracks. Father *wanted* me to marry Simon now? I would have some questions for my aunt when she arrived. "But who's going to look after him when he comes out of hospital?"

"That won't be for a couple of weeks at least and your aunt is going up to Caldwell Grange after your marriage."

"What sort of operation is it?"

Coralie shook her head. "I don't have any details, I'm afraid. Your aunt was a little vague. She kept correcting herself and finally said she didn't really know but it was necessary to stop him being in so much pain and discomfort. Above all, she stressed you were not to worry. You can ask her more about it yourself when she gets here tomorrow afternoon."

"I suppose so."

"Look, I know I'm the bearer of bad news, and I can't replace your father, but I'm here and I ain't going anywhere, honey. Cecilia has returned, I see."

"What? Oh, yes. She has. And she's being a total pain as always. Needless to say, the day after she returned, she had the housekeeper and the cook in, changed all the menus I had agreed to with Mrs. Hawkins, and complained about the beautiful flower arrangements all over the house, which I organized. She said they gave her hay fever. I haven't heard so much as a single sneeze from her but out they all had to go."

"And what about Simon? How is everything going there?"

Despite my fears for my father, I couldn't resist a smile. "Even now his sister's back he's still being warm and affectionate, just as he was before I first came here."

"And have the two of you…?" She raised an eyebrow.

"No. Simon wants to wait."

"Oh, does he? I wonder why."

Surely, she didn't think…. "He doesn't like chaps in that way, if that's what you're worried about. And, however close they have been and whatever you think, he and Cecilia are strictly brother and sister. No funny business. I don't think Cecilia actually goes for the physical stuff anyway. I may be wrong."

"No, I think you're right. I think sex and Cecilia are poles apart. As for Simon…. No, I don't believe he's homosexual."

"Of course, he may have dabbled a bit at Eton, I suppose."

"Eton?"

"The public school. A very exclusive private institution for the sons of nobility and the wealthy."

"Oh, I know what it is all right. I'm just interested as to why you would refer to Simon going to Eton."

"Because he went there as a boy."

Coralie stared at me, then blinked a couple of times. "Is that what he told you?"

"I think so. Yes, I'm sure he did. Or someone in this house did. Oh, I remember, it was Cecilia when she was arranging that infernal weekend where you and I first met. She said Lilo and Simon were at Eton together."

"I'm sure that will come as a great surprise to the head of that school because neither of them ever set foot there."

She must have been joking. But one look at her face and I knew she wasn't. "How do you know this? I mean, how do you know it's true?"

"Because I happened to bump into a mutual friend of theirs who was at Eton at the time they would have been there. I asked him about his schooldays and if Simon and Lilo had attended Eton as well.

He said Lilo was educated at home by a private tutor, and he hadn't a clue where Simon was educated but wherever it was, it certainly wasn't Eton."

Could I have got it wrong? Maybe Cecilia had said Harrow or one of the other prestigious schools, but I knew what I'd heard. "Why on earth would they lie about such a thing?"

Coralie shrugged. "Search me. Maybe he's ashamed of a poor education."

"Cecilia went to a finishing school in Switzerland with Fleur and Percy. That's where she met them. She said they were a few years younger."

Coralie laughed. "Most of those schools take girls from the age of sixteen up to around twenty. Cecilia would have hit sixteen in 1912, so she could have attended then but Fleur and Percy would have been too young. Two years later along came the war, and I can't see any of them traveling through war-torn France and Germany, where they would have been enemy aliens, in order to get to neutral Switzerland. By the end of the war, Fleur would have been twenty-two. It doesn't really fit, does it?"

I shook my head. "But why are they both lying about this?"

"I have no idea, but someone in this house must know the truth. The older servants. The butler, housekeeper, the cook even. Why not ask one of them?"

"I will."

Coralie reached for her purse, opened it, and pulled out a small, rectangular black velvet bag, which she laid on the side table between us. I watched, fascinated, as she undid the drawstring and removed an ancient pack of cards, which she then proceeded to shuffle. The design on the reverse glimmered and seemed to grow more vivid as she agitated the pack. After a couple of minutes, she laid the cards face down. "Grace, I need you to cut the pack four times."

I could see the design on the reverse of the cards appeared to be formed of interlocked letters in an arrangement resembling a vine. I duly cut the pack. The texture of the cards felt odd. Waxy, quite rough, as if the cards themselves had scales. I wanted to cease contact with them, as the longer they were in my hand, the more unpleasant the sensation became. I cut the pack quickly, creating four unequal piles, then withdrew my hand as if I had been burned.

Coralie smiled. "Not very nice, are they?"

"What are they made of?"

"If I were to say human skin you would be revolted, right?"

I backed away.

"Don't worry. They're not. They're actually made of a long-extinct species of reptile. A small but deadly creature resembling a lizard but with the most extraordinarily human-like face, or so those who saw it reported. They lived in Africa and were hunted to extinction for their skin. It's the luminescent quality that was so highly prized. Many died in the process of hunting them down. The creature exuded a deadly venom for which no antidote was ever formulated. It was always fatal, within twenty minutes of contact with skin. It also appeared that the venom, milked from the glands of dead animals, retained its potency for an unlimited time. Fortunes were made selling the stuff."

"And this pack. Are they tarot cards or...." I suddenly remembered. "These are the cards Fleur and Percy wanted you to use that night. You said they were in a safe place."

"That's right. They were and now they're here with me. I shall call on them right now. First of all though, where are Simon and his not-so-charming sister?"

"Out riding."

"Good. Let's get started." She picked up one pile of cards and fanned them out. "Take one and place it face down on the table."

I did so, and then repeated the action until there were four single cards lying face down. As I stared at them, the design on the back of each seemed to writhe snake-like as if trying to reach out to its neighbor. I closed my eyes for a moment, but all I could see behind my closed eyelids was a twisting and writhing vine.

"Open your eyes, Grace. You need to turn each card over. Begin with the one on the far left."

I did so. The illustration looked hand painted. A coiled snake with jewellike red eyes and a forked tongue protruding from its open mouth stared out at me, so lifelike I could swear it was moving, even though I could detect no change in its position.

"Now the next one."

The second card showed a thistle with vicious-looking barbs, so realistic they looked as if they could prick your finger. I turned over the next one. A teardrop-shaped bottle containing a liquid of greenish gold was positioned next to a human skull. Finally, I turned over the last card. A coffin with some unfamiliar symbols on it momentarily took my breath away. I had no idea what it meant but surely a coffin couldn't be a portent of good, could it?

"What does it mean?" I asked.

Coralie said nothing for a few seconds. She steepled her hands, her elbows resting on the arms of her chair. "Okay. First of all, don't be scared. I know that coffin card has upset you and, yes, it can be a symbol of impending death or some fatal disaster, but it's all in the positioning and the context. In this regard, these cards bear a passing resemblance to the tarot deck. What we have in this reading, when we take all four cards overall, including their positioning, direction the symbols are pointing and the context of your current situation here, are things to be cautious of and things to reassure us. We never read these cards singly, do you understand?"

I nodded.

"The reading tells us that you are surrounded by dangerous forces but – and this is important, Grace – you have the wherewithal to defeat them. You must tread with caution as there will be obstacles along the way. It will not be plain sailing but, with care and sound judgment, you will prevail."

"And the coffin? Where does that feature in all this?"

"As I said, we never read the cards singly. Of itself, it's nothing. When taken in conjunction with the other three cards, it produces the reading I have just given you."

I was hearing what she was saying but I couldn't tear my eyes away from that illustration. The way the card was positioned meant that the coffin stood upright with its narrowest end at the bottom. Was it meant for me? Had she omitted to say something she knew would upset me? Her expression gave nothing away.

She gathered the cards up, shuffled the entire pack again and replaced them lovingly in the velvet pouch, tied the drawstring tightly and slid the pack inside her purse.

We sat in silence until we heard a commotion outside the door. Voices and laughter. The door flew open, and Simon and his sister dashed in, still in riding gear. Cecilia's cheeks were flushed.

"Simply too divine out there today. Glorious sunshine, perfect riding weather and we stopped at this charming little hostelry I have never visited before. Had a glass of their own brew."

"It was pretty strong stuff," Simon said. "Good job the horses knew their way back."

Cecilia laughed. "You should have been out there," she said to us. "Put some color in your cheeks. Oh...." She laughed. "Not that *you* need it, Coralie."

I stared at her uncomprehendingly. Had she really said that?

Coralie said nothing and remained impassive. I bit my tongue, longing to speak out on behalf of my friend, but I got the impression she wouldn't have thanked me for it. No, Coralie was someone who knew how to get her revenge and possessed the means to do it. That thought alone sustained me and kept my mouth shut.

Cecilia, evidently wishing to maintain her level of alcoholic stimulation, poured herself a sherry from the decanter. "I hear your father isn't coming to the wedding, Grace."

How had she heard that? As far as I knew only Coralie and I were aware of it. I let it pass. "No, he has to undergo an operation."

"Such a shame. Still, too late to cancel now, isn't it? After all, the announcement's gone up in *The Times*. She's not having bridesmaids, Coralie, can you imagine? I did offer my services, but she declined."

"It's not all that long since your father died," I reminded her. "It didn't seem quite right to go all out with flocks of bridesmaids and page boys. Simon and I agreed to keep things as low-key as possible."

Cecilia took a sip of her drink. "One hundred and fifty guests *is* a little stingy, I must say. And who else would have been your bridesmaid? Coralie perhaps?"

Now I was sure Cecilia was goading me. She must know she couldn't wind Coralie up. Well, she damned well wasn't going to wind me up either.

"Where do you stop once you start?" I said. "I decided that when it came to bridesmaids it was better to have none at all."

Cecilia made a dismissive gesture with her hand, rather as if she were swatting a troublesome fly.

"There will be photographs, I daresay. Your father will have to content himself with those."

"I'm sure he will," I said. Out of the corner of my eye I caught Simon watching the exchange rather as he might witness a tennis match at Wimbledon. When he saw me looking, he slapped his thighs and stood.

"Time for my bath." He rang the bell and Buckingham appeared. "Tell Albert to draw me a bath, will you, Buckingham? I smell of horses. Better tell my sister's maid to get hers ready too."

"Very good, My Lord."

Buckingham held the door for Simon and he and the butler left.

Cecilia knocked back her drink and smoothed her riding crop through her gloved hand. "See you two slouches for cocktails at seven then."

Neither of us replied and she left.

"You can feel the atmosphere lift when she goes, can't you?" I said.

Coralie treated me to a broad grin. "I was thinking the same thing, honey. The exact same thing."

★　★　★

Aunt Penelope arrived the next day in a fluster of voile, oversize straw hat and tears. I greeted her in the hall.

"I'm so sorry, darling," she said as she kissed my cheek. "Your poor father is beside himself that he can't be here, but the doctor insisted, you know. He must have that operation right away."

"What exactly are they doing?" I asked. "Coralie didn't know."

"My dear, I'm not entirely sure. All your father would talk about on the telephone was how much he wished he could have waited until after the wedding. I daresay I shall find out all the details when I get up there. Then I can let you know. Or perhaps you will be able to speak to him yourself on the telephone once he's out of hospital."

Coralie had come up behind me and my aunt reached out to embrace her. "Coralie, my angel of mercy," she said, kissing her on both cheeks. "She's been wonderful, Grace. Simply marvelous. What a lovely friend for you to have."

"She is indeed," I said. "Coralie told me you two had become close."

"We have you in common, dear," Aunt Penelope said. "Of course, we would be friends."

"Your aunt has introduced me to traditional British food," Coralie said. "Roast beef and Yorkshire pudding, steak and kidney pie, and even kippers for breakfast although, I must confess, I draw the line at those. Oh, and that other concoction with fish and rice. What do you call it?"

"Kedgeree," my aunt and I said in unison and laughed.

"I told your aunt that one day I shall reciprocate by offering her catfish with grits and black-eyed peas. My cook's from the South like me and she makes a fine mess of grits."

Personally, I didn't think eating grit sounded at all appetizing, but maybe it lacked something in the translation.

"Let's go through to the drawing room," I said. "I'm sorry Simon isn't here to greet you, Aunt. He had some urgent business to attend to in London, but he'll be back later this afternoon."

"I sincerely hope so, my dear," my aunt said, linking her arm with mine as we strolled into the drawing room. Coralie followed close behind. "Wouldn't want him to be late for his own wedding, would we?" Aunt Penelope laughed but it sounded false for some reason. She also seemed to be speaking louder than necessary as if ensuring someone not immediately present could hear the conversation.

Once behind closed doors, she and Coralie bundled me over to the far side of the room by the French windows.

Coralie took my hand. "Grace, I want you to know that your aunt knows everything you do about me."

"You mean the stones, the cards, Beersheba...everything?"

Aunt Penelope nodded. "She didn't have much choice. She could see how worried I was that you were making a terrible mistake. Now I know the reason, I'm still desperately worried for you, but at least I think I am beginning to understand."

"And does Father know?"

"No," my aunt said. "I thought I would leave that up to you whether to tell him or not and, of course, he has rather too much of his own to contend with at the moment."

"He was so set against our marriage, but Coralie said he was adamant it must go ahead."

"Yes." I didn't like the way Aunt Penelope avoided my eyes when she said that. Instead, she looked at Coralie, who deftly diverted the conversation.

"There are only a few more hours before you officially become Lady Mordenhyrst," she said. "If Cecilia is planning to do anything to stop that she will have to get a move on. So far, I've seen no sign, but she's a deep one. Her aura has become difficult to penetrate."

Hearing her say that made me realize. "I haven't been aware of her aura for weeks now."

"She's probably managed to block you from seeing it. That means, of course, that she knows you have the power to see and that represents a threat to her. How are things with Simon?"

A warm glow filled me. "We're closer than ever. I'm sure he can't be tainted with the evil around here. I really feel I could trust him. If I told him—"

"*No!*" Coralie's exclamation was only a step away from a shriek. I jumped.

"I'm sorry," she said. "But don't be tempted to do that. He's still a Mordenhyrst and he's too close to his sister, even if he has backed off a little from her and grown closer to you. It's too risky."

"I understand," I said, wishing it didn't have to be that way, but I supposed the less Simon knew, the safer he would be. The safer we all would be.

Coralie squeezed my hand. "It's going to be okay, Grace. I reckon the three of us women are a match for any number of Cecilias."

"You really think she's at the heart of it, don't you?" I said. "I thought she was just a shallow society rich bitch."

Coralie laughed. "Oh, she's that all right and more. Let's see what tomorrow brings but, in the meantime, let's strengthen ourselves. Come and sit together round the card table and let's join hands. I'll make an invocation. It's one Beersheba passed on to me. Powerful and ancient."

Aunt Penelope and I joined her and the three of us bowed our heads.

"Let's make sure our hands touch each other's, fingers outstretched. Whatever happens, don't break contact. You can keep your eyes open or close them as you prefer, but please concentrate on my words. Your mind will understand their meaning."

"Even mine?" my aunt asked.

"Even yours, Penelope. Maybe yours more than anyone's. You're older, you see."

"Yes. I suppose I'm closer to the grave than either of you."

The way she said it, not in the least morbid. Practical. Coralie didn't respond.

The room grew darker as if a black cloud had passed over the sun. Out of the corner of my eye, something shifted. A figure moved close behind Coralie and laid its hands on her shoulders. In my head, I heard a familiar voice commanding me.

"Look at me."

"Beersheba," I whispered.

Her lips moved but her voice came out of Coralie's mouth. The ancient language of her ancestors poured into my brain, and I understood. Not the words themselves of course, but their meaning. Next to me, my aunt swayed slightly, and I knew she too was absorbing what we heard.

Beersheba spoke of an ancient and long-forgotten world where strange creatures roamed freely, and humankind was in its infancy. She told of a hybrid animal capable of walking on two legs like a man but equally at home in deep water. In my head a picture formed. A lizard-like reptile with a head not unlike a malformed human but its mouth longer and more pronounced. Its eyes were set to the front rather than at either side, its skin scaly and iridescent, reminding me of Coralie's pack of cards. Beersheba's words continued to flow, creating more images. These were more indistinct and hidden, until the fog cleared, and the visions coalesced into one human form.

Cecilia.

Coralie stopped speaking. My aunt's hand shook where her fingers touched mine. The figure faded from behind my friend, and she slumped forward. The room grew brighter again.

Coralie stirred. "Did you see her?" she asked me.

"Yes," I said.

"Who?" Aunt Penelope asked.

"Beersheba," Coralie and I said together.

"I had my eyes closed," my aunt said. "But I saw a horrible creature. Some sort of monster."

"Like a lizard?" I asked.

"Yes, but there was something badly wrong with it. Lizards don't look like that."

"Not the ones you see today," Coralie said. "But this one hasn't walked this earth in hundreds of years. And in the form Beersheba showed us, not for millennia. The last ones were the size of iguanas by all reports, although they were carnivorous and highly toxic, as I told you, Grace."

"Why did she show us this?" my aunt asked.

"Because, somehow or other, that is what we are dealing with. Or, at least, it is one of the things we're dealing with," Coralie said.

CHAPTER FIFTEEN

Simon made a brief appearance on his return that afternoon before jumping into his motor and speeding off to spend his last night as a bachelor with Lilo, who had leapt at the chance of being Simon's best man the following morning. As Simon drove off, I realized I had mentioned nothing to him about Eton. Indeed, I barely had a chance to give him a swift peck on the cheek before he left, and even then he had managed to wrong-foot me.

"I have a surprise for you," he said as he was leaving. "Pip has volunteered to give you away, so you won't have to traipse up the aisle on your own. Isn't that good of him?"

I mumbled something while inwardly wishing he hadn't bothered to do me such a favor. A man I didn't particularly like and hardly knew was going to stand in my father's stead? It hardly bore contemplating. Still, Simon obviously wanted to save me what he perceived might be embarrassment. In fact, I felt none at all and would have happily sailed up the aisle on my own.

"I shall look forward to seeing you at the altar," Simon said. "Don't forget. Eleven o'clock tomorrow morning." He took my hand and kissed it. "I love you, Grace. You will make me the happiest man alive when I slip that ring onto your finger."

And he was gone, leaving me with Aunt Penelope and Coralie. Thankfully, Cecilia had elected to stay with Fleur and Percy at their country estate ten miles away.

The three of us spent a quiet evening reading and lost in our own thoughts. Nerves started to jangle inside me. The strongest urge to call the whole thing off was almost all-consuming. But I had to see it through now. Besides, during yesterday's invocation, I had received a message loud and clear from Beersheba. Even if I ran, I would have to return. It was inevitable. I would be brought back, against my will if necessary, but whatever was to come was inextricably linked to my own fate.

Coralie seemed to read my dark thoughts and came over to me. Aunt Penelope had momentarily dropped off to sleep so Coralie spoke quietly not to disturb her. "It's only natural you should want to run away from this. The responsibility is a heavy one. To rid this place of the evil that infests it is not an easy challenge nor one that will go unresisted. But you're not alone. Remember that. Let it bring you strength. You have your inner power to draw on and Beersheba is connected to you through me. You have powerful forces at your side, Grace. Don't forget that."

"I won't." I was sure I sounded more confident than I felt. But still, as I watched a flight of swallows swoop and dive outside, I wished I could become one with them. Even more so when they suddenly took off in the direction of the setting sun. My heart soared with them. I envied them the freedom to fly wherever their fancy took them. But then I saw what had spooked them. The gyrfalcon glided effortlessly through the sky, a ghostly predator in pursuit of the swallows, and I knew that every one of their precious lives was in danger. I took it for the sign it represented. However tempting it might be to cut and run, I could never escape my destiny. My only choice was to make the best of it.

★ ★ ★

"Oh, dear me, miss. The heavens have really opened. What a shame." Nell turned back from the window, where streams of rain poured down the panes and the wind howled outside.

"Hardly fitting weather for late July," my aunt said as she watched Nell fix my veil onto the Mordenhyrst family tiara, which weighed my head down so that it was already beginning to ache.

"At least you won't have far to walk from the car into church," my aunt said. "The photographs will have to take place in the church hall or somewhere."

"They'll take some in church and the rest here," I said. "I just hope my dress holds up."

Needless to say, the weather did its worst. Coralie, Aunt Penelope and I arrived at the church with Nell in attendance. Two footmen were waiting with large umbrellas to shield us, but as I alighted from the Rolls, a sudden gust of wind drove rain and blown leaves directly at me, drenching my silk gown, which wilted, sagged, and then clung to me in a manner which, had she still been alive, my mother would have called 'unbecoming'. My veil billowed out in all directions before it came to rest on a large rose bush right by the entrance. The footmen were unable to provide any protection from the elements as their umbrellas had been simultaneously blown inside out and the force of the blast had sent them reeling, leaving all three of us at the mercy of the gale. I was stuck. My veil stubbornly clung to the thorns and the ripping noises it made as Nell and Coralie tried frantically to extricate me sent my spirits tumbling.

Finally, Nell wrenched it off me and I escaped into the church porch, there to inspect and try to rectify the damage.

I was soaked. The veil was ruined and there were dirty marks on the white silk of my dress that clung like a second skin. I could only hope the result still maintained some modicum of decency.

"That veil's had it and that's for sure," Aunt Penelope said, throwing the shredded tulle to one side.

"I can fix the tiara to your hair, miss," Nell said. "You'll see. It'll be fine."

The rector appeared, took one look at me and failed to hide the look of horror. "Oh, dear me, dear, dear me."

"Perhaps you could explain to the congregation why we haven't started yet?" I said, not wishing to hear any more of his anxious tutting. "No need to elaborate too much. Just say that the inclement weather has led to a slight delay."

"Yes, of course. Dear me, dear me." Finally he went away, and a few moments later his voice rang out, repeating much of what I had said verbatim.

I could hear a little shuffling but otherwise the assembled appeared to be placated.

The organist played suitable soft religious music while Nell and Aunt Penelope worked tirelessly to repair the damage.

"Trying to blot out the mud stains will only make it worse," Nell said. "I think we'd better just leave that. Everyone will understand. The tiara seems nice and firm now at any rate."

"Such a shame you haven't got your former lovely thick head of hair," my aunt said. "It would have had something to grip on to. The veil helped to keep it in place, especially the clever way Nell had gripped it. That short hair of yours...." She shook her head.

"If I had retained long hair, I would doubtless have had it styled in an elaborate way that would have blown to kingdom come and left me looking like a scarecrow," I said, unable to keep the annoyance out of my voice. "Has anyone seen my bouquet? Has that at least survived?"

"It's here," Pip said, emerging from the nave. "Oh my," he said, as his beaming smile fell on seeing me. "We have been in the wars, haven't we?"

"Don't make it worse, please, Pip," Coralie said. "Grace has had quite enough for one morning. Now, I think we're all done here. You look fine, honey. Trust me."

Pip took my arm. I held the bouquet of white gardenias, carnations and gypsophila, positioned it carefully so that it trailed over the worst stain, and stood up straight. Coralie and Aunt Penelope made their way to the front of the church and the wedding march started up.

As I proceeded up the aisle, past the rear pews, I was aware of how packed the church was. A few sympathetic murmurs floated past me and then I reached Cecilia's pew toward the front. There she was with Fleur and Percy, all three dressed in feather-trimmed black. I momentarily recalled the famous witches scene in *Macbeth*. As I passed them, they made no attempt to conceal their sniggers, and tears pricked my eyes.

I called on my inner power and drew strength from it. Ahead of me, Simon waited. He had come out of his pew, Lilo at his side. Both were smiling. Pip performed his duty with unexpected gravitas, for which I was grateful as well as a little surprised. Simon slipped the plain gold ring on my finger, we exchanged vows, two hymns were sung, prayers said, sermon delivered. It passed in a flash and then we were off down the aisle again.

Simon whispered in my ear. "You carried it off perfectly, Grace. Even with the weather and what happened to your dress, you still managed to behave every inch the lady. My Lady Mordenhyrst."

I stole a quick glance at him. His eyes were bright. Shining. He looked like a man in love, and I felt like a woman loved. The desire to escape Mordenhyrst Hall and all it represented had melted away and soon I would be rid of Cecilia's negative presence. In that moment I felt pure, unsullied happiness. If only we could stay that way forever.

Halfway down the aisle, I spotted *them* for the first time. Gathered together, like a flock. Men and women of the village who all bore a striking resemblance to each other. None of them smiled. All watched us, their eyes seeming to burn into me. With a shock I recognized Nell in amongst them. Only then did I see the family resemblance. Of all of them, the Mordenhyrst traits had been most heavily diluted in her, but here amongst her peers, it was unmistakable. In the days leading up to the wedding, she had been so helpful and friendly, I had grown to almost trust her. Now all my doubts about her came flooding back, tenfold. The villagers' faces were expressionless, even Nell's. If it wasn't so crazy, I would have sworn they were connected in some way, as if able to communicate with each other by some form of mental power. Telepathy. That was the word. I caught my heel in a small grating and stumbled a little. Simon steadied me, and I made it out of the church without further mishap. As we passed the back pews, I felt those eyes following me. Once outside in the fresh, windy air, I breathed rapidly and raggedly. Coralie was at my side in an instant, along with Aunt Penelope.

"Come on," Coralie said, "let's get you back to the Hall. You too, Simon."

"Of course," he said. "Too wet and windy for photographs here."

"Exactly." Coralie hustled me to the waiting car. "Let's get going. Those invited to the reception will follow on."

Inwardly I prayed none of the flock from the back pews followed. Nell would, of course, but on her own, I felt sure I could handle her. When she was with the others, she somehow became part of something much bigger.

Back at the hall, Mrs. Bennett seemed surprised to see us so soon but quickly rallied. The photographer arrived and, after performing some necessary repairs to my hair and makeup, while ensuring that my bouquet and careful positioning covered every stain on my now dry dress, we posed for photographs in the hall, the library, and the drawing room. Guests began to arrive, and the footmen handed out glasses of champagne. Simon and I, plus Aunt Penelope, formally greeted our guests, although Cecilia, Fleur, and Percy bypassed us, and made straight for more champagne while talking and laughing unnecessarily loudly.

A sumptuous wedding breakfast had been prepared by Mrs. Hawkins with some help from local cooks. As with the wedding itself, the reception passed in a blur – speeches, toasts, food and champagne.

It was time for Simon and me to adjourn and get changed for the evening's celebrations.

Up in our room, Simon took me in his arms. "You were magnificent today, Grace. I was so proud of you. Many other women would have crumpled under the weight of that awful weather, but you just rose above it."

"There wasn't much else to be done. Weather is weather. You can't control it. Anyway, it's done now."

"Yes, it is."

There was a faraway tone to his voice that made me look up from my position nestled against his shoulder.

I caught him gazing into space, over my shoulder, but unfocused on anything specific. He looked sad. "What's wrong, Simon?"

He shook himself. "Wrong? Nothing, darling. What could be wrong? I'm married to an amazing, resilient and beautiful woman. I can't believe my luck, if truth be told."

"I keep expecting Cecilia to do something dreadful. She's quite drunk, you know."

"Three sheets to the wind. With any luck, she'll pass out in a corner with her cronies and that will be that. I'll get one of the servants to clear them away."

It could have been a humorous remark, but he sounded so cold and callous I shivered. He saw me and laughed. "Don't look so shocked, Grace. My sister knows her time in charge is over and she's drowning her sorrows. She'll be out of your hair any day now. Off to Mayfair, where she will be far happier."

"And you're sure you don't mind that?"

"Whyever would I? I have you now. We have our whole lives in front of us."

But I couldn't help remembering Percy's words to me that first night. "She'll never let him go." Was that still true for Cecilia? Would she really allow Simon and me to build our lives together?

Simon left me so I could change into a beautiful scarlet and black silk and lace dress, accessorized with diamond and ruby drop earrings – my wedding present from Simon – and red silk-covered shoes with a Louis heel. Nell assisted me and she seemed a different girl from the one I had seen at the back of church. "You look lovely, miss…er…. My Lady," she said.

"Thank you, Nell, and thank you for all your hard work today. You really saved me so much embarrassment by your prompt and calm actions in sorting out my problems at the church."

"That's what I'm here for, My Lady. I wouldn't be much good to you if I couldn't fix a tiara."

"Nevertheless, I appreciate all your help."

"Thank you, My Lady."

I hesitated but I had to ask. I needed one last check, to be sure.

"Nell, those other people you were sitting with in church."

"Yes, My Lady?"

"Are you all related?"

"One or two are cousins and there was my aunt and uncle. My parents, of course. As for the others, I don't think so, although this is a small community, and we probably have some ancestors in common somewhere."

"The resemblance was more noticeable because you were grouped together. Were you told to sit like that?"

"Mr. Smythe-Leverton directed us to our seats. Not just us. Everyone. Bride's side, groom's side. The usual thing at weddings."

"So, Mr. Smythe-Leverton was acting as an usher as well as best man, then?"

"I suppose he was, My Lady. I didn't give it much thought at the time. It was fitting for us to sit at the back and that's where he directed us. He put us on the groom's side because we were from the village."

"That arrangement went out of the window almost immediately though, didn't it? I mean, there was hardly anyone from my family present, and the church was full. I saw people on my side of the aisle I had never set eyes on before. Villagers, members of society, all sorts of folk."

"But separated according to their place, My Lady. Mr. Smythe-Leverton was most scrupulous."

"I'm sure he was, Nell."

She was right of course, but I still wondered if his choice of seating arrangement hadn't been deliberately designed to throw me off kilter. And, annoyingly, it had succeeded.

I made my descent to find Simon waiting at the bottom, surrounded by friends…and his sister, who was holding a champagne glass at an impossible angle while somehow managing not to spill her drink. She gave me a sickly sweet smile and executed an unsteady, exaggerated bow. "My Lady Mordenhyrst. What a charming dress. So nice to see you without all that mud."

I ignored her comment and returned the smile with, I hoped, extra sugar. "Thank you, Cecilia, so kind of you to have noticed."

I then deliberately turned my back on her and spoke to Simon. "Shall we start off the dancing, darling? I think our guests are waiting."

"Of course." Simon attracted the attention of the conductor of the band he had hired for the occasion.

A roll of drums served to silence the chatter and the conductor took hold of the microphone. "My lords, ladies and gentlemen, the Earl and Countess Mordenhyrst will now take the floor in a Viennese waltz."

The strains of Strauss's *Wiener Blut* signaled our first foray of the early evening. I knew from experience that Simon was an expert dancer, me less so, but I followed him and managed not to tread on his toes, while keeping time with the rousing music. From time to time I caught Aunt Penelope's eye. She was watching us intently, alert perhaps for any sign that I was in danger. I gave her what I hoped was a reassuring smile and she returned it, but it was a half-hearted gesture that never progressed beyond her lips.

Simon held me as close as convention allowed. "I'm so sorry not to be whisking you off to Vienna tonight. That was to be an extra surprise for you, but I know you'll want to get up to Yorkshire as soon as possible to see your father."

"Thank you, Simon. What a lovely thought. When Father is recovered, let's do it then. It can still be our honeymoon. Just a little delayed, that's all."

"I shall look forward to that."

My thoughts drifted toward later that evening. What would it be like? Would it hurt? Some married women I knew had said it hurt terribly the first time but was better after that. I didn't welcome pain of any kind, but dancing so close to Simon, smelling his warm familiar scent, my body reacted with arousal. I wanted the reception to be done so we could be alone together. Truly alone.

When it was time for Simon and me to wish our guests good night, Aunt Penelope hugged me, and I felt a deep sigh shudder through her body. When she released me, there were tears in her eyes. I gave her hand a reassuring squeeze. No words were necessary.

I looked around for Coralie, realizing I hadn't seen her for some time. There was no sign. Maybe she had retired early. Odd that she hadn't said good night though.

A quick look in the study revealed that our guests and others had been most generous with their gifts. It would take a week to sort them out and another week to send the necessary 'thank you' letters. Under normal circumstances, they would have waved us off on our way, crowded round the doorway, spilling out onto the drive, especially now the weather had calmed and the evening had turned balmy. As it was, they all gathered in the hall to wish us well as we mounted the stairs. A few ribald comments wafted upward but I ignored them. There were giggles, excited chatter and, I was relieved to see, no sign of Cecilia and her friends. Maybe they had indeed passed out and been cleared up by the staff.

Once in our room, which had until that moment been Simon's alone, I stood by the bed, unsure of what to do next. I suddenly felt gauche and awkward, and waited for Simon to lead me.

He took off his tie and laid it over the back of a chair. I was surprised to see he was frowning.

"Grace, I hope you won't mind," he said, and I knew instantly that I would mind. Probably very much.

"I've had rather too much to drink, and I don't think I can...."
He nodded at the bed.

"That's all right." It was difficult to hide my disappointment, especially because I thought he had drunk very little. Certainly, no more than me, and I felt completely sober. "We can always lie in each other's arms. That would be romantic. We don't have to do anything."

"That is sweet and understanding of you but I'm going to have to beg even more patience from you tonight. I really need to sleep it all off and I can only do that if I'm alone. Do you mind awfully doing what the Americans call 'taking a rain check'?"

I stared at him, trying not to look incredulous. "If that's what you want," I said.

"Believe me, it's for the best. Your first time. Our first time together…should be special. It deserves to be perfect. We've waited all this time. Another night won't hurt, will it?"

I looked down at my hands, which I hadn't realized I had interlocked quite so tightly. "I suppose not, Simon. I'll go back to my room."

Before he could see the tears that had welled up in my eyes, I sped out of his room and down the corridor to mine, and closed the door behind me. I almost locked it, then decided not to. Why should I? I was married now. Maybe Simon would have a change of heart and decide to visit me in the night.

I clung to that thought as the hours ticked by. Finally, I began to drift off to sleep. On the edge of my dreams, I heard footsteps running up the corridor.

CHAPTER SIXTEEN

A rapid knocking on my door invaded my sleep. I opened my eyes and reached for the bedside lamp.

I rubbed my eyes, which protested at the sudden invasion of light. "Who is it?" I called.

"Coralie."

"It's open. Come in."

The door rattled and Coralie entered, closed the door, and turned the lock. She crossed the floor to my bed in seconds.

Still trying to rid my head of sleep, I took in her worried frown. "What is it? Has something happened? When we came up, I looked for you but you weren't there."

Coralie sat on the edge of my bed. "I had little warning and had to leave suddenly. My head felt as if it was exploding. So much negative energy in that one space…. As soon as I got back to my room, I lay down and Beersheba came to me in a dream. A waking dream. I couldn't sleep and I felt her presence. When I opened my eyes, there she was, standing next to me. She told me it was happening now. That I must come and get you and that I would find you here."

"I don't understand—"

"You will. You must hurry. Get dressed. There's no time to answer any questions now."

It was only then I realized that she was fully dressed. I scrambled out of bed, opened the closet and took out a jacket, skirt and blouse at random. "What time is it?" I asked, only aware that it was still dark outside or as far as I could tell through the closed curtains.

Coralie checked her wristwatch. "A little before five. The house will be stirring soon. We must leave before the servants are up or they'll give us away. We don't want Simon or Cecilia to know."

I didn't ask why. Somehow, I didn't need to. Since Simon's rejection, my fragile world had already begun to tumble. "You know about last night, don't you? That Simon and I…that nothing happened."

"I'm sorry, Grace. Come on, let's go, I'll tell you more on the way."

Together we moved as silently as possible through the still, dark house, down the stairs and into the hall. Coralie motioned me to follow her through the door to a world I had yet to discover at Mordenhyrst Hall – the world the servants inhabited by day and most of the night, but fortunately none of them slept down here. Unless the scullery maid had risen exceptionally early, we should be alone.

I let the heavy door close gently behind me before following Coralie down the stone steps. She had already lit a candle. The kitchen was, as I expected, spotless. Only the steady, rhythmic ticking of the large wall clock accompanied us as we pressed on in the uncertain flickering light, taking care to avoid bumping into furniture until we arrived at the back door. The key was in the lock and turned easily. The bolts were well oiled and drew back silently. I heard a noise. Someone was coming. Coralie pinched out the candle, holding the wick longer than necessary to try to contain the unmistakable odor.

Footsteps clattered down the steps.

Coralie had the door open and pushed me through. She closed it behind her. With any luck, the poor maid would say nothing about the unlocked door, believing it to be her own mistake. No doubt she would be relieved that it was she and not Buckingham or Mrs. Bennett that found it.

Coralie and I took off running through the kitchen garden, hiding ourselves under overhanging bushes and trees. Our route brought us out onto a lane rutted with the marks of centuries' worth of cartwheels. Clear of the house, I dared to speak, but even then, my voice was no more than a loud whisper. "Which way now? Are we making for the village? It's quite a hike."

"We don't need to go as far as that. Beersheba showed me. I just have to concentrate." We stood for a few seconds. The sky was growing lighter by the second although it was overcast, and rain was in the air.

Coralie stirred, spun round and pointed to a clump of trees a few yards away. "It's this way, but keep your voice down and try not to make a sound."

I nodded and followed her.

The trees quickly gave way to a clearing in the middle of which stood a fine old building big enough to house a small family. It was built in Palladian style with Grecian columns and must have been a striking building in its time. The original brilliant white of the marble still showed through in patches, despite showing all the signs of having been sadly neglected for decades. Ivy grew up its walls and wound itself around the columns like a serpent entwining itself around a tree branch.

The terrain was sparse grass and moss, littered with small white stones, sharp and uncomfortable to walk on. I bent down to remove one that had embedded itself in my shoe. It came away and I held it in the palm of my hand. I peered at it. "Oh my God." At least I had remembered to keep my voice low.

"What is it?" Coralie's whisper hissed in my ear. She took the offending object off my hand and turned it over in her palm.

"Is that what I think it is?" I asked, feeling my stomach churn.

She nodded. "Bone. It may be animal or human." She looked around her at the ground. The closer we got to the structure, the thicker the white shards lay. "This whole place is like a charnel house. That place was built as a temple. Sacrifices have been held here." She let the bone fragment drop from her fingers. "Come on, we've come this far. Let's see what's next."

I followed her. All the while I felt certain we were being watched. I glanced over my shoulder. We were surrounded by trees. No one could have seen us from the lane even though it was only a few yards away. Not a breath of wind ruffled the leaves. The ground crunched sickeningly as we walked over the carpet of bone.

We reached the foot of the short flight of wooden steps leading onto the porch of the 'temple'.

"Do we go in?" I asked.

Coralie looked at me. "I guess so. Be careful. I have no idea what we're going to find."

A creak greeted our first step upward. Then another and another. A wooden door stood ahead of us. Shut. Coralie went first. The feeling of being watched grew stronger. "Can you feel it?"

I didn't have to elaborate. Coralie nodded. "They're all around us."

My hands shook and I thrust them deep in the pockets of my jacket. I couldn't swallow and my throat muscles clenched. The hair on the back of my neck prickled as I felt a presence closing in on me. I grabbed Coralie's arm and we crept forward.

The door opened at her lightest touch as if someone on the other side had unlatched it. It swung back to reveal a dark room. The only illumination came from the early morning light filtering in through ivy-clad windows.

As we crossed the threshold the smell hit us. A rank mixture of rotting manure and body odor. There was something else too. An unfamiliar smell I couldn't make out. Like dead fish but with rotten meat added.

"Reptiles," Coralie said. "I've smelled dead alligators that stank like this."

We were in the heart of the building now. More light filtered in with the sun's rising.

And so did they.

It started with a shuffling, a rustling as of piles of dead leaves being whipped up by the wind, only there *was* no wind. The noise came from all around us, but we could see nothing. Only an empty, filthy room.

Then the voices. Whispering, chattering, growing louder with every second.

Another smell joined the miasma. Smoke. This time we could see it, curling up from the floor, wafting in from the walls, coating us in its greasy, sticky foulness, clinging to our clothes, hair, skin.

That's when we saw them. Only three at first. Three women, except they weren't any ordinary women.

These three were naked but where there should have been beauty, there was only a foul parody. Their skin was scaly, iridescent, like that of Coralie's pack of cards. Their limbs ended in long, reptilian claws, and when they came fully into view, I gasped.

The first was unmistakably Cecilia, but her face had the same scaly outer layer as the rest of her body. Her companions revealed their faces. Percy and Fleur. I watched in horror as they danced their macabre dance, and as they came closer, I realized something else about them. They had no external sex organs.

Light suddenly blazed through a window at the far end of the room, revealing the silhouette of another creature. I could make out no features, but instinct told me it was male. It hissed and the females hissed back. It stepped out of the light, into the shadows. I immediately thought of Simon but the body shape seemed too slight to be him. More like Pip. It even moved in a similar sinewy fashion. Yes. Pip. When he wasn't bounding around, he had that way about him, almost serpentine.

Next to me, Coralie began to chant. The words reached inside me and tugged at my inner core. Pain radiated from deep within me, nearly tearing me apart, and I bent double, retching but bringing nothing up. Only then was I able to join her in the chant Beersheba had implanted within us.

A loud, earsplitting screech from the creatures echoed around the walls and the three females ceased their writhing dance. They intertwined with one another as if trying to draw strength from each other and become one.

Coralie chanted louder. I echoed her. Together, we raised the volume until the walls were ringing with our voices.

The door slammed. All around us, shapes hemmed us in, drawing ever closer. They had no tangible bodies and they moved as one, but I knew there were many of them. There had to be many. One would not be able to function alone. It was as if they existed only as a colony.

The amorphous mass pressed closer. They pushed and crushed my body, my lungs compressed until I had to gasp for breath. I could no longer see Coralie and hadn't sufficient breath to call out for her. I felt my brain shutting down, losing consciousness, falling into darkness. In my head an image of my father appeared. He seemed tired, ill, but managed with his last ounce of strength to reach out to me.

"Hold my hand, Grace, lass, hold my hand." My inner spirit reached out to grasp his proffered hand. I couldn't quite get there. I touched his fingers but fell back. "Try again, girl, you can do it. Hold my hand."

With my last conscious breath, I willed my spirit forward and grabbed his hand.

I stopped breathing. Then a massive thrust from within me saw me gulping lungfuls of pure, fresh morning air. Beside me, Coralie was coughing. I opened my eyes and struggled to sit up. We lay on the grass on the edge of the clearing. The carpet of bone fragments lay between us and the 'temple'.

Coralie got to her feet and helped me up. My head swam and we staggered for a few moments. When I could trust myself not to choke, I spoke. "What was that? What just happened to us?"

"We were saved. You by your father, I'm guessing, and me by Beersheba."

"Did I really see Cecilia, Fleur and Percy, or was everything an illusion? And the male creature. I didn't see him clearly."

Coralie shrugged. "I really don't know. Maybe a mix of reality and illusion. Only time will tell."

My stomach lurched and I could tell Coralie was also feeling shaky. I had no idea how long we must have lain there but, with the sun directly overhead, we must have been gone hours. Someone by now had surely missed us.

"Let's get back," I said, anxious to get away from this hellish place. Despite the bright sunshine, which had seen off the earlier clouds, I felt cold, as if a penetrating chill had invaded my bones.

Arm in arm, Coralie and I stumbled back to the Hall.

We arrived to find the household in uproar.

Mrs. Bennett opened the door for us. I had never seen her flustered before, but her face was pale.

Simon shot down the stairs. "Grace! For heaven's sake, where were you both? And what happened to you? You're filthy."

Before I could speak, Coralie intervened. "We went for an early morning walk, Simon. Got ourselves a bit lost, I'm afraid. Then we got tangled up in some brambles and both took a tumble. We'll be fine once we get out of these clothes and have a nice hot bath."

Simon looked from Coralie to me. I nodded. The story sounded perfectly plausible.

An hour later, washed, dressed, hair and makeup expertly attended to by Nell, I decided against breakfast. It was nearly lunchtime anyway and my appetite was low. I had knocked on Aunt Penelope's door on my way down but there was no reply.

Simon was attentive, treating me like a precious porcelain doll. It was nice to be fussed over but a bit grating after a while.

"I'm all right, Simon. A slight tumble isn't going to break me. Do you know where my aunt is?"

He looked blank for a second, as if trying to remember who she was. "Ah yes. She went into the village. Morgan took her in the Rolls. That was before we knew you and Coralie were missing, of course. Come to think of it, she's been gone hours. I expect she got talking to someone. She seemed to be getting on rather well with the rector yesterday."

"Did she? I didn't notice."

The sound of a car engine drifted in through the open window in the drawing room where we now sat.

"That's probably them now." Simon went to the door. "Coming?" he asked. I nodded and joined him.

Aunt Penelope charged past Buckingham, her cheeks flushed. She barely acknowledged Simon. "Grace, I must talk to you. Alone." She glared at Simon, almost daring him to refuse her request.

"Of course," he said. "I'll go for a ride. I could do with the exercise. And so could the horse, I should imagine." He took the stairs two at a time while my aunt followed his every move. Once he had reached the top, she bundled me into the library and shut the door.

"Over there." She pointed to the far side of the room. "I don't want anyone in this house to hear what I have to say."

I followed her. My heart beat a little faster with each step.

"I've been having a most interesting conversation with the landlord of your local hostelry."

"I didn't think you ever entered such premises."

"I don't as a rule, but when someone comes up to you at your niece's wedding – a total stranger, mark you – and presses a note into your hand, mouthing 'I must talk to you', I am prepared to make an exception. He has, I believe, spoken to you on occasion. About the goings-on of the last earl."

"Yes. And Mrs. Chesterton. I thought she was your typical village busybody until he filled me in on her tragedy."

"Yes, poor woman. More sinned against than sinning, that one. And you need to speak to her, Grace. Urgently, before it's too late."

"Too late?"

Aunt Penelope nodded. "Everything Coralie has seen is true. There is an inherent evil in this place. Not merely the Hall but the village and the land in between. Do you recognize the type of trees that grow here?"

I shook my head. "I'm hopeless at that sort of thing. Mother was the gardening expert."

"I hadn't realized it either, but Mr. Sykes pointed it out. There's only one species of tree around here and it isn't found anywhere else. I asked him its name and he said that, as far as he knows, it hasn't got a name. No one has ever catalogued it. If you look closely at the leaves, you'll see something really strange. I picked one." She unclasped her handbag and, with a gloved hand, withdrew a sad, wilting tree leaf. "Look at that." She handed it to me.

I held it. It seemed damp and appeared to be dying. It curled into a tube and began to darken even as we watched it. I remembered the Russian Vine. But I had imagined that, hadn't I?

Aunt Penelope's voice held a note of triumph. "See? Now tell me that's normal, because I've never seen a leaf do that before, have you?"

"Certainly not as quickly. And they usually dry out and turn brown or something first."

"Exactly the same thing happened to one Mr. Sykes picked to show me. He said any form of contact directly with human skin will do that to a leaf off those trees."

"But what makes them grow only here? The soil?"

"Mr. Sykes said that's part of it but not the whole story. Years ago, some botanist came to study the local plant life and was astonished at what he found. He said this type of tree used to be everywhere before the last Ice Age. He gave it some Latin name which has been largely long forgotten. Somehow the ones here have proliferated but no other species will grow here."

"But there are plants, flowers. Grass." Somehow my experience with that Russian Vine didn't seem fanciful anymore. Nor did it appear that I had identified it correctly. Hardly surprising, even though the reason I had been so sure was that one wall of Caldwell Grange was covered in it.

Aunt Penelope was in full spate now. "Have you looked closely? The plant life round here is not the same as what we're used to. The botanist said they are all distant ancestors of the current varieties. Even the grass. It's spikier and grows more slowly. Oh, and Mr. Sykes also told me that the botanist was terribly excited by his findings. Sadly, he never lived to see them published. He died of a heart attack on the morning he was due to leave Cortney Abbas."

"That's a little convenient for anyone not wanting the story to get out."

"My thoughts exactly. And that's not all that's different about this place."

"True. We know a lot of villagers have Mordenhyrst blood in them but that's because of the appalling behavior of Simon's forebears."

"And that's where the story grows murkier than ever." Aunt Penelope drew me closer to her. "Mr. Sykes said there are problems with this latest generation. The ones the old earl fathered. Some of the mothers of these children have been talking. In private, of course. No one would dare speak about such things publicly, especially not when the earl was alive. But now.... You see, it's their...." She lowered her eyes in embarrassment. "Bodies. Not all of them, but some don't have...."

The image of Cecilia, Fleur and Percy dancing naked flashed in my mind.

"You don't need to be delicate, Aunt. You mean they have no genitals."

Aunt Penelope's eyes widened. "Why, yes. but how di—? Oh, of course, your wedding night." She looked downcast.

"Oh no, Simon and I didn't.... I mean, he said he had drunk too much so we agreed to wait. I had a dream...or maybe it wasn't a dream." I told her. Then it hit me. For some reason I couldn't fathom, it had never occurred to me that Simon would be anything other than a normal man under his Mayfair suits and Barbour jackets. But what if he was like his father? I had never so much as caught a glimpse of his body below the neck. I pushed the thought aside. My aunt was still talking.

"There's another thing Mr. Sykes told me. There's a belief in the village that the Mordenhyrsts aren't entirely human. Of course, he saved this bit till last, and I couldn't believe it. Everything else, but not that. I mean, it's the stuff of penny dreadfuls, isn't it? That's when he left me for a few minutes and went to fetch Mrs. Chesterton. She seemed unwilling at first. Well, it's an incredible story, isn't it? But.... Look, you need to hear it from her. I said I would come and get you. Will you come now?"

I didn't hesitate. "I think we should bring Coralie too. She's as much a part of all this as we are."

Aunt Penelope looked doubtful, then nodded.

"I'll get her," I said. "I think she's in her room."

Fifteen minutes later, with Morgan at the wheel, the Rolls glided into the village and stopped outside the church.

"Thank you, Morgan," I said, wondering how much I could trust him. At least he wasn't one who bore any resemblance to the Mordenhyrsts, for which I was grateful. I kept remembering how they had all congregated together in the church at our wedding. Had they really been directed there, as Nell insisted? Or had they already decided that's where they would sit? I had already lied to my maid, telling her my aunt wanted my opinion on a gift she was choosing for my father. Coralie exclaimed how much she would enjoy a trip to the village, and I had offered to give her a ride.

Aunt Penelope and I set off toward the village store, while Coralie took a different direction into the church. "I adore reading gravestones," she announced, loud enough for Morgan to hear. "And you have such ancient ones here in England."

"Enjoy yourself," I said. "We'll see you back here in a little while. Morgan, if you want to wet your whistle, I shan't object. Grab yourself some lunch as well."

He tipped his hat to me and smiled. "Very good, My Lady. Thank you."

Aunt Penelope and I went into the store and quickly selected a tin of assorted toffees. Cortney Abbas wasn't the type of place that attracted tourists and there was little to choose from. In less than five minutes we were back outside. No sign of Morgan.

My aunt had certainly spent a productive morning. She was all prepared for a little subterfuge. "Morgan will see us from the pub window if we go back the way we came, but we can double back on ourselves down this side street."

We scurried down the street, which wound to the right, leading us to a side entrance in the churchyard, hidden by a couple of those trees I suddenly noticed in more detail. A cursory glance at it didn't reveal anything of

THOSE WHO DWELL IN MORDENHYRST HALL • 213

significance, but looking closer, the bark *was* different. Neither smooth, nor gnarled, but more like scales. No time for nature study now though.

Coralie was waiting for us at the far side of the grounds where the grass grew tall. As we waded through it, bits of it stuck to our clothing.

"How vile," Aunt Penelope said, trying to brush it off and only making it worse. It stuck to her gloves as well, releasing a pale yellow sap.

I gritted my teeth and pressed on. We had to go that way or else run the risk of being seen from the pub and anyone traversing the village square.

"She's waiting for us," Coralie said, nodding toward a solitary cottage, where Mrs. Chesterton stood in the doorway.

"Come in," she said. "I've made some tea. I can't offer you anything stronger. Won't have the stuff in my house."

"That's quite all right, Mrs. Chesterton," my aunt said. "A nice cup of tea will be just the ticket."

The woman led us into her tidy parlor where we sat in upright wooden chairs. A white embroidered tablecloth covered the dining table and a tray awaited us with teapot, milk jug, sugar and crockery. Our hostess poured tea for us and distributed it. "I'm sorry there isn't any cake, I didn't have enough notice you were coming."

"Quite all right, Mrs. Chesterton," I said, taking a sip of tea. "We have rather sprung ourselves on you."

Mrs. Chesterton cast me a look. It wasn't exactly friendly but at least it wasn't the hostile glare she had treated me with in the past.

"I was talking to your aunt this morning, Your Ladyship, as I'm sure she has told you."

"Yes, Mrs. Chesterton, and I am most anxious to hear what it is you have to say."

She looked surprised. "So, you haven't told her then?" she said to my aunt.

"After what you told me, I really thought it was best she heard it from you directly. It's quite a story and I might have got some details wrong."

"Very well." Mrs. Chesterton looked as if she was deciding where to begin. She twisted a handkerchief in her lap. "I was only a young woman at the time, and had recently lost my husband. I was all alone with my young daughter to feed and clothe and no money coming in. When Lady Mordenhyrst – Lady Elise, that is – offered me the job of governess up at the Hall, I jumped at it. Not only would I have money, but she also agreed to let me have one of the cottages rent free as part of my salary. Sheila and I would have a secure roof over our heads for the first time since my Harry died."

"You couldn't have turned that down," I said.

Mrs. Chesterton said nothing. She carried on with her account. "At first, everything worked out really well. They already had a nanny, one who had known the family for years, so I wasn't involved in any of the day-to-day caring for the children. Also, the viscount was too young to need my services, so it was just Lady Cecilia and me. She was a willful child, as I'm sure you can imagine, but a lot of them are. It was nothing I couldn't deal with.

"I can't remember when it all began to change. It started with the earl paying unexpected visits to the schoolroom when Lady Cecilia was in the middle of her lessons. She would throw down her pencil and race to her father, who would pick her up and whirl her around. Needless to say, I got no sense out of her for the rest of the day, so eventually I asked him if he would delay his visits until we had put the books away for the day. I remember he gave me an odd, annoyed sort of look. His eyes bulged. It was most peculiar. And quite unpleasant. It made my skin crawl. But he did as I asked.

"Time passed and the nanny caught an especially bad cold. Lady Mordenhyrst didn't want Cecilia to catch it and asked if I might stay overnight in the Hall to be on hand should either of the children need me. Sheila was still very young, so I made up a bed for her in my room and she went to bed, good as gold. But then the earl heard of the arrangement, and he was angry. So angry. He said my little girl would have to stay in the cottage on her own. When I asked why, he said it wasn't for me to question his decisions. He made it clear that if I didn't do as he ordered, I would find myself out of work and homeless." Mrs. Chesterton gritted her teeth. "He knew he had me over a barrel. My daughter was nine years old. Far too young to be left alone overnight. But I had no choice.

"I remember it was around eleven-thirty at night. I was getting ready for bed when my door flew open. There was the earl in his night attire, drunk, of course. He lurched towards me. I tried to get away, but he was too powerful and much, much stronger and bigger than me. He threw me on the bed and ripped my blouse. His nails scratched my skin, drawing blood. Then he held me down with one hand and stuffed something in my mouth to keep me from screaming. Once he had gagged me, he fumbled with his dressing gown and it fell open. He knelt above me, and I saw...I saw...." Mrs. Chesterton dissolved into floods of tears. Coralie and I exchanged glances while my aunt put her arms around the sobbing woman.

"It's all right, my dear," Aunt Penelope said. "You're nearly there now, but Grace needs to hear the rest."

Finally, Mrs. Chesterton blew her nose and raised her tear-streaked face to me. "He wasn't as my husband had been. As far as I know, he wasn't like any man. From the neck up, he looked perfectly human, but...it started partway down his chest. Scales. Shiny, glittering scales." The tears began to flow again. "He reached between his legs and this...thing. It was like a thick worm. It twitched and grew as he held it. He was pointing it at me and laughing. That laugh. I'll never forget it till the day I die. And this thing, it grew. He stroked it, fondled it.... I swear the thing took on a life of its own, a serpent or snake of some kind. Its...its...head parted and something slithered out of it. It was like...like a tongue. It flicked like a snake's would...." Her voice tailed off.

I stared, horrified and speechless. My mouth dried and seconds ticked by, but Mrs. Chesterton hadn't finished.

When she resumed, her voice was so quiet, I had to strain to hear. "I lay there, desperately trying to get away. The...*thing* was in charge now. It was straining to get at me. The earl was blocking my escape.

216 • CATHERINE CAVENDISH

This big powerful creature, I can't call him a man anymore. But that *thing* was controlling him, and it wanted to get at me. It had grown so long now and writhed so much, he needed both hands to steady it and direct it. In a minute it would drive its way into me. It was only inches away and I knew he would force my knees apart if I didn't act now. I saw my chance. I don't know where I got the strength but with both his hands occupied, I managed to bring my knees up and kick him. Hard. Between his legs, and I swear it was that thing and not the earl that let out a scream. He fell to the floor, still clutching it, and I ran. I raced down the corridor and out into the night. I didn't stop until I reached my cottage. I half-expected him to follow me and I packed everything we had, which wasn't much. Mercifully my daughter slept on. The sleep of the innocent, I suppose. I stayed up all night, bags at the ready. I watched out of the window, but he didn't come. When it was a decent hour, I took my daughter and we made for the church. When the rector arrived for Communion, I threw myself on his mercy. He was a good man, Canon Pennywright. He helped me get this cottage."

Coralie coughed. "Mrs. Chesterton, would you say the late earl was human?"

The older woman shot her a look. "No, I would not. As a God-fearing woman I would say he sprang from the depths of the Devil's inferno. Him and all his brood."

"But," I said, "couldn't you have left here? Started a new life elsewhere?"

Mrs. Chesterton blew her nose. "Where would I go? I had no money, my only home was right here, thanks to the canon's generosity. Oh, I did consider it. Seriously at first. After it...all happened, I was ill, you see. My mind collapsed, you might say. Poor Sheila had to nurse me. She had to grow up quickly. Too quickly. And then the canon...he died suddenly. Poor man fell from the church steeple. The churchwarden found him lying on the ground. He had something in his hand. Part of the guttering I believe. That's how they knew where he had fallen from. He must have grabbed hold of it to save himself, only it was rusted through."

"What was he doing up there in the first place?" Aunt Penelope asked.

Mrs. Chesterton shook her head. "We'll never know, will we? Anyway, after he passed away, the present rector arrived, and he continued the arrangement that allowed me to live in the cottage rent free in return for duties around the church. To me they're not duties though. It's my life now. Especially since Sheila left."

"Wasn't there some rumor that you had another child?" Coralie asked. I flashed her a warning look. It seemed so direct, insensitive. But Mrs. Chesterton seemed unfazed.

"This is a small village. People make things up. I wasn't with child. I was ashamed. I thought that, somehow, I had brought it on myself. Maybe I dressed too provocatively. I hid myself away, made new clothes that couldn't possibly attract a man. I wouldn't go out until I was sure I was presentable and respectable. And I said nothing. I never told anyone what happened with the earl. I reckoned as long as I stayed silent, he would leave me alone, and he did. Maybe he thought no one would believe me anyway. I was hardly in the first flush of youth – unlike his usual conquests – and not the prettiest either. Poor Sheila. She had a lot to contend with. I'm not surprised she doesn't want anything to do with me anymore."

"I hope you now know it was nothing you did wrong," Coralie said, and I nodded. "That man, the late earl, was an evil bastard. Sorry about my language."

"Privately, I have called him far worse. And all his family. Like I said, publicly I've been like all the rest and never talked about what happened.... But I'm tired of keeping quiet. That man is dead and I want to speak out."

I sat forward. "Mrs. Chesterton, we're aware that there's something terribly wrong with Mordenhyrst Hall and this entire village. Coralie has ways of...." How to explain something pagan to a committed Christian without frightening her off. "Coralie has contacts.... She...." I looked at her helplessly.

218 • CATHERINE CAVENDISH

"What Grace is trying to say," Coralie said, "is that I know a bit about how to deal with the evil that is all around here. I believe that, with your help, we can work to get rid of its manifestations and influence altogether."

"Somehow, I don't think it will be as easy as you may think," Mrs. Chesterton said. "Others have tried...and failed."

"What happened to them...these others?"

"All dead. Just like the canon. And Lady Elise. Suicide, they said. If that's true, this village must have the highest suicide rate in the country. There have been at least twenty to my knowledge. Others have gone missing. It's not too difficult to hush things up here. Cortney Abbas is at the end of a lane going nowhere. It's isolated. No one comes here unless they intend to."

"I can't think it will stay that way for much longer," I said. "There are a number of major roads being constructed not far from here, connecting the smaller towns and villages so that people can get to the cities. It's only a matter of time before someone looks at the map and wonders why Cortney Abbas is sitting there by itself. Houses are being built. There's some pretty countryside around and people may well want to come and live here."

"I'd like to see them try," Mrs. Chesterton said. "*They* don't take kindly to incomers, not unless they've invited them in themselves." She looked directly at me as she said this.

I had to ask. "When you were up at the Hall and looking after the children, did you ever see either of them in a state of undress?"

"Grace!" Aunt Penelope's shocked voice rang round the room.

"It's quite all right," Mrs. Chesterton said quietly. "I know why she's asking. Only once, Your Ladyship. I came in on them early one evening. I was quickly shooed out of the room and Nanny was furious. The present earl was still in his cot, so I didn't see anything other than a chubby pair of legs kicking and a sweet little face. Nanny was in the middle of preparing him for bed. Lady Cecilia was putting on her nightgown and she turned toward me. It was only a fleeting glance, you understand, but it did disturb me."

"Why was that?"

"Because she didn't...I mean to say, between her legs, instead of what you and I have, she simply had a mass of glittering skin that covered her from the top of her legs up to her chest, maybe a bit higher, although you could never see it when she was dressed."

Coralie cleared her throat. "What you're telling us backs up what Grace and I saw in the grounds of the Hall. We weren't sure if it was illusion or reality. Now I think you've confirmed it. There's an ancient abomination in this village. It infested it generations ago and has bred here ever since. Thankfully though, it seems nature has managed to find a way of at least partially circumventing it or we would surely be overrun by these creatures by now but, thankfully, it seems not all are capable of reproducing, Possibly very few in fact, especially with the current generation."

"Dear God," Aunt Penelope said. "That such creatures could exist at all is beyond me."

Mrs. Chesterton exhaled audibly. She looked exhausted. "I'm sorry, but I'm going to have to ask you to leave now. I feel a little... unwell."

"Is there anything we can do?" I asked.

She shook her head. "I just need to get to my bed and sleep for a while. I'll feel better then."

We all stood and thanked her for her help. "I can't imagine how difficult this has been," I said. "Talking about this after so long."

"On the contrary, I feel like a burden has been lifted," Mrs. Chesterton said. "Thank you."

We said our goodbyes and left. This time we openly walked together back to the car as Morgan emerged from the pub, buttoning his chauffeur's uniform. We had agreed to say nothing until we got back home.

When we arrived, Simon was waiting for us. He looked serious.

"Grace, please come into the drawing room, I have some news for you." The others made to follow but he stopped them. "Later, please. This is for Grace's ears only."

Once inside, he shut the door and led me to a settee. My heart was jumping wildly. From his expression, whatever he was going to tell me wasn't the best news.

"It's your father," he said. "Grace, I'm so sorry but his condition was worse than we were told. It wasn't gout. It was gangrene caused by an injury when he fell recently. They had to amputate his leg just above the knee, but poison had entered his bloodstream and he died early this morning. It was very quick, and he was in no pain."

I sat there, numb. I heard his words, but they seemed to hang in the air as if directed at someone else who wasn't there. Simon held my hands and stroked them. Tears filled his eyes. What I had learned about Cecilia couldn't apply to him. This was Simon. I had had my doubts. Grave doubts at one time, but seeing him there, so emotional on my behalf.... No, here was no monster. He couldn't be.... I let him put his arms around me. I laid my head on his shoulder and wept my heart out. Memories of Father flooded my brain – of being carried on his shoulders when I was maybe three years old. My first pony, Nutkin, and how my father had led me around the paddock. I had sat there, so proud in my new riding attire. These and many more reminiscences ran like a reel of film. One day they would sustain me but for now they added to the awful pain of loss that weighed on me like a millstone. Worst of all was the realization that he had been dying, or even dead, when I had experienced that vision of him, holding out his hand to me.

Eventually, my tears dried. I had none left. "I must go to Yorkshire," I said.

"I'll come with you."

I didn't argue. "I have to tell Aunt Penelope. And Coralie."

"I'll ask them to come in. I shouldn't think they've gone far." He rang for Buckingham, who arrived in a moment.

Aunt Penelope burst into tears. Coralie put her arm around her. Mrs. Bennett arrived with a pot of tea and left after saying, "We all wish to express our sincere condolences, My Lady."

"Thank you, Mrs. Bennett," I said.

★   ★   ★

It was late evening when we arrived in Leeds. Father's chauffeur was there to meet us in the Bentley, which had been my father's pride and joy. Like everyone else connected to Caldwell Grange, he wore a black armband. Aunt Penelope, Coralie and I were all dressed in black, and our journey was a mostly silent one.

Mrs. Earnshaw, the housekeeper, had made up beds, but I had neglected to inform her that Coralie was joining us. "Oh dear, I need to change things around. I'm so sorry, Miss Grace…I mean, My Lady. I do hope Miss Duquesne won't mind sleeping in the attic, only Mr. Sutcliffe's room is…. What with all the repairs. You heard about the roof? All the trouble in the gales we had."

I had indeed. It had taken around a third of the roof slates off, exposing the upper rooms to the elements. Tarpaulin covered the damage for now, but it had led to a distinct shortage of bedrooms.

"And all the others is taken."

"I won't hear of Coralie sleeping in a drafty attic," Simon said. "I shall be perfectly happy there. Grace, you and Coralie won't mind sharing a bed, will you?"

"No, of course not," I said, and Coralie agreed.

Mrs. Earnshaw raised an eyebrow that was quickly lowered again. "That's settled then. Thank you, My Lord."

The undertakers had placed Father's coffin in his bedroom, and I made my way straight there, Simon, my aunt and Coralie following close behind me. Despite my aversion to open coffins, I had to see my father one last time. I had to say goodbye.

"He looks so peaceful," I said, my voice a whisper. He lay on a white satin pillow, a matching sheet pulled up to the top of his chest. His hands lay on top of a royal-blue cover, also made of satin. I touched his left hand, squeezed it, tried to pretend it wasn't as cold as I knew it to be. "Goodbye, Father. Rest in peace," I said. I touched my fingers to my lips and then to his forehead. A solitary tear tracked its way down my cheek. In the background Aunt Penelope softly wept. Coralie muttered an incantation but this time the words didn't penetrate my brain and I had no sense of what she was saying.

Later, I lay next to Coralie, but couldn't sleep. My head swirled with the events of the past few days. Every time I closed my eyes, visions of my father reaching out to me swept into view. His sudden change of heart over our wedding had disturbed me. He had been so insistent that our marriage take place when, up to that point, he would have welcomed me home with open arms. Now, as I lay there, I began to wonder. Had something got to him? Memories of that night down by the Thames came back to me. That strange ethereal bird that had manifested itself. Could it have somehow been sent to frighten my father? Acton Sutcliffe had never been known to fear anything in the corporeal world, but a force from beyond?

A deep groan sliced through the darkness. I sat up. At first, I wasn't sure where it was coming from. Then I knew. Next door. My father's room. I looked across at Coralie, who was sleeping soundly. I mustn't wake her. Besides, it was probably nothing.

I pushed the covers back and slipped my feet into my slippers, listening intently.

The groan came again. This time, louder.

Out in the corridor, all was silent. The groan came a third time. No question as to its origin. It echoed off the walls. I padded to Father's room and turned the door handle. Another groan. Like someone in pain. My mouth ran dry. I pushed at the door, and it opened.

Inside, silvery moonlight penetrated the gaps between the curtains. It focused like a beam on the coffin mounted on its trestles.

I wished I had woken Coralie. Maybe I could go back and get her. I hesitated. No. I must see this through myself. She was only next door after all.

Another groan. So close. I was within inches of the coffin, but it wasn't coming from there. I took another step. Looked down at where his body....

I gasped.

The coffin was empty.

A movement from the bed grabbed my attention. Someone was over there. Why hadn't I brought a lamp with me? A candle? Anything? "Grace." It was my father's voice. "Forgive me. I couldn't stop them. I couldn't stop them." His voice grew fainter. The shadowy figure seemed to dissolve in front of my eyes.

I looked back down in the coffin. This time I screamed.

My father was back. But not as he had been.

CHAPTER SEVENTEEN

Simon did his best to calm me, but I couldn't stop shaking. Aunt Penelope stood motionless and disbelieving of her own eyes. I kept staring down at the face that had been my father's but was now hideously twisted and discolored. Earlier he had been serene and at peace, his skin and lips pale and bloodless but unmistakably Acton Sutcliffe. Now a deformed creature with a rictus grin and blackened skin that looked as if it had been charred by fire stared up at us, its eyes wide open and fearful.

"Something must have gone terribly wrong in the embalming process," Simon said. He tugged at the lid and closed the coffin. "I'll get on to the undertakers in the morning and give them a piece of my mind."

"I don't think that will do any good," I said.

"Why? This is unacceptable."

"I don't think they're responsible for it, do you, Coralie?"

She shook her head.

Simon looked from one to another of us. "Do you two know something I don't? If so, I wish you would tell me."

I spoke. "We don't think what happened here is anything to do with the embalming process."

"Really? Then what is it to do with?"

"We don't know," Coralie said. "Do you?"

With three pairs of eyes on him, I wasn't surprised Simon shifted uncomfortably.

"You've lost me, I'm afraid. Look, I'll get on to the undertakers and ask them to remove your father's body and take it to the Chapel of Rest. I think that might be the best thing all round, don't you?"

I agreed. Of everything that had happened in the past hours, this made the most sense. I did have pangs of uncertainty about Coralie's words to Simon. They amounted to an accusation. But I was too exhausted and overcome to deal with them now. I kissed Simon good night, ignoring the fact that it was already after four in the morning, and went back to bed.

★ ★ ★

For once, and despite everything, my dreams were pleasant. Maybe my unconscious mind was trying to give me some kind of respite. A walk in the sunshine, birds singing, blue sky and fluffy white clouds, a rare sense of peace that was all too soon shattered by a vigorous shaking. I awoke with a start to find Coralie bending over me. She put her finger over her lips and motioned for me to follow her. Tying my dressing gown around me, I followed her out of our room and into the corridor.

Coralie opened my father's door. His coffin was still there but the lid was once again open. I thought we were alone until I caught sight of something moving in the shadows. I couldn't make out who, or what, it was until Coralie produced a small flashlight from her pocket and shone it right at him.

"Simon!" I exclaimed.

He looked shocked. His eyes wide and frightened, as if he had been caught stealing. "Get out of here, both of you," he said, his voice a low growl. "This isn't for you."

"This isn't Mordenhyrst Hall," I said. "This is *my* house. *My* home. What are you doing in here?"

He moved closer and I saw he was dressed in pajamas. A silk dressing gown in a paisley pattern hung loosely around him. In his hand he held a silver dagger.

"Put that down, Simon," Coralie said.

He ignored her.

I moved swiftly round to the bedside table and struck a match. I picked up the candle in its holder. Now I could see Simon in more detail.

He stood impassively, glaring at Coralie. For the time being he seemed to have forgotten my existence. I took in the firm set of his jaw, his neck, which seemed a little longer than usual, maybe because he wasn't wearing his usual high collar. Part of his upper chest was visible, hairless and....

"Oh God, no." I almost dropped the candle. The top of his pajama shirt revealed a hint of skin. Iridescent skin.

Now he remembered my presence. "I'm so sorry, Grace. You know, don't you? You know about us. Who told you?"

"That doesn't matter right now," Coralie said. "The fact is that, yes, we do know. We know about your charnel house in the woods. We know your family is part of some hybrid race and that the entire village is either part of it or complicit in keeping your secrets. How do you get them to do that? Torture? Bribery?"

Simon shook his head. "Nothing like that. Oh, what the hell, it will be a relief to let it all out. I'm tired of all the secrets, all the subterfuge and lies. I can't do this anymore." He sank down on Father's bed. We waited as he collected his thoughts. After a few moments, he looked up. "Cortney Abbas has always been isolated. In the past, so many stories circulated about strange things that went on there that people stayed away naturally. Children were warned never to go there. If they did...some of them never returned. That was sufficient to stop others from following. But then it wasn't enough. Some of us went further. It's becoming harder and harder to keep our secrets. My family has always been adventurous anyway. Those who can reproduce haven't always exercised sound judgment. My father was one of the worst. He sowed his seed far and wide. Not just in the village either. But when he got older, he mellowed, until the young women he was with were merely dressing. A pretty face to grace his arm and provide companionship. Nothing more. Needless to say, none of them lasted long." Simon laid the dagger on a bedside table. Coralie grabbed it. He made no effort to reclaim it.

My throat was parched, but somehow I found my voice. "Why did you marry me, Simon?"

He looked at me, tears filling his eyes. "Because I did the unthinkable, Grace. I fell in love with you. I was only supposed to find a suitably well-connected girl to replenish our coffers and provide an acceptable face for society and marry her. I wasn't supposed to fall in love. Our sort isn't supposed to have feelings. Do you see Cecilia having any feelings? Or Fleur? Percy?"

Coralie spoke up. "Grace and I saw them. In that place in the woods. Lilo and Pip are too, aren't they? You're all related, then. And you were there, weren't you? You let us go."

Simon nodded. I wanted to hold him and comfort him but a part of me felt revulsion at what I knew him to be.

"And you didn't attend Eton, did you?" I asked.

"Yet another lie to make us fit in. No. We were all educated at home. Very well educated of course, but it would have been impossible to attend public school. We would have been found out on the first day. Any male friends or acquaintances we had outside our own kind were educated at Harrow or Marlborough, any public school but Eton, so the truth wouldn't be discovered. I became adept at avoiding awkward questions from any former Etonians. All I had to do was change the subject back to *them*. I became adept at deflection. Besides, they love nothing more than talking about themselves. I have all the certificates and school reports, of course. Perfect forgeries. Money can buy you almost anything. Except happiness." He looked down at his hands, then as if remembering his relative state of undress, tied his dressing gown tightly around him, hiding all trace of his ancestry.

"Oh, Simon, when were you going to tell me?" I asked. I sat down on a nearby chaise longue. Coralie sat beside me and took my hand.

"Would you believe me if I said I hadn't a clue?" he said. "I kept trying to plan for it. Why do you think we haven't spent the night together?"

"But it would have had to come out sooner or later, and the longer it went on, the worse it would have been."

"Do you think I don't know that? God, Grace, I wish I'd never met you. Before then, I was living a perfectly carefree life. I was among my own people, doing stupid useless things in between making money for the bank. It was all so simple. Then Papa reminded me of my duty. Even if I couldn't father an heir, I should at least marry someone who would keep Mordenhyrst Hall alive. The upkeep of this place is crippling but it cannot be allowed to die. This house is the focus. *We* are the focus. We're the leaders, you see. All the rest look to us for decisions. Papa did his duty and now it was my turn, to the best of my capabilities at any rate. When I first met you, I thought you were a strong, practical down-to-earth girl who could probably cope with pretty much anything. That was important, you see. My mother.... She wasn't strong. She hated the physical side of things with my father. She couldn't stand to look at him when he came to her at night. Oh, she loved Lia and me, but when Papa insisted she must produce another child, because it was clear from the moment of our births that neither Cecilia nor I would ever be able to...Mama couldn't stand it. Things got worse and worse. She went mad. Then she hanged herself in her room when everyone else was out for the afternoon. She clambered up on top of a massive chest of drawers and threw herself off, managing somehow to send it crashing to the floor. It must have taken her a long time to die. She slowly strangled, you see." He raised his tear-stained face and the pain in his eyes scythed through me. "She haunts that room to this day. Oh Grace, I'm so sorry. As soon as we get back to Mordenhyrst Hall, I'll consult with my solicitor and draw up the papers for an annulment. You'll be free within weeks."

"What were you doing in here with that dagger?" Coralie asked.

"It's part of the ritual. You're right about the Garden House." He gave a half-smile. "Pretty name for such a grim place, isn't it? I have to take your father's heart back there with me as an offering to the spirits of our ancestors."

"*No.*" I would never allow him to desecrate my father's body.

He stared at me as if I had just shot him. "I have to, Grace."

"You will not touch his body and that's final. Get out of this room. Now. You're leaving for Mordenhyrst Hall on the first train. Now, *get out.*"

He stood, hesitated as if about to say something, decided against it, and left.

"Where's the bloody key?" It wasn't in the door. Coralie and I searched.

I pulled open the top drawer of Father's tallboy and there it lay on top of a pile of pristine white handkerchiefs. "Got it. I'm locking myself in here."

"I'll stay with you."

I was so relieved she had said that.

We lowered the coffin lid again. I tried to avoid looking at the hideous parody of my father's face for the last time. Outside, a man's footsteps sped down the corridor.

"Guess he's not waiting for morning," Coralie said.

I opened the curtains a crack, and then wider. "It *is* morning." I looked down to the driveway. Simon was climbing into the back of Father's car. The chauffeur closed the door and got into the driver's seat. In seconds, the engine revved and they set off.

"Grace, I want to do another reading with you," Coralie said. "With the stones this time."

I nodded. "Perhaps, as Simon has gone, we should get dressed and go downstairs. We can use the table in the morning room. I'll still keep this door locked though."

Coralie frowned as she looked at the coffin. "I think that's a good idea. We can't be too careful."

Downstairs, the house was quiet except for the distant sounds coming from the kitchen. The scullery maid was up and about her duties, stoking the range.

I drew back the curtains in the morning room and Coralie produced the velvet bag of stones. She scattered them on the table and they glittered, changed color, and finally settled into an array of blues, greens and black. Blacker than the first casting had produced.

"What do you see?" I asked, aware that the room was growing darker.

"Danger. It's all around you, Grace. It's around us both."

"And Aunt Penelope?"

"She must leave here. Today. She must take the first train back to London and stay there. She must never come back here or set foot in Mordenhyrst Hall. Her life depends on it."

"But why?"

"She knows too much. Grace, can you feel nothing?"

I could. The darkness was undeniable, although Coralie seemed unaware of it. "I can barely see across the room," I said.

"Then she has come for you."

Coralie had barely uttered the words when a hand gripped my shoulder. I cried out. The grip tightened. Another hand gripped my other shoulder and clung on, digging what felt like claws into my skin, opening up the wounds that were only now healing. I could feel the presence's breathing, sense its feelings of dread and finality.

Coralie closed her eyes. "Beersheba," she whispered.

Thoughts flew into my head, transmitted by the being that held me in its grasp. Images of death and burning. Flames shooting ever upward, the cracking of bones, the sound of hundreds of voices making invocation to their deity. A scalding bright white light seared through the blackness. A creature, without form or substance, manifested itself in thought waves and blurred images. A huge crowd of people swayed, bowed, then raised their hands in supplication. The gleam of a dagger like the one Simon had held. Screams of anguish, cries of rapture. And blood. So much blood.

The image faded and I fell forward as Beersheba released her hold. My shoulders smarted and stung.

Coralie opened her eyes. "That's what we're dealing with. Beersheba has shown us."

I nodded.

Coralie pointed to my shoulders. I looked. Droplets of blood stained my white blouse.

★   ★   ★

The undertaker's face was at least as pale as any of the bodies he had prepared for their funeral.

"I can only offer my most sincere and humble apologies, Lady Mordenhyrst. In all my years in the business, I have never seen anything like that. I cannot imagine how such a thing could occur."

"I understand, Mr. Farrar. I doubt that you will ever see it again either. At least, I pray that you don't." Despite my best efforts the poor man refused to be mollified. His assistants carefully took my father's coffin downstairs and the staff lined up to pay their last respects. The next time they saw him would be in church and the casket would be firmly closed at all times from now on.

★   ★   ★

The church was packed with Father's employees, local dignitaries, and a handful of family and close friends I hadn't seen for years. Aunt Penelope had been in floods of tears when she learned she wouldn't be attending.

"But he's my brother. My only brother."

"Yes, and you're my only surviving aunt," I said. "I want it to remain that way. Father would too."

She had capitulated eventually, and we packed her off to the station. I hadn't told her it would probably be the last time we ever saw each other.

When it was my turn to leave, I thanked every deity imaginable for the wonderful household of servants at Caldwell Grange. They would look after the house and grounds and ensure work continued on the repairs. As yet I had no idea when I would be returning, or even if that would happen.

All I knew now was that I had to return to Mordenhyrst Hall.

Cecilia was back.

CHAPTER EIGHTEEN

With Aunt Penelope safely at home in Belgravia, I could turn my attention to what had to be done at Mordenhyrst Hall. I don't know what I would have done without Coralie to guide me. She knew so much, and I felt like a child on her first day at school.

Morgan hardly spoke a word on the drive from the station. Mrs. Bennett was polite. Buckingham was polite. Nell was polite. But their eyes never focused on mine. When I tried to engage them with eye contact, they looked away, or down as if something interesting had suddenly appeared at their feet. Simon was out somewhere. He didn't appear to have told any of the servants where he was going. Either that or they had been told not to tell me.

"Did you notice how empty the village seemed?" Coralie said.

I nodded. I also noticed that only those villagers who bore no resemblance to the late earl were in evidence. Mr. Sykes stood at the door of his pub. It looked as if the place was deserted even though it should be busy with lunchtime trade, while the rector seemed even more troubled and flustered than usual. No sign of Mrs. Chesterton. I resolved to check up on her.

Nell put my things away efficiently but without conversation. I decided to resolve this. "You seem unusually quiet, Nell. Are you feeling well?"

She jumped at the question. "Me, My Lady? I am very well, thank you. The weather has been fine and sunny and...I've been very well."

She turned back to her task of hanging my dresses in the wardrobe. I struggled for another topic of conversation. "How have things been here in my absence?"

This question seemed to startle her even more. "Here, My Lady? Oh...same as usual."

"Nothing peculiar going on at all? Strange noises? Marks on the wall? Nothing like that?"

"No, My Lady. It's been very...quiet."

There couldn't have been a greater distance between us if someone had extended the Great Wall of China. I gave up.

I told Coralie about it as we sat in her room a little later. "It's as if she's been told not to say anything. Or maybe she's too scared anyway."

Coralie looked out of the window. "We may get our answer. Cecilia's back from her ride. She doesn't look too happy either."

We left Coralie's room and met Cecilia down in the drawing room, where she was engaged in lighting a cigarette. No holder this time but then she was dressed in her riding clothes. Perhaps that made a difference. She snapped her lighter shut as soon as she saw us.

"So sorry for your loss, Grace," she said, the words meaningless as they were devoid of any hint of sincerity.

I ignored her comment. "Is Simon around?"

"He's...somewhere...." She stared at her cigarette as if it had suddenly become a fascinating object.

"Do you happen to know precisely where?" I asked, keeping my voice even.

"Walking in the grounds, I should expect. There are a few thousand acres to choose from."

"Have you spoken to him since your return?" Coralie asked.

Cecilia looked her up and down as if she were some peasant, unworthy of her time or attention. "Not that it's any of your business, but yes, as a matter of fact I have." She switched her attention to me and fixed me with a long, hard gaze. Around her, the air darkened. Once again, I could see her aura. Dark gray, rapidly morphing into black. I sensed Coralie could see it but tried to keep my expression bland.

"Enjoy your cigarette," Coralie said. "Shall we go for a walk, Grace?"

"What a good idea," I said. "It's a beautiful day. Shame to waste it indoors. Maybe we could go for a ride as well."

"Oh, I shouldn't do that if I were you," Cecilia said.

"Whyever not? I'm sure Dulcie would appreciate a pleasant canter across the fields."

"So she might. I wouldn't know. She isn't here anymore."

"What? Where is she?"

"Same place they all are. Sold. One of my late father's last wishes. He felt the cost of maintaining a stable was unjustifiable in these difficult economic times. He foresaw that death duties would be crippling and that we would have to sell off certain assets. An Irish owner bought the entire stable. Even took the staff. I have just enjoyed my final ride on Pearl Fisher. I saw him off a few minutes ago, with all the others. Shame you weren't there. You could have kissed Dulcie goodbye. I think she was the most distressed of all. Probably wondered why you hadn't bothered to turn up."

"Why wasn't I informed?"

Cecilia looked wide-eyed. "Weren't you? Simon was supposed to tell you. Oh well, I imagine with everything else, it must have slipped his mind."

"More like you didn't bother to tell him either."

Coralie took my arm. "Come on, Grace. It's done now. No point in arguing over it."

I glared at Cecilia. A faint smile played around her lips.

Once outside and out of earshot of the Hall, I spoke to Coralie. "I want to go to the stables."

"Very well."

The stables were empty. Morgan was polishing the car. He seemed surprised to see us. "Is there anything I can do for you, My Lady? Do you want to go somewhere?"

"Not just now, Morgan. Tell me, did you see the horses being taken away a short time ago?"

"Yes, My Lady. Nice feller. Captain O'Leary. He used to be in the cavalry. Loves horses, breeds some good racers too. Even has some trophies in his collection. Our horses will be well looked after there."

"Where have they gone?" I asked.

"Somewhere in County Antrim, I believe. I'm no good with geography but I think that's where he said it was."

"Thank you, Morgan," I said. "Oh, just one more thing. Did Captain O'Leary employ Harper and the stableboys as well?"

"Yes, My Lady. Oh, all except Barnes. He didn't want to leave the village so he's going to be a footman. Mr. Buckingham's taking him under his wing."

"Thank you, Morgan."

Coralie and I moved away, continuing our walk in the direction of the Garden House.

"That's a little irregular, isn't it?" Coralie asked. "Employing a servant without your say-so."

"Entirely irregular. Unless perhaps Simon approved it, but in this place Cecilia's word still becomes law, and she clearly approved all this. The sooner she leaves, the better."

Coralie nodded. "One way or the other."

*　*　*

We came to the clearing and the sea of bone fragments that made my flesh crawl. "We have to go in there, don't we?" I whispered to Coralie.

"I'm afraid so. We're not alone though. I've brought protection." She tapped her purse. What would it be this time? Stones or cards? Maybe both.

The sickening crunch of the bones under our feet made my stomach churn. It was a strange relief to step onto the porch of the building that should have been a place of beauty but now seemed instead to form a focal point for everything that was vile about this place.

Coralie opened the door, and we were met with the familiar stench of death and decay we had experienced before. Once inside, the atmosphere thickened.

We made our way forward. The whispering started. Indistinct but repetitive, growing louder by the second. This time we made it to the back of the room. In front of us, a long table held a collection of mirrors, candles, and a mask.

Coralie lit a couple of candles with her lighter. A strange silhouette formed, growing more distinct as the flames grew stronger. She lit a couple more, then a couple more.

I cried out. A hideous face swam into view. The candles burned brighter. I staggered back, yet its presence grew larger. A reptilian face, yet with human features around the eyes, nose, even the mouth. It hovered a little above the table. It didn't blink or move its mouth. It stayed there, staring at me, while its stench made me gag.

"Coralie, get away from it."

But she ignored my plea. Instead, she reached forward. The creature seemed to swallow up her hand, then her arm. I screamed.

Coralie's laughter echoed around the still room. "It's a trick, Grace. None of it's real. Look, I'll show you."

She stepped away from the altar. The image faded and I saw immediately that she was holding some sort of mask in her hand. She held it out. "See? It's made of some sort of rubber. Quite effective, actually. The effect is all achieved with mirrors. It could easily fool anyone if they weren't right up close to it. And, of course, no one ever is. Only those in the know. For the rest? A handy device that helps keep them in check. Rule by fear."

From the darkness at the far side of the room came the sound of someone clapping slowly. From the shadows, a figure emerged. Simon. In sharp contrast to the man who had sat with tear-filled eyes in my father's bedroom, this Simon looked bitter, dejected, unkempt. Maybe it was being back here – the force of Mordenhyrst Hall and Cortney Abbas feeding the evil within him. "You two should be detectives," he said.

"It didn't take much," Coralie said, waving the mask at him. "Anyone could have discovered your little...secret here."

"But that's where you're wrong," Simon said. "No one else would ever dare to. Only you two, and my family, of course. None of the villagers for sure. Also, I'm interested to know how you got in. The place is always kept locked. Only Lia and I have keys. She wouldn't have let you in and I certainly didn't. I followed you here. I saw you turn the handle and walk in. How did you do it?"

I cast a quick glance at Coralie. "Looks like we had some help," I said.

Simon's expression changed. In his eyes, the man who had told me he had fallen in love with me returned. The swiftness of the transformation from one personality to the other was startling. "You must leave here. Leave this place and never come back, do you understand?"

"Leave Mordenhyrst Hall?" I asked.

Simon shook his head. "It's much too late for that. They'll find you wherever you go. At least at the Hall you can see them coming. No, you must leave this building. Burn it to the ground if you have to. At the Hall, you can fend them off. They'll all come back, you know. They have to. In time, each of us must return here. And when we do, there's one thing you must do." His voice faltered and he sank to his knees in the dirt of the floor. His face contorted as if he was battling some agonizing inner force.

I touched his shoulder. "What must we do, Simon?"

Tears streamed down his face. He spoke behind gritted teeth. "Kill us. Kill us until not one of us remains. Or we will kill you. We have to, in order to survive. It's all about that, you see. All about protecting the race. We were contained here for millennia but now we're spreading. Not just in this country but by sea and now air. The whole world is out there for the taking and we have the means to go wherever we choose. More and more of those of us who can breed will leave and ensure the survival of our species, by force if we have to. We must be stopped before the roads come.

Before more and more cars make it easy for us to go far from home, always with the knowledge that one day we must return, in greater and greater numbers as we enhance the stock with more and more of you. Greater diversity will mean fewer deformities. You have the power, Grace. You and Coralie. You can sense our presence without any physical evidence. Lia told me. Now go, please. I must prepare."

"Prepare for what?" And then I saw his aura forming before my eyes, shimmering around him like a mirage. Gray-black, yet tinged with a pale pink that I didn't understand.

Coralie gripped my arm and pulled me away. "Come, Grace, we must do as he says. *Now*. Can't you hear it?"

Footsteps, coming closer. Simon wailed. "It's too late! They're here."

Cecilia arrived first, closely followed by Fleur, Percy, Pip and Lilo. Behind them a cluster of villagers poured into the small room. I recognized some. My heart sank when I saw Nell among them. I guessed that every single one of the Mordenhyrsts' local progenies were here.

Next to me, Coralie dropped her stones and they landed with a clatter on the floor. Even in the dirt and gloom, they glittered. They rolled impossibly despite their sharp angles. Some of the assembled drew back from them.

Cecilia laughed. "Don't think your circus tricks will work here, Coralie. We have methods of our own."

"You sure do, honey," Coralie said. "We've seen them. Mirrors, rubber masks. You should get a job in Hollywood designing special effects for the movies."

The smile died on Cecilia's face. She reached behind her and pulled something from the back of her riding dress. She held it aloft. A gleaming silver dagger. "Hardly a Hollywood prop," she said, a smile curling her lip. "Now we shall make a sacrifice to our god."

Coralie laughed. "You have no gods here. *I'll* show you the power of a spirit."

The crowd murmured as Coralie began to chant her ancient invocation. As before, the words reached for my inner core. This time it was stronger, more powerful. I felt my spirit joining with Coralie's. The stones glowed, pale at first, then stronger as the spiritual chain between the two of us joined and grew ever firmer.

Behind Cecilia two shapes glimmered. At the same time, the auras of Cecilia and her friends emanated darkness, curling smoke-like upward and then outward, spreading over the villagers. Some staggered. Some fell.

The door slammed shut. The lock engaged. People screamed. Coralie and I stood firm, spiritually bound together side by side.

The room grew lighter. The figure of Beersheba emerged from behind Cecilia, who cried out in agony as the spirit's skeletal claws dug into her shoulders, ripping the clothes off her back. Beersheba was joined by another – by her ragged clothing, a woman from a much earlier time. I knew instantly she had to be Clothilde. Cecilia had no choice but stand there. Beersheba and Clothilde joined their spirit forces and raised her a few inches from the ground. Cecilia's body, devoid of all visible sex organs, was covered from mid-torso to thigh in iridescent reptilian scales.

Cecilia screamed and tried to break free of the hold the two women exerted but they were too strong for her. Coralie began to chant the ancient verses. The villagers whimpered, some cried, none moved to help their stricken leader. Coralie ended on a high, shrill note that bounced and echoed off the walls as Beersheba threw Cecilia aside like a discarded toy she crumpled and lay silent and unmoving.

One by one, Clothilde and Beersheba grabbed Fleur, Percy, Pip and Lilo. All tried to escape but none could. They were held fast in an unbreakable force field. Each went through the humiliation meted out to Cecilia, with the same result.

Simon watched from his kneeling position, weeping softly. I wanted to stop this. He wasn't like the rest. Yes, he had deceived me, but he wasn't cruel like Cecilia or as complicit as the others. As for the villagers, they were surely victims of circumstance.

Beersheba seemed to sense my hesitation. So did Coralie. She called out to me, "Don't be deceived again, Grace."

I tried to concentrate, but I knew my resolve was waning. Beersheba hissed at me.

Coralie shook me hard. "This has to be done. They have to be stopped. Don't you see?"

"They're not murderers."

"Aren't they?" Coralie indicated the pile of unconscious naked bodies. "Every one of those is guilty of murder. Fleur, Pip, Lilo, Percy...they are all acolytes of the Mordenhyrsts. But, you know.... Simon, I truly believe you're in love with Grace. For that, and that alone, I pity you. But your kind cannot be permitted to continue."

Fresh tears fell freely down Simon's face.

Beersheba made a sudden move to grab hold of him, but from out of nowhere, Cecilia was faster. She leapt at him, dagger in hand. A bloody flower bloomed in Simon's chest. He fell forward, driving the weapon through his body to the other side.

She spat at me. "You'll never have him. He is mine forever."

The link between Coralie and me broke, and Beersheba and Clothilde faded. The villagers stood in silence. Watching. Waiting.

I realized they were looking to Cecilia to give them direction. I couldn't let her do that. There were far more of them than there were of us. My friend seemed momentarily out of it. The strain of the past minutes? The suddenness of the break in our link? I had no time to speculate. I only knew I had to act, and I had to do it now.

I leapt forward, grabbed the dagger with both hands and, with strength I had no idea I possessed, dragged it out of Simon's lifeless body. I flew at Cecilia, bringing the weapon down hard into her chest. She saw what I intended a fraction too late. Maybe she didn't think I would actually do it. For once her arrogance served her ill.

She fell back with a cry. Her breath rattled in her body once, twice, three times and then she was dead, her eyes open, staring at a world she had quit.

Fleur, Percy, Pip and Lilo stirred. At the sight of Cecilia and Simon, their expressions turned ugly. Coralie came to and grabbed up her stones in one handful. As her fingers touched them the doors flew open. Fresh air blew in.

So did the smell of burning.

And a rushing sound, as of the beating wings of a thousand giant birds.

Coralie nudged me. "Come on, Grace, we have to get out of here. Now."

I grabbed Coralie's outstretched hand and together we pushed through the crowd, drawing strength from our inner spirits. As soon as we emerged from the building, the doors once again slammed shut. We raced over the bone fragments and paused on the edge of the wood.

Overhead, the sky filled with giant gyrfalcons. Their ghostly plumage caught the morning rays of sunlight. They swooped and soared and stirred up the ground. With no building to shelter in, Coralie and I dived into the bushes, shielding our eyes from the raging dust storm whipped up by the flapping wings of ever-increasing numbers of the falcons. This was no natural phenomenon. The sheer size and numbers of these birds belied that. The noise of the ghostly storm deafened us. Only distant cries and screams from the tortured and damned broke through. Coralie and I clung together, each of us knowing we should be swept up by this gargantuan force, but something protected us.

"The land is being cleansed!" Coralie yelled above the cacophony.

She didn't have to say it. I knew. As suddenly as it began, the storm died. We watched the birds soar high above us and disappear as if evaporated by the sun.

But the fire raged on, burning at full pelt, unnatural flames of blue, purple, green, yellow and orange. From inside, the shrieks and cries of the dying made me retch. I slammed my hands over my ears to try to block out the awful sound. It didn't work. I hear it still.

"Clothilde's fire," Coralie said. "It will not be seen outside the village. Let's go. There's nothing to stay here for now."

"No, I want to stay," I said. "I have to make sure no one gets out. You heard Simon. I believe that's the one time he told me the truth."

Coralie nodded. "That, and the times he told you he loved you."

Yes, I could see that. I also understood that he wanted to die. Finally, he was at peace. Or at least, I hoped so. His torment had always been that he had far more of his mother than his father in him – a cruel trap from which he could never extricate himself.

Overhead, a bird circled. The Montagne gyrfalcon was back, but this time it was alone. I prayed it hadn't come to claim Simon's soul.

CHAPTER NINETEEN

1965

All these years later, life goes on in the village. No one looks like the Absent Earl anymore, and as for Mrs. Chesterton.... She was found dead in bed the same day of the fire. A massive stroke apparently.

Coralie and I stay on at Mordenhyrst Hall, and the gyrfalcon has never returned. The staff changes over the years. Nell perished in the fire along with Joseph and some of the others. As for the rest, Morgan, Mrs. Bennett, Mrs. Hawkins and Buckingham elected to stay with us, and Nancy joined us too. When staff become too old to work, I give them a cottage on the estate and, in return, they keep us in fresh eggs, vegetables and fruit all year round. Of course, our produce is a little different than what you might get in these newfangled supermarkets. I couldn't even tell you the names of some of them, so Coralie and I tend to call them after the foodstuff they most closely resemble. Our raspberries are darker and more elongated, our apples smaller and sharper than most but only need a spoonful of sugar to sweeten them.

Strictly speaking, I have been the dowager countess since Simon died. There isn't an earl, and the title is now dormant. The legal people managed to trace an heir, but he turned it down flat. He also turned down the opportunity to live at Mordenhyrst Hall. He told me, through his solicitor, that I was welcome to it and everything in it. I presume he meant the ghosts but, since that day back in 1928, I have only ever glimpsed Elise out of the corner of my eye. I feel she is at peace now. Mostly, anyway.

I still haven't tackled the attic. I doubt I ever shall now. From time to time, Coralie and I venture up as far as the door leading to it, but something always puts us off. The stones tend to behave oddly when Coralie casts them anywhere near, and the cards are not propitious. We hear noises coming from up there but prefer to think a family of bats may have moved in. Of course, that wouldn't explain the odd-looking stains on the ceilings of some of the upper bedrooms.... So, all the portraits of Lady Elise remain up there, unloved and unseen. When Coralie and I have passed, no doubt someone will investigate. I wish them luck.

From time to time someone appears in the village who we must deal with. Mr. Sykes usually alerted us in the beginning but now that task has fallen to his son and, in due course, his grandsons, who also help us with some of the heavier jobs around here. Of course, only Coralie or I can have the final say, because we are the only ones who can see the aura. Quite what will happen when we're gone is something we battle with. So far, we have no answer. Maybe scientists in the future will be able to help. Of course, we can't trust anyone with our secret, or it would cause a frenzy in the newspapers and television. We subscribe to *Scientific American* and *The Lancet* and any other journals we can find to help us locate even one clever scientist to carry on our work. But there has been no one so far.

What do we do when we find one of the creatures? We dispatch them, of course. It's always humanely. Doctor.... Oh, I had better not say his name, had I? He'll get into such trouble if the British Medical Association finds out. Anyway, this doctor we found administers a nice big dose of morphine and that's that.

Coralie assures me that the earth beneath our feet and all around Cortney Abbas is cleansed. Since the gyrfalcons performed their sterling task, it has taken a lot of hard work, many fires and numerous summonses to achieve that, but the first sign was when a single snowdrop appeared one January. This was followed by a small patch of bluebells. In the past ten years, all sorts of wildflowers have been appearing, of the sort you would find in your garden. Nature is responding.

Aunt Penelope died during the last war. In 1941, it was. A bomb fell near her home, and she suffered a massive heart attack, dying in her bed. I couldn't attend the funeral. You see, I cannot leave the village. Neither can Coralie. It simply won't let either of us go. Or maybe it's Beersheba, or Clothilde. We have long resigned ourselves to our fate. We could live in much worse surroundings, after all.

As for the bodies…we burn them until nothing remains but ashes. These we then scatter to the four winds. Are we murderers? Some might say so. We see ourselves more as guardians. There's been talk of a large council estate they want to build only a couple of miles away. It's on land we don't own, or we could probably stop them, although other landowners have fallen victim to compulsory purchase orders so maybe not. Either way, it seems it will go ahead one day, probably even within our lifetimes. So, you see, we have a duty to protect these future inhabitants. They too will call Cortney Abbas their home because the extent of the building work will join up with the current boundary of the village.

No, we're not murderers. We have to ensure that these creatures, whose race should have been extinct long ago, die out, and never walk this earth again.

It is our destiny.

ACKNOWLEDGMENTS

As always, where would I be without Julia? Julia Kavan, my trusted friend and fellow writer who – just when I think I've cracked the case and written the story – never ceases to find the errors of my ways. Without her guidance goodness knows what Don would make of it.

Which leads me on to editor-extraordinaire Don D'Auria. A legend in his own (and many other people's) lifetime(s). It's been a few years now since I got that first email from him accepting a story I had written, and many thousands of words later I am still as thrilled as ever to be part of his 'stable'. There's quite a few of us these days and I count it a great privilege to be among that number. Huge thanks also to Nick Wells and everyone at Flame Tree Press, with a special mention to Mike Valsted, who spotted a couple of factual errors of the potentially embarrassing kind. It is such a pleasure working with you all.

My longsuffering husband, Colin, suffers 'the slings and arrows of outrageous fortune' shared by any partner of a writer – especially when that writer is bogged down in a plot twist that threatens to scupper the entire story. There were a few of those in this story, as always. Thank you for not murdering me, Colin. A big thank you to my extended family – Lisa, Howard, Daniel and Fabian – and wonderful friends who support me even though horror isn't really their 'thing'.

Major thanks to everyone at the Shippy Writers group. We have a blast every month – and somehow also manage to get some great writing/designing done. As at the time of writing, an anthology is in the creation stage. When you read this, it will hopefully be out there in the wild.

James Lefebure, step up and take a bow, for being by my side through my book launches, ready to enter into the spirit of all my daftness, and for being an amazing friend and supporter. Phil Larner – thank you so much for all your friendship and support and the use of the most appropriate venue any author could have. Ramsey Campbell – thank you for being such an inspiration and you and Jenny for your friendship.

Thank you to my fellow Flame Tree writers for being so supportive and to all the other writers I have encountered over the years whose help, advice and support has been immense. If I start to mention names, I will go on for pages and still omit someone so, thank you one and all.

To all my readers, please know that I appreciate every single one of you and am thankful for your continuing support. If you are new to my stories, I hope you stick around. There are plenty out there and others to follow. I hope to keep you deliciously scared for a few more years to come.

Catherine Cavendish
Southport, 2023

FLAME TREE PRESS
FICTION WITHOUT FRONTIERS
Award-Winning Authors & Original Voices

Flame Tree Press is the trade fiction imprint of Flame Tree Publishing, focusing on excellent writing in horror and the supernatural, crime and mystery, science fiction and fantasy. Our aim is to explore beyond the boundaries of the everyday, with tales from both award-winning authors and original voices.

•

Other titles by Catherine Cavendish:
The Haunting of Henderson Close
The Garden of Bewitchment
In Darkness, Shadows Breathe
Dark Observation
The After-Death of Caroline Rand

Other horror and suspense titles available include:
Thirteen Days by Sunset Beach by Ramsey Campbell
Think Yourself Lucky by Ramsey Campbell
The Hungry Moon by Ramsey Campbell
The Influence by Ramsey Campbell
The Wise Friend by Ramsey Campbell
Somebody's Voice by Ramsey Campbell
Fellstones by Ramsey Campbell
The Lonely Lands by Ramsey Campbell
Dead Ends by Marc E. Fitch
The Toy Thief by D.W. Gillespie
One By One by D.W. Gillespie
Black Wings by Megan Hart
The Playing Card Killer by Russell James
Demon Dagger by Russell James
Will Haunt You by Brian Kirk
We Are Monsters by Brian Kirk
Hearthstone Cottage by Frazer Lee
Those Who Came Before by J.H. Moncrieff
Stoker's Wilde by Steven Hopstaken & Melissa Prusi
Stoker's Wilde West by Steven Hopstaken & Melissa Prusi
Land of the Dead by Steven Hopstaken & Melissa Prusi
Whisperwood by Alex Woodroe

•

Join our mailing list for free short stories, new release details, news about our authors and special promotions:

flametreepress.com